CLAUDE RANGER
CANADIAN JAZZ LEGEND

MARK MILLER

Also by Mark Miller

Jazz in Canada: Fourteen Lives (1982)

Boogie, Pete & The Senator: Canadian Musicians in Jazz, The Eighties (1987)

Cool Blues: Charlie Parker in Canada, 1953 (1989)

Such Melodious Racket: The Lost History of Jazz in Canada, 1914-1949 (1997)

The Miller Companion to Jazz in Canada and Canadians in Jazz (2001)

Some Hustling This! — Taking Jazz to the World, 1914-1929 (2005)

A Certain Respect for Tradition: Mark Miller on Jazz, Selected Writings, 1980-2005 (2006)

High Hat, Trumpet and Rhythm: The Life and Music of Valaida Snow (2007)

Herbie Nichols: A Jazzist's Life (2009)

Way Down That Lonesome Road: Lonnie Johnson in Toronto, 1965-1970 (2011)

Front cover photograph, Festival International de Jazz de Montréal, July
1986, by Mark Miller

Back cover photograph, Basin Street, Toronto, October 1983, by Mark Miller

Title page photograph, Basin Street, Toronto, October 1983, by Mark Miller

Index: Mark Miller

Tellwell Talent
www.tellwell.ca

ISBN
978-1-77302-561-2 (Hardcover)
978-1-77302-559-9 (Paperback)
978-1-77302-560-5 (eBook)

TABLE OF CONTENTS

CLAUDE RANGER
CANADIAN JAZZ LEGEND

ACKNOWLEDGMENTS

I first heard Claude Ranger one afternoon in the summer of 1972 at a Toronto Musicians' Association Trust Fund concert on the plaza of the Toronto-Dominion Centre. I would have recognized him by name at that point but I did not know him by sight. Nor, for that matter, was I aware that he had recently moved from Montreal to Toronto.

He was playing with trumpeter Bruce Cassidy, perhaps just sitting in; the circumstances were not clear. Cassidy's regular drummer, Terry Clarke, was also there, as were tenor saxophonist Alvin Pall, pianist Bernie Senensky and bassist Don Thompson.

Ranger's kit looked like nothing I had ever seen before. His drums were very small, his cymbals high and almost vertical; he had tied his hi-hat and bass drum to his drum stool with a piece of rope so that they would not slip away from him when he played, which was no more than intermittently — a few bars, a chorus at most, and then he would stop, leaving Clarke to continue alone.

There was an apparitional quality to Ranger's presence that afternoon, but when he did play, it was obvious that there was something quite magical about his drumming. I was puzzled but intrigued and made a point of hearing him whenever I could in the months that followed.

I finally met him in 1974 while preparing biographies for the *Encyclopedia of Music in Canada*, an early assignment in my career as a writer, and I eventually interviewed him at some length on three occasions, the first in 1978 for *Down Beat* and the second and third in 1981 for projects of my own.

I came to know him reasonably well during his Toronto years, and we remained in casual contact after he moved to Vancouver in 1987. When our paths crossed in 1993 at the Festival International de Jazz de Montréal, where he was appearing with P.J. Perry and I was on assignment for *The Globe and Mail*, I offered to send him my own Ludwig "Jazzette" drums, vintage 1973 and latterly collecting dust in my basement, as a kind of personal *hommage*. He accepted and, as I understand it, refinished and eventually sold them. I saw him for the last time, by no more than chance and for just a brief conversation, one grey afternoon in the fall of 1994 on Robson Street in Vancouver.

Our relationship was cordial if perhaps guarded — the result on one hand of his nature and on the other of my profession as a journalist and critic which, as I practiced it, required that I maintain a certain distance, socially, from musicians. I nevertheless appreciated his trust at the time, and I thank him for it now. *Claude Ranger: Canadian Jazz Legend* could not have been written without the foundation offered by the interviews that we did and, more generally, by the contact that I had with him over that period of about 20 years.

Ranger's remarks in an interview *en français* with John Gilmore in 1982 echoed, corroborated and expanded on many of his previous comments to me in English; I thank John for his permission to quote from that interview and also from interviews that he did with Pierre Béluse and Léo Perron for his ground-setting *Swinging in Paradise: The Story of Jazz in Montreal* and *Who's Who of Jazz in Montreal: Ragtime to 1970*, both of which have been important to the preparation of this book.

My thanks as well to Laurence Svirchev for permission to quote from the interview he did with Ranger in Vancouver in 1990, and for his photographs of Ranger at the piano and with the Jade Orchestra during that same period. Thank you also to Lani Ranger for the photographs of her father as a young musician, to Ron Sweetman for permission to use his photograph from *Coda* of Aquarius Rising, and to Bill Smith for his photograph of Ranger with the Jane Bunnett in 1988.

My thanks particularly to the many people who have been willing, either in person or by telephone, to share their memories of Ranger: Ken Aldcroft, Buff Allen, Ron Allen, Ray Ayotte, Jonnie Bakan, Ivan Bamford, Lilly Barnes, Ed Bickert, Joe Bjornson, Seamus Blake, Roland Bourgeois, Jane Bunnett, Bruce Cassidy, Terry Clarke, Lili Clendenning, Coat Cooke, Larry Cramer, Steve Donald, Michel Donato, Sean Drabitt, Phil Dwyer, Kevin Elaschuk, Barry Elmes, Jane Fair, Dave Field, Nick Fraser, Rob Frayne, Bruce Freedman, Gregory Gallagher, Sonny Greenwich, Steve Hall, Kate Hammett-Vaughan, François Houle, Yves Jacques, Terry King, Gerry Labelle, André Lachance, Michel Lambert, Janus Lebo, Pierre Leduc, Peter Leitch, Daniel Lessard, Dave Liebman, Kirk MacDonald, Jacques Masson, Spike McKendry, Bob McLaren, Mike Milligan, Michael Morse, Bob Murphy, Lorne Nehring, Kieran Overs, Alvin Pall, Charles Papasoff, Danny Parker, P.J. Perry, Ken Pickering, Greg Pilo, Lani Ranger, Clyde Reed, Vito Rezza, Barry Romberg, Ron Samworth, Dave Say, Bernie Senensky, William Stewart, Michael Stuart, Neil Swainson, Pierre Tanguay, Don Thompson, Kevin Turcotte, Dylan van der Schyff, Norman Marshall Villeneuve, Steve Wallace, André White, Michael White, Perry White, Tony Wilson and Rene Worst.

My thanks moreover to those who responded to my queries by email: Miles Black, Coat Cooke, Michel Côté, John Doheny, Raynald Drouin, Frank Falco, Richard Ferland, Brian Hurley, Joe LaBarbera, Geoff Lapp, Ranee Lee, Peter Leitch, Brian Longworth, Chris McCann, James McRae, Nilan Perera, Sylvie Perron, Richard Provençal, Jeff Reilly, Vito Rezza, Pierre Richer, Ron Samworth, Roy Styffe, Guy Thouin, Rikk Villa, Gavin Walker and Jack Walrath.

My thanks similarly to those who offered a variety of other personal and professional courtesies that assisted my research: Bernie Arai,

Joe Bjornson, Greg Buium, Bernard Dionne, Gordon Foote, Oliver Jones, Diane Kadota, John Korsrud, Pat LaBarbera, Mike Murley, Ron Sweetman, Rob van der Bliek and Jim West, as well as S/Sgt Alex Bolden and Cst. Amanda Smith of the Langley, B.C., detachment of the Royal Canadian Mounted Police, Marijka Asbeek Bruuse and John Orysik of the Coastal Jazz and Blues Society, Natalie Hodgson and Caroline Sigouin at Concordia University Archives and Special Collections, Maureen Kennedy and Carole Warren at CBC Toronto, and Jill Townsend of the Vancouver Musicians' Association.

My thanks as well, for their interest, encouragement and support at important points in the conception, research and writing of this book, to Stuart Broomer, Greg Buium, Samantha Clayton, Nou Dadoun, Dr. Robin Elliott, Dan Fortin, Nick Fraser, Janus Lebo, David Lee, Fern Lindzon, Jack Litchfield, Barry Livingston, Katie Malloch, Lorne Nehring, Elaine Penalagan, Tim Powis, Lani Ranger, Janis Rubenzahl, Ron Samworth, Julie Smith, Alan Stanbridge, Laurence Svirchev, Rob van der Bliek, Dylan van der Schyff, Steve Wallace, Carole Warren and John Wilby.

My thanks finally to Greg Buium, Dan Fortin, Nick Fraser, Fern Lindzon, Jack Litchfield, Bill McBirnie, Lorne Nehring, Tim Powis, Janis Rubenzahl, Steve Wallace, John Wilby and especially Stuart Broomer, all of whom read, and have commented on, the manuscript.

The research and writing of *Claude Ranger: Canadian Jazz Legend* was assisted by a grant in 2014 from the Writing and Publishing Section of the Canada Council for the Arts.

Mark Miller, January 2017

Preface

On a cold December afternoon in 2013, I met Ivan Bamford at l'Escalier, a café-bar in a warren of small, randomly furnished rooms over a Maison de la Presse Internationale on St. Catherine Street in Montreal's east end.

Bamford had purchased Claude Ranger's last drum set in Vancouver in 1997 and taken it to Montreal in 2001. He kept it for several years in the basement of this same St. Catherine Street building, where he was free to play late at night without fear of disturbing his neighbours.

Bamford remained in touch with Ranger between 1997 and 2000, even as Ranger, 35 years his senior, drifted out of music and eventually moved away from Vancouver. On occasion, Bamford would pick him up — at first in the West End and latterly in Aldergrove, southeast of the city — and take him back to his own place in Burnaby for dinner. Ranger was unusually expansive on what proved to be their final evening together, speaking sardonically and at times severely about his life and how he would be remembered.

As Bamford sat down at l'Escalier, setting his coffee cup on one of the café's old, thrift shop tables in anticipation of my first question, he recalled a comment that Ranger had made that night.

"Claude said that you would want to talk to me. And here we are, all these years later…"

INTRODUCTION

On or about November 2, 2000, Claude Ranger left his one-room apartment in a subsidized housing complex on 30th Avenue in Aldergrove, never to return.[1] He was 59. More than 16 years later, his fate is unknown; the investigation launched by the Royal Canadian Mounted Police in early 2001 remains open.[2]

Ranger's disappearance followed a period of several years in which he had gradually disengaged from all of the things that had sustained him as a musician, including — finally — music itself.

It was, moreover, a period marked by a degree of reflection and regret. After 30 years of playing jazz — and, in truth, of living life — with a remarkable sense of immediacy, a love of risk and no particular concern for consequence, he began to assess his legacy.

He was still playing in 1996 when bassist Kieran Overs, visiting from Toronto, encountered him one late summer afternoon at the corner of Denman and Robson streets in Vancouver's West End.

"I asked him how he was doing," Overs remembers. "He said he was doing really well. Then he said, out of the blue, 'I don't want to be remembered as that guy with the cigarette in his mouth. That's what everybody always talks about.'"

Overs understood. "He wanted to be known for his drumming.

The thing that he didn't realize is that he *was* known for his drumming, of course, but he was justified in his concern."[3]

Indeed, the cigarette perpetually tucked into the left corner of his mouth, no less than the bottles of beer within easy reach at his side, were, in their way, tools in Ranger's particular approach to his trade. Inevitably, they also became the trappings of his legend.

He expressed similar regret to Ivan Bamford in 2000 about the effect of those trappings on the way he was regarded by the public. "He felt he was famous because of *those* things at least as much as because of his accomplishments as a drummer and musician. If he had been more of a 'straight' guy, he wouldn't have had all the notoriety."

And yet there was an element of cultivation to Ranger's notoriety. That cigarette, for example, with its impossibly long ash burning ever more impossibly longer. "It was a symptom of the absolutely disciplined carelessness that he had," suggests the Toronto saxophonist Ron Allen, who worked with Ranger in 1980. "The way it would hang, defying gravity — he knew it was intimidating, he knew it was attractive, he knew how to seduce."[4]

Ranger had in fact stopped smoking by 1996, an act of remarkable willpower for someone who — in the words of a friend from as far back as the mid-1960s, Montreal bassist Michel Donato — "just needed one match in the morning; one match, that's it."[5]

He had also stopped drinking, at least for a time, and he had been diagnosed with bipolar disorder. He sold his drums to Ivan Bamford in 1997 and made his final public appearance at Vancouver's du Maurier International Jazz Festival in 1998. Long the ladies' man, he moved to Aldergrove alone.

If Ranger's demons and his dependencies, and their effect on his career, are necessarily a part of his story, it is nevertheless his skill as a musician, his impact on the jazz scenes of Canada's three largest cities, Montreal, Toronto and Vancouver, and his influence on many of the country's younger players that make that story worth telling.

Pears Restaurant, Toronto, June 1981.
Photograph by Mark Miller.

It is a story of passion, dedication, compromise and intransigence, of generosity and negligence, of hurt both felt and caused. It is also the story of jazz in Canada more broadly during the 30 years in which Ranger was a significant force, a story that reflects his contrarian perspective in face of the conservatism and commercialism that characterized the music as it was played by its most popular figures — many of whom he worked with, if only in passing and in some dismay.

• • •

He was a small, handsome man, five-foot-seven or so, portly for a time in his early thirties, but trim in later years, the result of a passion for cycling. His eyes were his most arresting feature, "blue like the ocean," in the words of one friend. His gaze, especially toward women, could be penetrating.

His French accent also helped in that respect, the mark of a Québécois abroad, as in effect Ranger was for the last 25 years of his career, first in Toronto and then in Vancouver. He was nevertheless conflicted about the language itself and, more specifically, about the way he spoke it.

"I don't like French," he once admitted in accented English. "I have this against French — it's not that I hate it, it's us Québécois, like me. I don't speak very good French, you know? When guys from overseas come and start speaking French, it's so beautiful, I hate it."[6]

He was not, in any event, very talkative in either language, communicating most comfortably instead through music, a man for whom — as the Toronto bassist Mike Milligan observes — "a gig wasn't just a gig, and a concert wasn't just a concert, it was a major life event."[7]

Beyond music, Ranger lived in a state of restless creativity. He melted wax crayons into sculptures, he drew, he did jigsaw puzzles, he took up photography for a time, he refinished drums and he made furniture, seeking in each of these activities an opportunity to lose himself to the immediacy of the task at hand — much as he lost himself in music.

In his preoccupation with the moment he gave no thought to his legacy until his career was all but over. But the fact that he left very little to show for his life in music is also a reflection of the Canadian jazz scene, which went largely undocumented in the 1960s and 1970s and only gradually less so in the 1980s and 1990s.

The Ranger discography comprises some 20 LPs or CDs as a sideman and none as a leader, an altogether random, incomplete and often poorly recorded survey of a career that lasted nearly 40 years. About 30 of his compositions, including his best known piece, *Le Pingouin*, survive on commercial or private recordings, as airchecks from Radio-Canada broadcasts or as lead sheets that have inadvertently remained in the possession of a very few of the many musicians who played them with him. The exercises that he so freely and generously wrote out for his fellow drummers are similarly, if more widely scattered across the country, copied and passed down through three or four successive generations.

The recordings are difficult to find, the compositions rarely performed. The exercises continue to have currency, but orderly patterns of eighth notes on score paper convey only Ranger's discipline as a musician, not the spirit of his playing — the spirit that made him such a compelling figure on the bandstand to those who rose to the challenges that went with it, as many musicians across the country did, whether for a night or two, or over a period of years.

The scant documentation of his legacy notwithstanding, he remains a compelling figure in the history of jazz in Canada, all the more for his disappearance, a scarcely conceivable turn of events that has had the effect of elevating him beyond legend into myth — in the words of the Montreal artist and essayist Raymond Gervais, "an enigma bordering on fiction."[8] His story is nevertheless real enough, even in the absence of a formal conclusion. It simply stops, an unresolved narrative that has left those who knew him — whether personally or professionally, intimately or from a distance — without closure.

It was not until November 2012, a dozen years after his disappearance, that some 20 Vancouver musicians finally gathered to pay their respects with two concerts at the Ironworks Studios under the banner "Feu vert: A Tribute to Claude Ranger."[9]

One of those musicians, drummer Dylan van der Schyff, visited Toronto a few months later for an engagement at The Rex. By then, I had undertaken the preliminary research for *Claude Ranger: Canadian Jazz Legend*, but had not decided whether to make it the basis of a book; van der Schyff supported the idea immediately.

"Don't just do it for Claude," he suggested, as if speaking on behalf of all the people whose lives Ranger had touched. "Do it for us."[10]

CHAPTER ONE

Rosemont

Claude Ranger[1] was born on February 3, 1941, in Montreal, a city of two solitudes, as novelist Hugh McLennan described it for the ages just four years later[2] — French to the east and English to the west, separated symbolically by The Main, St. Lawrence Boulevard.

A small black community, whose significance in the history of jazz in Canada has far outstripped its size, thrived in the south-central down-town neighbourhood of Little Burgundy, near the Canadian Pacific Railway lines that offered the heads of its households their primary source of employment. Other groups — Greeks, Italians, Jews — also lived among themselves in pockets around the city, sub-solitudes as it were, although not as clearly demarcated as French and English or, for that matter, black and white.

Typically, Ranger's father, Aurèle, and his mother, Lucille (*née* Richer), raised their family east of St. Lawrence Boulevard. They lived during the 1940s on *rue* de Bordeaux, below Masson, at the north-east edge of the Plateau Mont-Royal, and then — around 1951, when

Aurèle, theretofore employed as a labourer, took a job with l'Imprimerie Desmarais as a driver — moved a short distance farther east to 1st Avenue, above Masson, in Rosemont.[3]

De Bordeaux and 1st Avenue were working-class streets lined with red, brown and yellow brick row houses built in the first decades of the 20th century to designs that were functional but of no particular aesthetic distinction. The Rangers' 1st Avenue address — a two-storey, semi-detached duplex with a shallow setback from the street, a slightly deeper rear yard and a narrow back lane — would scarcely have been large enough to accommodate a family that grew in due course to six with the arrival of Claude's younger brother and sisters, Jacques, Gisèle and Murielle.

Ranger rarely spoke of life at home and then only to suggest evasively that it had been very difficult. The Rangers kept their secrets, but could not counter suggestions of Lucille's infidelity or conceal Gisèle's marriage to a member of the Montreal criminal underworld, each an indication of a household in some disorder.

It was not a promising environment for anyone inclined toward a career in music, much less a young French-Canadian who wished to play jazz. The most successful jazz musicians of Ranger's generation in Montreal, and of generations before him, were Anglophones — pianists Oscar Peterson and Oliver Jones from Little Burgundy, trumpeter Maynard Ferguson from Shaughnessy Village due north of Little Burgundy, and pianist Paul Bley from Outremont, above Mount Royal. Among French Canadians of the same era, only bassist Michel Donato would have as significant a career in jazz, and none would have Ranger's impact outside of Quebec. His achievement, moreover, was entirely his own, a triumph of sheer will, given the apparent personal and cultural isolation in which he spent his early years as a musician.

Oscar Peterson had been the product not only of an active musical family, but of a rich musical community that included the choir at Union United Church on Delisle Street and the entertainers who worked in the black nightclubs on The Corner, across Little Burgundy, at Mountain Street and St. Antoine. Oliver Jones, in turn, had studied for several years with Peterson's sister Daisy, and played as a boy both at Union United and at the Café St. Michel on Mountain Street. Paul Bley and Maynard Ferguson, sons of white, middle-class families, had each studied formally by or during their teens, Bley at the McGill Conservatory and Ferguson at the Conservatoire de Musique du Québec à Montréal. All four, prodigies to one degree or another, were performing publicly, if not professionally, by the age at which Ranger was only beginning to show an interest in music.

• • •

"There was no music at my place, at my mother's and father's," Ranger once recalled. No music, save on one occasion when Aurèle played harmonica, an instrument found in many working-class Quebec households.

Small, inexpensive, and relatively easy to master, the *musique à bouche* was popularized in the late 1920s and the 1930s by Henri Lacroix and other French-Canadian recording artists who shared with Quebec's *violoneux* and *accordéonistes* a repertoire of reels, jigs, waltzes and other dance pieces. Theirs was essentially a *musique folklorique*, but even after popular tastes had shifted in Québec toward more sophisticated styles of music from Paris and New York, it retained a certain resonance for many in Aurèle's generation.

"I only heard my father play once," Ranger continued, marvelling at the memory, "but he was flying! He was so shy, he didn't want to do it. He played just for a minute, and never again, but he had *something*."

Ranger's real introduction to music, and to drums in particular, came instead at school, where he found himself a member of a cadet corps — likely the 977th, which was affiliated with the Régiment de Maisonneuve and which marshalled, complete with marching band, on the grounds of the École Louis-Hébert, an elegant, three-storey Art Deco building on 6th Avenue near Beaubien.

"In school, in those days," Ranger explained, "you had to be in the army. It was called cadets. A little discipline. You got a uniform, like cadets in the army. I was one of those guys walking around and wondering, '*What* am I doing here?' I didn't know *why* I was doing it; I thought maybe *everybody* had to do it."

Although instinctively uncomfortable with regimentation, as he would be throughout his life with direction and conformity of any kind, Ranger was drawn to the power of the band — and in particular of one of its members — to compel, if not indeed to inspire.

"There was this guy who was playing this drum, just by himself. A bass drum. And everybody was marching to it! I couldn't believe it. Just one guy playing, and everyone was marching! I thought, 'I want to be a drummer! I'd like that!' I think I was 13. After that, I was just grabbing anything and hitting it, like everyone else does. But I really *worked* at it."

Starting with "pots and pans around the house and the garbage can tops in the alley,"[4] Ranger in time acquired a proper — and quieter — practice pad made of rubber and began to study at the École de Musique Thibault-Levac, three blocks south of home on Masson, between 2nd and 3rd Avenue.

Already in character — already determined, already impatient — he quickly grew frustrated with the limitations of his three-dollar, half-hour lessons, likely once a week. "I thought I'd like to go back the next day," he admitted, "instead of waiting so long."

With money earned from working on weekends at a local grocery store, and with further assistance from his father, Ranger bought his first drums; a family photograph shows him playing what appears to a blue and silver Ludwig kit of early 1950s vintage. He soon stopped taking lessons and entered into a period of intense study on his own, already convinced that he had found his calling.

The extent of his preoccupation is apparent in another family photograph, this one of the Rangers on an outing in the country. Surrounded by Gisèle in a light summer dress, Aurèle stripped to the waist and Jacques in a cowboy suit, Ranger lies in the long grass, his back against a tree, a sailor's cap angled on his head and a drum stick incongruously at the ready in each hand.

Montreal, c1957.
Courtesy Lani Ranger.

"At 14 or 15, I really got into it. I said, 'I think this is it, I think this is what I'm going to be doing.' Or maybe I wasn't even thinking it; it just happened. I lost all of my friends. There was no one anymore and I found myself alone with a set of drums. 'What can you do with it?' I was just banging on it. I quit school — actually, I was thrown out — and I quit work. I just tried to play. I was 16. I sat there for two years, all day long, and just hit the drums."

Ranger later told another, younger Montreal drummer, Jacques Masson, that it was Aurèle who had instilled in him the disciplined work ethic that put music above and before all else. In Masson's words, the senior Ranger told his son, "'Okay, if you want to be a musician, now it's your *job*. So you get up at seven in the morning, you eat breakfast and you start practicing — *all* day. You're not going to be a musician just to loaf around, to bum around. You've got to be serious.'"[5]

As indeed Ranger was and, to a fault, would be. He played at 17 — "just before really starting" — with a guitarist at a resort spot north of Montreal, then began working in earnest at 18 with a trio at the Lantern Café on the corner of Masson and 2nd Avenue, not far from the École de Musique Thibault-Levac.

There, his career barely underway, he came face to face with the practical reality of the calling that he had accepted. "The guitar player was a fireman," he remembered, "and he was a body builder — a 'Mr. Montreal' and a 'Mr. Canada' a few times. The accordion player was a mailman. And *me*, what *I'm* doing is practicing drums. That's all I know. So I'm thinking, 'Am I going to have to do something *else* in life?'"

CHAPTER TWO

Showbars

Rosemont remained Claude Ranger's world as a musician, save for the summer spent up north, until he was 18 — 1st Avenue, the École de Musique Thibault-Levac and the Lantern Café. It was, all told, a relatively sheltered existence, one that changed quickly and dramatically when he travelled in late 1959 to St. John's, Newfoundland, with an ice show, the first of countless variety acts that he would accompany in one setting or another over the course of the next 10 years.

He went to St. John's with a trio — piano, bass and drums — that played for a troupe of a dozen or more skaters. "It lasted two weeks," he remembered. "One day the [manager] left. Didn't pay anybody. I woke up one morning sick like crazy. No money, nothing. Go to the Salvation Army, get some food. I remember that. Oh yeah!

"We were lucky that the three of us got a gig on New Year's Eve, a paying gig. I got a hundred dollars. I flew from Gander to Montreal; stopped in Quebec [City]. My first trip on a plane. Watch out! Watch out! What a thrill: all this adventure with music, all this adventure with reality!"

Ranger was clearly not discouraged by the turn of events. Instead, he saw them as a challenge. "That's when the trouble started," he admitted, "because I was *not* going to give up. I was *going* to play. The most difficult part was then, when I was 18. There were no girls at that time. Usually a young boy has girlfriends. There was not such a thing in my life."

* * *

That's when the trouble started. It was just a passing comment, one that Ranger made perhaps wryly or in mild self-deprecation during an interview some 21 years later, but it betrayed a conflicted perspective on the events of the two intervening decades, a perspective that carried over into the two decades that followed.

"The trouble," he had said. Not "the fun." Music was always a serious matter, not a diversion — not something to be taken lightly in the least.

When asked in that same interview about the point at which he had become interested in jazz, Ranger bristled at the very question. "I'm not 'interested' in jazz. I was *never* 'interested' in jazz. I just... *love* it."

There was, moreover, something palpable — something physical, perhaps even addictive — about that feeling.

"To me," he added, "my body doesn't want to do anything else. I will play anything, but it seems as though there's nothing else but jazz."

There must have been a time, of course, when Ranger became "interested" in jazz, if only in the sense that there must also have been a time when he was not. He offered two overlapping accounts of the point at which he first made its acquaintance, one that began with Gene Krupa and Dave Brubeck, followed by Max Roach and Miles Davis, and another that started directly with Roach and Davis. The former version, which Ranger related to Montreal jazz historian John Gilmore in 1982,[1] seems the more plausible, at least to the extent that it is consistent with the general timeframe of his early and impressionable years as a drummer, the mid-to-late 1950s.

Gene Krupa had been something of a matinee idol in jazz since the mid-1930s, first with clarinetist Benny Goodman's orchestra and quartet and then as the leader during the 1940s of his own big band. His frenetic drum solos on *Sing, Sing, Sing* and *Drum Boogie* — all flash and flourish, albeit in the flailing, rather ungainly manner of a man possessed — captured the public's imagination during and after the Swing era.* His celebrity was reaffirmed in 1959 with the release of *The Gene Krupa Story*, a Hollywood film that starred Sal Mineo as Krupa onscreen, with Krupa himself playing on the soundtrack.

Dave Brubeck was effectively Krupa's aesthetic opposite, a pianist and composer whose intellectual bent found expression in a formalist approach to the "cool" jazz of the early 1950s. But Brubeck enjoyed similar celebrity, to the point of appearing in 1954 on the cover of *Time*, an achievement that may or may not have been noted on newsstands in Montreal's east end.

The drummers in Brubeck's quartet during this period were, in turn, Joe Dodge and Joe Morello; when the latter agreed to join the band in 1955, he insisted on playing solos, and did so in an efficient and orderly manner that — given Brubeck's popularity — was also influential on younger drummers of the day.

If Krupa and Brubeck — and Morello — were indeed Ranger's introduction to jazz, he was soon looking further afield for inspiration.

"The first two drummers I heard were Jimmy Cobb and Max Roach," he suggested in an earlier, variant account of his formative years. "I had two records. I was listening to them all of the time: *Max Roach + Four* and [Miles Davis' *In Person*] *Friday Night at the Blackhawk*. That was very nice. Then there was Elvin [Jones], and finally I just listened to *whoever* was playing. I used to go crazy when I heard Tony Williams."

The Roach recording was released in 1956, but likely came to Ranger's attention later, inasmuch as he remembered listening to it at the same time as Davis' *Blackhawk* LP, a San Francisco club recording from 1961

---

*   As employed here, Swing ("S" majuscule) refers to the genre popular in the 1930s and 1940s; swing ("s" minuscule) refers to the predominant rhythm, or rhythmic quality of jazz.

with Jimmy Cobb at the drums.

Roach had been central to the revolution in jazz drumming inspired by the emergence in New York during the early 1940s of bebop, a daring new style that challenged the tenets of Swing by giving precedence to small groups over big bands, to the individual musician over the ensemble and to improvisation over the written note. At the same time, it advanced the harmonic, melodic and rhythmic language of jazz to new levels of complexity that demanded correspondingly higher degrees of virtuosity from those musicians who would play it.

To complement bop's melodic and rhythmic innovations in particular, its drummers — Kenny Clarke first, then Roach, Art Blakey, Roy Haynes and others influenced by Clarke — adjusted the roles of the bass and snare drums, the hi-hat and the ride cymbal in ways that allowed for a more flexible approach to keeping "time" than had been the case with Swing.

Swing stylists had marked each quarter-note beat of a four-beat bar explicitly, often rigidly, on the bass drum. Roach, after Clarke's example, shifted the second and fourth beat less emphatically to the hi-hat and subdivided all four even more subtly into repeated patterns of variously grouped eighth or sixteenth notes on the ride cymbal, freeing the bass drum for accents — for "dropping bombs," in bop parlance — and employing the snare drum for counter figures and other rhythmic shadings.

As Ranger would have heard on *Max Roach + Four*, Roach was an extremely disciplined and technically adept drummer whose playing, for all of bop's new freedom, retained an implicit awareness of form and melody. Miles Davis' drummer, Jimmy Cobb — five years younger than Roach and also, by the time he appeared on *Friday Night at the Blackhawk*, five years further along in the evolution of bebop — was rather scrappier and more impulsive.

Both men would leave their mark on Ranger's drumming. So, too, in time would Elvin Jones and Tony Williams, who were to Roach in the mid-1960s what Roach and Kenny Clarke had been to Gene Krupa 20 years earlier — Jones, through his work with the John Coltrane

Quartet from 1960 to 1965, and Williams, still a teenager, as Jimmy Cobb's replacement with the Miles Davis Quintet in 1963.

Jones and Williams, each in his own way, defined a style that was at once freer and yet, in its layering of rhythms and tempos, internally more complex than strict bop drumming had been. They were otherwise at some distance aesthetically, between Jones' loose, embracing swing, his power and his imposing, at times almost brutish presence on one hand, and Williams' taut, insistent cymbal ride, his tightrope sense of risk and balance and his imaginative play of shadow and light on the other — no less than Jones' rounded eighth-note triplets and Williams' skittering straight eighths and sixteenths. Both men could be explosive; Williams, for his audacity, was the more likely to surprise, indeed to startle — lightning, in effect, to Jones' thunder.

Even as Ranger was inspired by Roach and Cobb, and especially by Jones and Williams, he was also troubled — or so he told John Gilmore — by the knowledge that they were all African-Americans, a point of fact that only underscored how far removed he was, culturally, from the music that he wished to master.

"'*Câlisse*,'" he remembered thinking, "'how can I do this? I'm white!' That bothered me for a really, really long time. I thought you had to be black to play."

• • •

Montreal's distance from New York, geographically, and the perspective that it offered, if only symbolically, left Ranger free to choose his influences without being pressured to conform to the specific example of any one of them at any given time. That same distance had allowed Oscar Peterson to draw at the piano on models as disparate in the early 1940s as Art Tatum, Teddy Wilson and Nat King Cole; like Peterson, Ranger was less the product of a style or a trend than simply of an era, the early-to-mid 1960s. And no less than Peterson's 1940s, a period in which Swing was giving way to bebop, Ranger's 1960s were a time of transition between post-bop's structuralism and the avant-garde's relative freedom, a tension explored by — among others — John Coltrane with Elvin Jones, and Miles Davis with Tony Williams.

At the same time, the Montreal scene had a dynamic of its own, albeit one rather dated in the larger scheme of jazz history. According to Pierre Béluse, five years Ranger's senior, there was a stylistic division among the city's drummers that ran along east/west lines.

"To me," Béluse remarked to John Gilmore in 1982, "in the east end, they all got [the] Buddy Rich and Louis Bellson [Swing] style first. In the west end, they didn't have the technique to play like Buddy Rich, and they were playing more like Kenny Clarke, Art Blakey, you know, more bebop, none of the Swing, less of the technical aspect of it."[2]

Ranger, already going his own way, belonged stylistically, though not geographically, with the city's modernists, as did, for that matter, Béluse himself. But the generalization survived its exceptions: the legendary Guy Nadon, who epitomized the city's east-end drummers, answered precisely — if idiosyncratically — to Béluse's description, as confirmed by a third Montreal drummer, Keith (Spike) McKendry, who identifies another east/west dichotomy on the city's jazz scene.

"Guy Nadon could play those fast single-stroke rolls like Buddy Rich. He had good time, too. Excellent time. But he didn't do jazz gigs. The guys in the east end stayed in the east end and did their work. The jazz clubs were in the west end. And those guys never came to the west end."[3]

• • •

According to rankings in the Canadian section of a poll conducted by the Canadian Broadcasting Corporation's weekly FM radio show *Jazz at its Best*, the country's two finest drummers in 1960 and 1961 both lived in Montreal — Donat Gariepy and Billy Graham.[4]

Gariepy had been touted as the "Gene Krupa of Canada"[5] when he worked during the mid-1940s with alto saxophonist Stan Wood at Belmont Park in north-end Cartierville and at the Auditorium downtown on Ontario Street. By 1960, however, his style had dated badly. Len Dobbin, writing for the Toronto jazz magazine *Coda*, dismissed him as "at best a fair society band drummer."[6] Taking Gariepy as a case in point, Dobbin was in fact openly critical of the poll's Canadian results, which were skewed toward Montreal and Toronto musicians who enjoyed a profile on CBC radio or TV, as Gariepy did through his work over the years with pianist Neil Chotem, guitarist Gilbert (Buck) Lacombe and others — and as did, to a lesser extent, Billy Graham, a deft bop drummer in the style of Max Roach and, as such, perhaps worthier of his *Jazz at its Best* showing.

Until the advent of *Jazz en liberté* in 1965, CBC Montreal, no less than CBC Toronto and CBC Vancouver, generally solicited its jazz content from the musicians who worked in its studio orchestras and on its variety shows — musicians who were conversant with jazz, but not necessarily, and in truth rarely, in the vanguard of the local scene, where the prevailing bop, hard-bop and post-bop styles of the day would in any event have been deemed by the CBC to be too modern for the general audience that it served. Thus the faces of jazz most recognizable in Montreal, Toronto and Vancouver were not always the faces of those cities' most interesting or most dedicated jazz musicians, a false reality that would limit the broader public recognition that Claude Ranger, among many others, received during his career.

Moreover, the *Jazz at its Best* poll results inevitably perpetuated themselves, giving additional credence to the winners, however well or poorly chosen, by the inadvertence of pushing everyone else further into the shadows. "We have few enough inventive jazzmen in Canada," Len Dobbin observed, of the poll's shortcomings, "and it is sad to see that people aren't getting out to hear them."[7] Sadder still, they would not have been at all encouraged by the poll's results to do so.

From Dobbin's perspective as someone who was "getting out" frequently — most notably to the Vieux Moulin, Little Vienna, la Tête de l'Art, the Penthouse and the Black Bottom in the course of the early 1960s — the hierarchy on the Montreal jazz scene looked rather different. His columns for *Coda* during that period point to the pre-eminence of Pierre Béluse among the city's drummers, both with his fellow Montreal musicians and with visiting American stars.

Béluse was rivalled in those respects only by Emile (Cisco) Normand, who stood a distant third to Donat Gariepy and Billy Graham in the *Jazz at its Best* poll for 1961, just months after his arrival from Windsor, Ontario, via Detroit.[8]

• • •

Claude Ranger's name would not begin to appear in the pages of *Coda* until 1967. For the first several years of his professional career, he purposely kept his distance from the jazz scene in the west end and played instead for floor shows at a succession of nightclubs in the east end — the Rainbow Café, the Mocambo Café and the Casa Loma, each one a little closer, both geographically and symbolically, to the jazz scene downtown.

Montreal's fabled nightlife, which supported thousands of musicians and their families, faced a number of challenges during this period, some political and some economic. It had already survived the reformist zeal of the city's mayor, Jean Drapeau, who came to power in 1954 on a promise to confront organized crime and tackle its attendant problems of civic corruption, gambling and prostitution; the latter two in particular had brought Montreal the reputation of being "wide open" in terms of the welcome it offered equally to those who sought such "illicit" pleasures and to those who would provide them, dating back to the days of Prohibition in the 1920s.

Although Drapeau lost his bid for re-election in 1957, he was returned to office in 1960 — there to remain until 1986 — and immediately renewed his campaign. Its success, together with the incipient and competing popularity of television, placed new financial pressures on the city's nightclubs, which responded in many cases by reducing the number of musicians in their employ and in other cases by replacing floor shows with strippers and, in time, dropping bands altogether in favour of recorded music.[9]

Montreal's nightlife held loosely to the general pattern of Montreal itself, save in one respect. There were cabarets both to the east and to the west of St. Lawrence Boulevard, as well as several right on The Main itself in the vicinity of St. Catherine Street. To the extent that these two worlds were mutually exclusive, it was inevitably to the disadvantage of the city's French musicians.

"I was in the east-end crowd and wasn't allowed to play the nice shows," the alto saxophonist Léo Perron told John Gilmore in 1982. "Yeah, because I was French. And the French didn't mix with the English, and the English had the best jobs because the west end had the nicer hotels, and the bigger shows and the nicer music. So we grew up with [Québécois star Michel] Louvain and they grew up with Frank Sinatra."[10]

There was, moreover, a third line running through the city's nightlife, one that set the black cabarets on The Corner in Little Burgundy apart from the other nightclubs in the west-end. Rockhead's Paradise, which had competed directly in the late 1930s and the 1940s with the storied Café St. Michel across Mountain Street, was still in operation during the 1960s. Most of the musicians who worked on The Corner were black, many of them Americans who found Montreal's comparatively mild racial temper to their liking.

In each case — whether the east end, the west end or The Corner — cabaret work served as a point of entry and, absent the availability of anything more formal, offered a practical education for young Montreal musicians who had set their sights on careers in jazz or in the city's recording and broadcasting studios.

"You'd learn your craft right on the bandstand," notes one of those young musicians in the mid-1960s, guitarist Peter Leitch. "It was part of the culture of becoming a professional. When somebody new came along — when some kid came up — musicians would say, 'Well, can he cut a show?'"[11]

• • •

Ranger would have been just such a kid in 1960 when he went into the Rainbow Café, a small cabaret on *rue* Notre Dame East at Théodore, near *rue* Viau, deep in the east end. He had long since taught himself to read music, but to that point — just turned 19 — he had played only for dancers at the Lantern Café and for ice skaters in St. John's. At the Rainbow, however, he and his fellow musicians under the leadership of guitarist Aurèle Lacombe accompanied a floor show whose acts relied in particular on his skill as their drummer to highlight the nuances of their performances, whether with a drum roll, a rimshot, a choked cymbal or, simply, silence. His was a significant supporting role, one that required close attention, precise timing and, technically speaking, the independence of right hand from left, one foot from the other, and both hands from both feet.

As an older Montreal drummer from that period, Dennis Brown, explained to John Gilmore, "You caught punch lines on comedians' jokes, jugglers, a dancer's kick — everything that moved, you accented it, pointed it up. And all this had to happen while you still knew where you were in the context of the music. You still had to swing, or, if you were playing Latin or Afro, you still had to maintain that feel."[12]

Soon enough, Ranger had "cut" enough shows at the Rainbow to move up and west in the cabaret world to trumpeter Robert Lavoie's showband at the Mocambo Café on Notre Dame East at the corner of du Havre. The Mocambo was one of the largest rooms in the east end, and also one of the few to advertise its weekly attractions in the English-language *Montreal Gazette*. As well it might: although it presented established Quebec stars during the period in which Ranger worked there, notably singers Alys Robi and Jen Roger, it also imported many American rhythm and blues performers, including Ruth Brown, Chubby Checker, Fats Domino, the Drifters, Clyde McPhatter and, in May 1964, a 14-year-old "Little" Stevie Wonder.

Ranger told Jacques Masson that he relied on a photographic memory when faced with the music that each new act brought to the Mocambo, a claim that Masson subsequently verified. "They would have the rehearsal on Monday and some musicians who played with Claude told me that he would read the show at the rehearsal and after the rehearsal he'd close the book and throw it on the floor. He wouldn't open it up for the rest of the week and he wouldn't miss a punch."

Montreal, c1960; the guitarist may be Aurèle Lacombe.
Courtesy Lani Ranger.

Ranger would not necessarily have backed all of the Americans — some travelled with their own musicians — but he accompanied the other acts that completed each week's bill, an assortment of singers on their way up or down, dance teams, comedians, magicians, ventriloquists, acrobats, unicyclists and trained animals.

He took this passing parade in stride. "*Ben* fun," he told John Gilmore in French. "It was good for me. It didn't matter what, I was learning all the time." But, he scoffed in English on another occasion, cabaret work had "nothing to do with jazz, man, nothing at all."

At some point in the summer of 1964, however, he moved still farther downtown to the Casa Loma, just two blocks east of St. Lawrence Boulevard on St. Catherine Street and unique among Montreal cabarets by virtue of having a jazz club on its second floor — a jazz club with a weekly lineup of American stars unrivalled by any other room in the city's history, either before or in the 50 years since.

Jazz Hot, as it was known, opened in December of 1963 with Oscar Peterson and, over the course of the next 15 months, presented many other major figures of the day, including Dizzy Gillespie, Bill Evans, Coleman Hawkins, Thelonious Monk, Erroll Garner, Max Roach and Abbey Lincoln, Art Blakey, Gene Krupa, Miles Davis, Horace Silver, the Modern Jazz Quartet, the Woody Herman and Duke Ellington orchestras, John Coltrane, Cannonball Adderley and Wes Montgomery.

Ranger worked downstairs with pianist Marcel Doré's showband, once again accompanying variety acts, but did not often venture upstairs to hear the artists who were defining the aesthetic of the music that he so passionately wanted to play. Instead — according to Spike McKendry, who was a member for a time of pianist Pierre Leduc's trio opposite the American stars at Jazz Hot — Ranger spent his breaks in the band room two floors below.

Ranger did see and briefly meet Max Roach at Jazz Hot in September of 1964, but he shunned the Miles Davis Quintet, with Tony Williams, in November of that year and the John Coltrane Quartet, with Elvin Jones, in January of 1965, just three weeks after

Coltrane had made his most celebrated recording, *A Love Supreme*. Ranger's explanation for avoiding Coltrane was revealing and, in the harsh light of retrospection, unforgiving.

"I was too scared," he conceded. "So I didn't go up. I never saw Coltrane live, never saw McCoy Tyner live, never saw Jimmy Garrison live... What a fucking mistake, eh? *Not* to go and see *Coltrane!* I don't know what I was afraid of. Maybe *my* thing was waiting to come out, and I was afraid to get badly hurt. So I didn't go."

Indeed Ranger, by then 23, was just starting to make himself known on the local jazz scene, at first simply by going to hear other Montreal musicians after he had finished work at the Casa Loma, and then, in due course, by sitting in with them. His friend Norman Marshall Villeneuve, who played drums at Rockhead's Paradise under the name Norman Griffith in the mid-1960s, noticed his initial hesitance.

"There would be a lot of times when he wouldn't want to sit in. He'd just want to listen. In the early years, he was a good listener. He would rather listen than play. He didn't want to play until he was ready."[13]

Ranger himself recalled eventually sitting in at the Black Bottom, a coffee house that had opened in October 1963 on St. Antoine Street, one block west of Rockhead's Paradise, with Nelson Symonds usually its attraction. Once the Americans who were appearing at Casa Loma began to drop by after hours to listen or to sit in, word quickly spread about the modest Canadian guitarist whose roughshod virtuosity and startling intensity had little precedent stateside. No less than Wes Montgomery, who played at Jazz Hot in February 1965, left Montreal duly amazed, having been alerted to Symonds' presence at the Black Bottom by Oscar Peterson, John Coltrane and Horace Silver. "If he ever come here," Montgomery later told an American television interviewer with some finality, "it's *over*."[14]

Symonds, who would in fact never leave Montreal, employed several drummers during his time at the Black Bottom, including an American, Charlie Duncan, and the African-Canadians Norman Griffith, Clayton Johnston and Billy McCant, as well as Ranger's fellow Québécois Bernard Primeau. It was Johnston who bade Ranger welcome on the bandstand. Ready or not, Ranger finally accepted the invitation.

"Before then," he admitted, "I could only *think* about sitting at a set of drums with all of these guys. I would need a beer for sure! And then I would sit there and drop sticks! I was very shy."

Shy, yes. And after several years exclusively of cabaret work he was still adjusting to the freedom in jazz to play an *active* role in shaping a performance even as it unfolded, using the very same means — attention, timing, independence of movement — but to very different ends, which changed rather than repeated from night to night.

Ranger remembered well the first time he felt as though his years of preparation had been rewarded — early one morning at another after-hours spot, likely the Café Pascale on Stanley Street, which hosted jam sessions during the summer of 1966. A good friend, tenor saxophonist Alvin Pall, with whom Ranger had worked for Marcel Doré at the Casa Loma, was on the bandstand.

"I walked in after a gig in my B-flat suit — that's black — and I was asked to sit in. There I am, stuck, with this set of drums, and I'm thinking, 'What *is* this shit?' But I played, and suddenly my practicing and my listening came out, and I was told, 'Oh man, you started to sound like Elvin.' I was pleased, very pleased."

CHAPTER THREE

Jazz en liberté

Claude Ranger was still working at the Rainbow Café when he began to study theory and harmony in the early 1960s with Frank Mella, travelling by bus across Montreal from Rosemont to Mella's studio on West Broadway, near Loyola College, in the farthest corner of Notre-Dame-de-Grace.

Ranger did not drive, then or ever, which would have been a decided enough disadvantage for any musician whose workplace often changed from one night to the next and from one quarter of the city to another, let alone for a musician routinely burdened with three or four drums and at least as many cymbals, as well as hardware and accessories. In later years he was an avid cyclist, but throughout his career Ranger relied for transportation to and from work on the good will of his fellow musicians, his friends and his fans.

He had no need for his drums, of course, on his weekly visit to Frank Mella's home in N.D.G. "Mr. Mella," as Ranger still referred to him years later, played violin in CBC studio orchestras and taught music privately, offering lessons — in English — based entirely on classical principles. He was not doctrinaire, however, and made allowances for the possibility that his students' interests might ultimately lie somewhere other than in classical music. As a result, he attracted several jazz musicians to his studio in the 1950s and 1960s, among them Ranger, Guy Nadon, saxophonist Gerry Labelle and trumpeter Alan Penfold.

According to Labelle, Mella insisted that the rules of music be properly understood as the prerequisite for breaking them,[1] a philosophy that would have suited well Ranger's sense of discipline on one hand and his love of freedom on the other.

"He's why I know music," Ranger said of Mella, by way of reviewing the full, if limited extent of his formal studies over the years. "He is my teacher, my only teacher. I never had any other teacher. Well, I had a drum teacher, and then I had another drum teacher. The first drum teacher lasted four months and I found out he couldn't read music. That was even before I had a set of drums. After that, I had a set of drums — many years after — and I was stuck, like, 'Oh, what's happening, why can't I understand that?' So I went to another teacher to study. It had to do with reading. It took me three lessons to understand what I wanted to find out."

Thus reading. But Ranger had also started in his late teens to compose at the piano. Again, at about 20, he remembered, "I found I was stuck." And so began the commute — down to Sherbrooke Street, across to West Broadway and back.

"I went every week and studied. Without the piano, just with manuscripts. Riding the bus. Studying harmony: 'That makes sense; that does *not* make sense.' He was a very good teacher, like right away. He was a little old man, played violin. A pro. He knew everything about music. His violin was in a canvas bag, like what you throw out garbage in. When he wanted me to hear a few notes he'd pick up the bag. *Boing, boing.* 'That's the way it sounds.'"

Ranger's composition *Challenge*, written in 1963,[2] dates to a point at or near the end of his studies with Mella. Remarkably, and uniquely, it was still in Ranger's working repertoire, with some adjustments, more than 40 years later, an angular blues constructed on a single ascending phrase — more a motif than a melody — repeated seven times with slight modifications. Its directness and urgency defied the prevailing norms on the Montreal scene of the early 1960s and signalled a bold start to the body of work that Ranger completed during the next five years — a body of work, *Challenge* aside, that has been largely lost.

• • •

Claude Ranger and Denyse Desilets met briefly in their mid-teens and again a few years later. They were married in the fall of 1962 and lived for a time on *avenue* de la Salle below Notre Dame East, just eight blocks west of the Rainbow Café. Ranger had moved to the Mocambo by the time their first daughter, Danielle, was born; he was working at the Casa Loma when Suzanne and Sylvie, twins, followed.

In practical terms, Ranger's responsibilities to his family were at odds with the career he hoped to have in jazz. Showbands offered relative stability; even though the number of musicians in their employ from one nightclub to the next was in decline through the 1960s, a drummer of Ranger's skill would have remained in demand. Engagements in jazz clubs, on the other hand, tended to be casual, transient and poorly paid.

Nevertheless, Ranger was understandably ready to put the Casa Loma behind him. "A showband," explains Peter Leitch, "is like the closest you can come to having a day job in music. You go in at the same time every night and you play exactly the same music the same way."

Ranger stayed at the Casa Loma through 1966, possibly into 1967. But his description of his daily routine during this period makes clear his frustration. Before he went to work each night, he noted, he spent his free time writing and arranging music with an eye and an ear to the day when he would be leading his own jazz band.

"When I came back from the Casa Loma," he recalled, "and it's three in the morning, I'd practice until five or six in the basement on my practice pad. That's how much I was angry at myself."

That anger found expression in his drumming when the occasion allowed, as it did when, finally, he began to play jazz. Looking back in a remarkably revealing moment of candour years later, he admitted, "I wanted to play like a fighter. I wanted to play drums like *this*."

He made the sound of an explosion.

"Like *kill* everybody. But not really. It's just that I wanted to make a big fist, like *this*! To play like that means practicing very, very hard. Like really *hit*. Make sure that everything is strong, like Elvin Jones. Elvin's wrists are big; they don't have to work as hard. But me, I'm not as big. Have you seen Max Roach? Max Roach's hands are like *this*!"

He held up his hands, palms wide apart.

"And that's just one hand! That's Max Roach. Tony Williams, he's little, like me. He's bigger here."

He patted a bicep.

"That's all. So it doesn't matter too much, I know, but it used to bother me — being little."

• • •

The year 1967 marked the turning point in Claude Ranger's career. To whatever limited extent he had played jazz in local clubs in 1966, he had done so informally. The scene, in any event, was relatively quiet, with the Black Bottom facing only sporadic competition from the Penthouse, at least until the Barrel Theatre opened its Jazz Workshop in the fall and la Jazztek followed at Café la Bohème toward the end of the year.

As 1967 began, Ranger was heard for the first time with his own band, a quartet whose other members' identities have been lost to history, on CBC radio's *Jazz en liberté*, a weekly series of concerts usually recorded at l'Ermitage for broadcast locally on CBM-AM and CBF-FM and in due course across Canada on the CBC's

French network.

L'Ermitage, a hall built between 1911 and 1913 on the campus of the Collège de Montréal at Sherbrooke Street and Côte-des-Neiges, had been used since the 1940s by various classical ensembles for concerts and by the CBC for such programs as *Radio Carabin* and *Nos futures étoiles*. With the debut of *Jazz en liberté* in 1965, it also became an important showcase for Montreal jazz musicians, offering their fans a comfortable alternative to late nights in small, smokey restaurants and nightclubs.

Ranger's appearance on *Jazz en liberté* vaulted him rather suddenly into the ranks of Montreal's better known jazz musicians, among them trumpeter Herbie Spanier, saxophonists Nick Ayoub and Lee Gagnon, pianists Pierre Leduc and Armas Maiste, vibraphonist Yvan Landry, vibraphonist and drummer Cisco Normand, and bassists Michel Donato and Don Habib, all of whom were heard frequently on the program — as Ranger himself would be during the next few years, both as a leader and a sideman.

So it was that he was back on *Jazz en liberté* in May of 1967 with a septet led by alto saxophonist Maurice Mayer, a septet that was actually Ranger's own in all but name. The compositions and arrangements were his — in order, *Chapitre deux*, *Distortion*, *Entre ciel et terre* (Between Heaven and Earth), *Friday*, *Latin Blues* and *La Machine* — as was the format, one that he would favour for the rest of his career.

"It started when I heard Archie Shepp," he later explained. "Do you remember that band with no piano? Just horns, bass and drum?" Indeed Shepp led several New York bands that answered to that description in the mid-1960s, a succession of sextets, septets and even an octet variously heard on the tenor saxophonist's recordings *Four for Trane*, *Fire Music* and *Mama Too Tight*, each in its way a classic of the New York avant-garde.

Ranger also cited the influence at this time of alto saxophonist Ornette Coleman who, even before Shepp — and in fact for virtually all of his career — worked without a piano. Coleman's recordings from Los Angeles and New York in 1959, *Tomorrow Is the Question*,

The Shape of Jazz to Come and *Change of the Century*, were no less classics of their time, albeit in ways more personal to Coleman than typical of the avant-garde.

Shepp, with his caustic improvisational rhetoric, like Coleman, with his unique melodic conception and his rather personal intonation, would have been constrained by — if not altogether in conflict with — the harmonic framework that a pianist could not help but outline. Ranger, too, was drawn to the same freedom.

"Guys," he remarked, plainly, to John Gilmore, "can go further." But he also spoke appreciatively of one of Coleman's drummers from this period, Ed Blackwell, and in particular of Blackwell's "loose, dancing sound," a sound that would have been a lot less loose and dancing had bassist Charlie Haden not been the only other member of the rhythm section.

The influence of Shepp, Coleman and their contemporaries in the burgeoning avant-garde was new to jazz in Montreal at the turn of 1967, although Cisco Normand had played some of Coleman's compositions at le Mas as early as 1961[3] and Shepp himself would make his presence felt at the Barrel Theatre later in 1967.

In looking forward to Shepp and Coleman for his lead, Ranger was also challenging a tradition that went *back* many years in Montreal, where the piano had come to define the sound of jazz, from the novelty ragtime of Willie Eckstein and Harry Thomas in the late 1910s and the blues of Millard Thomas in the early 1920s to the Swing and bop stylings of Harold (Steep) Wade in the 1940s. With the emergence of Oscar Peterson in the mid-1940s and of Paul Bley in the early 1950s, the tradition was set, Peterson drawing with extravagant virtuosity on everything that had gone before and Bley looking more modestly to what might lie ahead.

Ranger's decision to depart from that tradition apparently did not go unnoticed among Montreal's pianists in the mid-1960s. "They did not like it," he told John Gilmore, dryly. "They were not happy."

At the same time, though, Ranger's attraction to the Shepp and Coleman bands did not mean that his own music in 1967 was comparably avant-garde. Even if Ranger's musicians were able to "go further," they did not in fact go very far. The primary soloists on Maurice Mayer septet's *Jazz en liberté* broadcast were all still following the tenets of bebop — Mayer himself with brimming passion, baritone saxophonist Jean Lebrun with predictable, though dramatic bluster, and trumpeter Herbie Spanier with remarkably detailed clarity and facility.[4]

Ranger's writing was similarly beholden to convention. Two of the pieces on the program were blues, *Chapitre deux* and *Latin Blues,* and two were ballads, *Friday* and *Entre ciel et terre*. Taken altogether, they reveal an unsorted range of influences, from the functional nature of dance band "stocks" and showband arrangements to the colour and counterlines — though not the shapely melodic contouring — of "West Coast" jazz and on again to the near edge of chaos where Charles Mingus often worked, with and without a pianist.

Then, as later, lyricism did not come easily to Ranger. His jazz themes were generally severe and typically brief, his ballads rather plain in their sentimentality. That severity was nevertheless effective on *Distortion,* 24 bars of rhythmic punches, one per bar, with simple four-bar motifs introduced at the fifth, 13th and 21st bars. It also served well the darkly programmatic, dystopian implications of *La Machine*, which was Ranger's most ambitious composition — and substantially his most dissonant — of the broadcast.

The real revelation, however, was his drumming. Less than a year after he was pleased simply to be told that he had started to "sound like Elvin," he was now playing with a degree of assertion and authority that was very much his own. Moreover, the clear, resolute pattern of his cymbal ride — his signature for the next 30 years — was securely in place from the first bars of *Chapitre deux*.

• • •

Maurice Mayer's septet was heard on *Jazz en liberté* in May, not from l'Ermitage but from the Youth Pavilion of Expo 67, the "Universal and International Exhibition" presented between late April and late October of that year on Montreal's St. Helen's and Notre Dame islands as the focus of celebrations honouring the centennial of Canada's confederation.

Mayer was one of many Montreal musicians seen on various stages around the Expo site; *Jazz en liberté* regulars were heavily featured, along with a few noted Canadians from other cities, including Ron Collier, Moe Koffman and Phil Nimmons from Toronto and Lance Harrison from Vancouver. Maynard Ferguson returned home from the United States for concerts with Montreal musicians, and several American stars also made the trip north, among them Dave Brubeck, Duke Ellington and Thelonious Monk, each with his own band.

Claude Ranger, meanwhile, spent much of this same period downtown — west of St. Lawrence Boulevard, finally — with Lee Gagnon at la Jazztek, his first steady job as a jazz musician. He was 26.

"When Lee Gagnon asked me if I wanted to play with him at la Jazztek," he later explained, "I quit showbands. I decided I never wanted to work again except for jazz. That's when I decided, which was very hard."

Quite so. No less than his first club engagement of *any* sort eight years earlier at the Lantern Café, la Jazztek immediately revealed the realities and attendant compromises that lie ahead, a variety of commercial imperatives at odds with the integrity of the music that Ranger had been preparing himself to play.

La Jazztek, a second floor room at the Café la Bohème on Guy Street just above St. Catherine, attempted initially, and with some success, to be both a jazz club and a discotheque. John Norris, whose comments in *Coda* reflected the perspective of someone on the jazz side of la Jazztek's business equation, described the club as "a curious place," and noted with implicit disdain that it "plays hit parade discs between sets for the gyrating customers of the club."[5]

In truth, a nightspot in Montreal — or Toronto, or Vancouver — whose sole attraction was jazz could not hope to be financially successful for very long, any more than a musician whose sole focus was jazz — at least a musician without an international profile.

La Jazztek and its bandleader were both cases in point. Lee Gagnon had as high a profile as any jazz musician in Montreal during the 1960s, but left the club in 1968 and, for all intents and purposes, put jazz behind him a few years later. La Jazztek continued less ambitiously with Nelson Symonds, late of the Black Bottom, through 1971.

Gagnon's two-year run at la Jazztek was nevertheless eventful. Many musicians came and went, Ranger staying as long as any of them, although not without interruptions. He was in place by April of 1967, alongside pianist Art Roberts and bassist Michel Donato, when Gagnon recorded the LP *Le* [sic] *Jazztek* for Capitol Records.

Few were the recordings by Montreal jazz musicians during this period, and fewer still by jazz musicians elsewhere in Canada. In the years after Oscar Peterson made his first 78s for Victor in the mid-1940s, the city's jazz scene was represented on commercial LPs only by the Canadian All Stars with saxophonist Al Baculis and others in 1955, pianist Milt Sealey in 1957 and 1961, Nick Ayoub in 1964, Pierre Leduc in 1965 and Yvan Landry in 1966 and 1967.[6]

Le Jazztek was the first of three Gagnon LPs between 1967 and 1969. It also marked Ranger's debut on record, and a most confident debut it was, at times almost rambunctiously so. He held little back as Gagnon, moving plainly, if rather shrilly between tenor saxophone, alto saxophone and flute, led the quartet through two of his own compositions and the jazz standards *Take Five*, *Summertime*, *How Insensitive* and *Con Alma*.

Le Jazztek also captured Ranger and Michel Donato at a very early stage — scarcely months along — in what would become a formidable partnership that continued until the mid-1970s. Like Ranger, Donato, 18 months younger, had worked in Montreal showbands at the outset of his career, but moved on to jazz in 1964, when he joined Pierre Leduc's trio at Jazz Hot. His style was propulsive, his technique spry, his ideas audacious and his sound deep and dark, combining elements of his acknowledged influences, Oscar Pettiford, Scott LaFaro and Charles Mingus, to very personal effect.

He and Ranger were quick to establish a rapport. "We had a ball together," Donato marvels. "We *knew*. We could feel each other — in half a bar. I liked to fool around, because that's what he liked. But then we always ended up landing on our feet — like a cat — at the same time."

Reviewing *Le Jazztek* for *Coda*, Len Dobbin had little praise for Gagnon, but identified Ranger as "one of the very best drummers in town" — this, after only a few months actively on the scene — and suggested that the record was "definitely worth having for the rhythm section." While he regretted the fact that Roberts, Donato and Ranger were not backing a soloist "the calibre of, say, Herbie Spanier," he added, pointedly, "the fact that Gagnon is a better business man than jazz soloist is probably the reason the LP exists at all."[7]

John Norris, who visited la Jazztek shortly after the recording was made, also found much to like about Gagnon's rhythm section, which by then had Pierre Leduc in Roberts' place. Gagnon himself was absent that evening, offering Norris "an opportunity to hear the brilliance of pianist Pierre Leduc and the integrated and sparkling support of bassist Michel Donato and drummer Claude Ranger." Comparing their "rhythmic feel and approach" to that of Herbie Hancock, Ron Carter and Tony Williams — the Montreal musicians' counterparts in Miles Davis' rhythm section of the day — Norris noted, "there was much the same flexibility and ease of change in the music of this threesome."[8]

Gagnon recorded his second LP, *Je Jazze*, in September of 1968, with Ranger, Leduc, trumpeter Ron Proby and bassist Roland Haynes. *Je Jazze* was rather more substantial than *Le Jazztek*, if only for its emphasis on original compositions by Gagnon, Proby, Leduc and the Montreal guitarist Richard Ring in a variety of modern styles. Proby's affinity for hard-bop rang especially true, both in his tunes, *Visage* and *Strut,* and in his playing, while Ranger was again an aggressive participant, at times almost to the point of belligerence — "like a fighter," as he would say later, "like *kill* everyone."

Ranger had long since left la Jazztek by the time *Je Jazze* was released in November of 1968, but his tenure there established him on the scene as both a player and a personality. His exposure with Gagnon, at la Jazztek and on record, was compounded by his appearances on *Jazz en liberté* with his own bands, as well as with Leduc, Proby, Herbie Spanier, alto saxophonist Bob Roby and others.

His work with Gagnon also brought him to the attention of two musicians who would play important roles in his career during the 1970s and 1980s, pianist and bassist Don Thompson and guitarist Sonny Greenwich, both newly arrived in Montreal during the summer of 1967 after working stateside with the popular American alto saxophonist John Handy.

Thompson, like Ranger a product essentially of his own invention, has been a marvel among Canadian musicians for his mastery of two instruments that have little in common procedurally, piano and bass, and his skill on two more, vibraphone and drums — all played with an unassumingly adaptable sensibility that extends over a wide range of styles, from mainstream jazz to the near avant-garde. Once settled in Toronto, as he was by 1968, he became a cornerstone of the local studio and club scenes; in the most venturesome aspects of that role, he often employed or played alongside Ranger. Their first encounter, however, was in Montreal.

"Sonny and I were playing with Lee at the Jazztek," Thompson remembers, harking back to a point later that year when Ranger was not working at the club. "Lee just happened to mention that he was rehearsing a big band. Maybe we'd like to come by the next day? He told us where it was — it was in a school. When we got there, we couldn't find the room. We could *hear* the band playing, but we couldn't find it. But as we were getting closer, the band sounded great, and I thought to myself how good the rhythm section was, because it was *really* swinging. And then, when we finally found the room, and looked in, there was no bass, there was no piano, there was only Claude. And I think he might have had his little bass drum — a tom-tom on its side — and one cymbal, a snare drum and a hi-hat. That was it, that's all he had. He was the whole rhythm section."[9]

CHAPTER FOUR

Aquarius Rising

"If I get one good horn player, I'm straight," Claude Ranger once remarked. "The thing is, it's hard to find someone who can improvise their own way, not the way everyone does it on record, but new, fresh."

His search, which he undertook repeatedly throughout his career, had something of a Diogenean quality to it. Ranger's "honest man" was a saxophonist unreservedly of his or her own mind — a rarity in Canada, where jazz musicians looked for their lead precisely to the way their American counterparts did it "on record," as indeed he himself had initially looked to Max Roach, Elvin Jones and Tony Williams.

At some point in the summer of 1967, however, he met Brian Barley at la Jazztek.[1] "Right away," he remembered, "the first time I played with him — I was working with Lee Gagnon — I said, 'Lee, I'm joining Brian, we're making a band!'"

As in fact they did, although neither as quickly as Ranger seemed to imply, nor at the expense of his place with Gagnon's quartet at la Jazztek; Ranger would continue to work there intermittently well into

1968. Whatever the timing of events, he had found in Barley a saxophonist who was willing and able to "go further" — someone, moreover, who knew about Archie Shepp and Ornette Coleman, as well as about John Coltrane, Eric Dolphy and especially Sonny Rollins.[2]

Barley was not unique in Montreal during the 1960s in his openness at least to Rollins and Coltrane. Wimp Henstridge had been influenced by Rollins, as had Alvin Pall by Coltrane. Ron Park, who moved between Toronto and Montreal in this period, had listened closely to Rollins and Coltrane in turn, although primarily to their late-1950s, hard-bop recordings. Barley, never comfortably a bebopper, looked instead to later Coltrane, and to the 1960s avant-garde more generally, retaining something of Rollins' syntax in his solos but finding his own voice in the expressive extremes explored by Coltrane, Coleman and Shepp.

Barley and Ranger had spent most of their respective professional lives to that point on very different paths. Barley — younger by almost two years, originally from Toronto and the son of a United Church minister — seemed destined for a career as a clarinetist in classical music. He had been a member for three seasons of the National Youth Orchestra of Canada and had played on occasion in the Cleveland Orchestra and the Vancouver Symphony Orchestra, all the while dabbling in jazz as a secondary interest.

In May of 1966, however, he suffered a severe head injury in an automobile accident en route back to Vancouver from a concert by pianist Bill Evans in Seattle. The epileptic seizures that followed, and the medication that he took to control them — no less than the recreational drugs that he used to offset the side effects of the medication — left him increasingly at odds with the formalities of the classical world, and they with him.

Although he continued to work from time to time in that realm after he moved to Montreal in the fall of 1966, he found more comfort, musically and socially, with the city's jazz community. He established himself quickly enough to take his place in the bands that Maynard Ferguson staffed locally for concerts at Expo 67, a sextet in May and a big band in June.

Though gentle by nature, a man of fashion and quite humorous, he could be headstrong on the bandstand. His sense of purpose and his intensity as an improviser brought him opportunities to work with Pierre Leduc, Ron Proby and Herbie Spanier, all of whom valued such qualities in a bandmate. He also played in the fall of 1968 with the American drummer Charles Moffett, lately of the Ornette Coleman Trio.[3]

But those same qualities also came at a price. "Brian had quite a hard time," Ranger notes. "He really wanted to play. Every time he had a gig, he wanted to play so much, really *play*, that he kind of *over*played it. So he was never hired very often. It seemed as though there was only one kind of music for him, one kind of playing, and that's what he did."

Ranger might well have been describing himself in the later years of his own career. For the moment, though, he and Barley, kindred spirits, worked in each other's bands on *Jazz en liberté*, crossed paths in Lee Gagnon's absence at la Jazztek — evidently Barley was not welcome otherwise — and appeared together with Proby and Spanier at the Black Bottom.

"Brian is probably why I play jazz," Ranger once observed. "It was with him that I went 'outside' a little bit." On another occasion he admitted, "It seems to me that Brian's the one who taught me how to play jazz, because he was a 'heavy' and I was very fortunate to play with him."

At the very least, Barley affirmed the viability of Ranger's determination to strive for a level of freedom and expression that went beyond the norm in Montreal. Together, they formed a trio in 1968 with Michel Donato and committed themselves to rehearsals that could run seven or eight hours a day at Barley's residence on Lincoln Avenue. And even that, apparently, was not enough for Ranger.

"Michel, he would drive me nuts," he complained later. "He used to stop and go off for *lunch*."

And if not lunch, Donato would break away no less pragmatically for studio work; he, alone among the three musicians, played in Montreal's radio, television and recording orchestras. Ranger and Barley simply continued on without him.

"We had more fun, just Brian and me," Ranger remembered. "Just drums and tenor. We used to play outside on the street — for nothing. But lots of people. The music was something very scary for Montreal, but everybody loved it. We used to play for nothing! Five dollars, two dollars, six dollars!"

Jazz en liberté broadcasts aside, opportunities for all three musicians together were scarce. "I believe that we were the only ones to play this type of music in Montreal," Donato told Alain Brunet of *La Presse* in 2003, noting the inspiration that they had taken from Sonny Rollins' trio with Oscar Pettiford and Max Roach, which had recorded *The Freedom Suite* in 1958, and pointing to the latitude that they enjoyed in the same format. "In this sense, we were a bit ahead of our time."[4]

Ranger positioned the Barley trio in similar, if more general terms. "It was a good band," he suggested in 1981. "Stronger than any bands coming out today. Stronger, as in crazy — not knowing where we were going. We just kept going. 'OK, what's *next,*' *yo*u know?"

For *Jazz en liberté*, Ranger, Barley and Donato took turns as the trio's nominal leader; they also served on occasion at l'Ermitage as the core of other bands — a Ranger quartet with Pierre Leduc in May 1968, for example, and a Donato quartet with trumpeter Alan Penfold in May 1969. The latter band's performance was issued on CD under Donato's name 35 years later as *Jazz en liberté*, along with a piece by the trio from another broadcast in the series.[5]

More formally, the trio recorded eight compositions in January 1969 at the Studio André Perry in Brossard, across the Champlain Bridge from downtown Montreal. Barley was responsible for five of the themes, Ranger for one — *Showbar* — and Donato for one. The eighth was George Gershwin's *Liza*.

Ranger later claimed that he stopped writing once he met Barley. "I started to change things up. I just felt like not working so hard anymore, not writing all day. So I just stopped — and started playing drums again."

Indeed, *Showbar*, if only by its title, harked back to an earlier period in his career; like another Ranger composition in the trio's repertoire, *Challenge*, from 1963, it is a rather sly piece, just a vaguely sinister, eight-bar melody thrice repeated, the second time modulated a half step up.

In any event, it was — no less than Barley's *Ready by Three*, *Mystery*, *Loneliness* (or *Oneliness*), *Tri-Tonality* (or *Try Tonality*) and *Hazel*, Donato's *Aimé* and even Gershwin's *Liza* — of rather incidental consequence, so widely did the three musicians range from the skeletal structure that it implied and the motifs that it offered for further development.

Barley, Donato and Ranger improvised together in a way that was open rather than free, at least in the sense that "free" has been understood in the context of avant-garde jazz. Their explorations were rhythmically grounded but melodically impulsive, their interaction both suggestible and immediately responsive. Barley's exuberance as a tenor saxophonist and — on *Aimé* and especially *Mystery* — as a bass clarinetist, set the temper of the music; Ranger, very much in his element, responded in kind, his small drums tuned tight — hard, unyielding surfaces sharply struck — and his cymbals brash. He swung fiercely or not at all, playing tension against release with crescendos that exploded in a clatter of sound, as though his drum set had collapsed beneath him with a shudder and a crash.

It was heady stuff for Canada in 1969, had Canada only known. The recording, more than sufficient in length for an LP, was never issued.

• • •

If Ranger had in fact stopped writing during the period in which he was working with Brian Barley, he nevertheless had an outlet for his older compositions on *Jazz en liberté*. Pierre Leduc presented *Showbar*, as well as Ranger's *Soir d'automne* ("Autumn Eve") and

Wizard Spice with a septet in October of 1968. Ranger led his own septet at l'Ermitage on a number of occasions and in January 1969 supplemented a quintet with two trumpets and three trombones to play what were effectively big band versions of his compositions *Réflexion*, *La Machine*, *Beau temps, mauvais temps* (Good Times, Bad Times), *Shelah* and *Le Revenant* (The Ghost).[6]

Réflexion and *Le Revenant* were fairly conventionally in the big band tradition; Ranger's playing was an idiomatic match — assertive yet precise in a way that suggested that he had listened to Guy Nadon and his fellow East-end drummers, with their Swing styles, even as he himself was drawn to the bop style that flourished in Montreal's west end.

La Machine, heard previously on *Jazz en liberté* as played by the Maurice Mayer Septet, turned even more ominously dystopian — more severely dissonant — with the additional horns. Ranger typically reworked his compositions over time, always looking for something new or more — always wanting to "go further."

Ultimately, however, he arranged the five pieces around the quintet and gave three of its members, Pierre Leduc, Ron Proby and saxophonist Léo Perron, the lion's share of the hour. He clearly revelled in the weight and drama that the brass section — the trombones especially — gave his lines and counterlines, but he stopped shy of developing each composition into a fully orchestrated work. Understandably so, given the effort involved; the *Jazz en liberté* broadcast may well have been the tentet's only performance.

• • •

Ranger, Barley and Donato remained sporadically active as a trio until Donato left for Toronto late in 1969, discouraged in part by the insistence, especially in Montreal studios, that he should put aside the acoustic bass — an instrument on which he had few, if any Canadian peers — in favour of the bass guitar.

"They told me the acoustic bass was finished," he explains. "That's why I left. I was mad. I said, '*I ain't* finished!' And the first gigs I got when I moved to Toronto were with Don Thompson and Terry Clarke and with Sonny Greenwich. So I stayed. Then I met a guitar player there. I went and knocked on his door.

"I said, 'My name is Michel Donato. I play bass.'

"He said, 'Come up.' Lenny Breau. Amazing."

Ranger and Barley, meanwhile, continued into 1970 with a new bassist, Daniel Lessard, and a new name, Aquarius Rising. Lessard, six years younger than Ranger, had recently arrived from Quebec City after two years stateside at the Berklee College of Music in Boston. Like Donato, he found little call for acoustic bassists in Montreal; unlike Donato, he switched more willingly to an electric, even to the point of playing it — a Hofner, the instrument made famous by the Beatles' Paul McCartney — with Aquarius Rising.

The trio came by its name honestly. Ranger and Lessard were both Aquarians. Barley was a Sagittarian with Aquarius rising, a planetary aspect that he used as the title of the composition that became the trio's theme. Coincidentally, the song *Aquarius* from the epochal rock musical *Hair!* was an international hit in the spring of 1969, introducing astrological references into everyday conversation.

Whatever commercial considerations may have gone into the decision to adopt the new name, they went no further. "The group title," Ron Sweetman observed in an admiring review that appeared in *Coda*, "conceals not a mess of electronic jangle, but three dedicated young jazz musicians who would cut less ice with today's audience if they were known as the Brian Barley Trio, or Le Trio Claude Ranger."[7]

As it was, Aquarius Rising scarcely cut much more, although it did find some work in 1970 at a spot on Crescent Street known as Oliver, and a coffee house in suburban Dorval, the Shire, as well as the Café Baudelaire in Quebec City and Meat and Potatoes in Toronto.

Aquarius Rising, The Shire, Dorval, Quebec, July 1970.
Photograph by Ron Sweetman, as published in Coda, *October 1970.*

It also made its first and only recording in June of that year for inclusion under Barley's name in the series of Radio Canada International transcription LPs that the CBC used to promote Canadian music abroad via diplomatic missions, radio networks, libraries and music schools in other countries. Some of these recordings were leased domestically to commercial labels in Canada, including sessions by Lee Gagnon and Don Thompson in 1969 and Sonny Greenwich in 1970;[8] others were available more obscurely to the public on a mail-order basis for all of two dollars, postage included.[9]

In the years around 1970, the RCI program under the direction of Edward Farrant supplemented and ultimately surpassed Canada's commercial recording industry in the documentation of the country's jazz musicians; *Brian Barley Trio* stands among the classic recordings in the Canadian jazz discography, along with other RCI albums from that period by Greenwich, Paul Bley and Pierre Leduc.[10]

Barley recorded five compositions, four of them his own — *Plexidance, Schlucks, Two by Five* and *Oneliness.* The fifth was Ranger's *Le Pingouin,* a variant blues whose descending, chromatic four-note bass vamp evoked a penguin's waddle, with a rather jolly melody on top to heighten the comic effect and a series of short single-note glisses to suggest, perhaps, slips and slides on the ice.

Ranger enjoyed writing descriptively, at times programmatically. In that regard, his explanation of the concept behind another of his compositions, the unrecorded *Kono,* holds equally well for *Le Pingouin.* "Inspiration can hit you anywhere," he explained in an interview with Greg Gallagher for *Canadian Composer.* "Many times I'd just be looking outside at what was around me and it would happen. Then there are those pure moments of imagination, like my tune *Kono.* It's a musical fantasy about an elephant and it uses a particular rhythmic idea to communicate the elephant's presence."[11]

Beyond its inherent charm, *Le Pingouin* also served as a showcase for Ranger's drumming. Twice in the 10-minute performance on the Barley LP — once to introduce the theme for the first time and again to reintroduce it for the last — he played at length off that brief bass vamp, setting out a deft pattern of counter figures on snare, bass drum, hi-hat and ride cymbal in the manner of Max Roach, and then breaking into a brisk, galloping sort of swing irresistibly his own.

Le Pingouin was one of at least six Ranger compositions in the trio's broader repertoire,[12] along with *Challenge, Showbar* and three pieces included on a *Jazz en liberté* broadcast under Barley's name in June of 1969, *Soir d'automne, Monking Bird* and *Blues pour vous.* The apparent allusions in *Monking Bird* to Thelonious Monk and Charlie Parker were not supported by the piece itself, which was — no less than *Blues pour vous* — simply another of Ranger's typically short, functional themes of the sort that served the trio's sense of immediacy so well.

Brian Barley Trio would prove to be the only recording of the trio in either of its forms, with Donato or with Lessard, to be released publicly. In 1972, Edward Farrant deemed it "by far the most popular" of the LPs that RCI had made available by mail-order, but added realistically, "we are not expecting huge sales."[13]

• • •

Brian Barley and Claude Ranger were not alone in challenging the status quo on the Montreal scene during the late 1960s. If anything, they were eclipsed in that regard by the Quatuor de Jazz Libre du Québec, familiarly known as Jazz Libre — literally, "free jazz."

Jazz libre came together during the eventful summer of 1967, when tenor saxophonist Jean Préfontaine, trumpeter Yves Charbonneau, bassist Maurice Richard and drummer Guy Thouin fell under the sway of the New York avant-garde of the day, drawing on the immediate influence of the African-American musicians who were appearing at the Barrel Theatre, which operated as a coffee house in the basement of a former Canadian Legion building on Mountain Street, below St. Catherine.

Unlike the fashionable Jazztek at Café la Bohème, just four blocks away, the Barrel was decidedly downscale, reflecting the modest prospects of a new style of jazz with little commercial appeal. Geoffrey Young, writing in *Coda,* described the club as inexpensive, dimly lit, with barrels for tables and a diffident waiter who "operates as if you want nothing but the music."[14]

The Barrel's lineup during the summer and fall included the bands of Archie Shepp, alto saxophonist Marion Brown, drummer Sunny Murray and Shepp's fellow tenor saxophonists Albert Ayler and Frank Wright, all of whom gave fierce expression to the spirit of the civil rights movement that was roiling the ghettos of America's major cities — a sentiment with which Jean Préfontaine and Yves Charbonneau, in particular, felt some kinship from their own disaffected socio-political perspective as *independentistes* in Quebec.

Jazz Libre itself worked fairly obscurely at the Barrel during the winter of 1967-8, then saw both its profile and its notoriety soar in 1968 and 1969 when it appeared with the iconoclastic singer and songwriter Robert Charlebois in his revues *Peuple à genoux, l'Osstidcho* and *l'Osstidchomeurt*. The quartet played rock music in support of Charlebois and his fellow singers Louise Forestier and Mouffe, but returned to character when it was featured on its own in Préfontaine's *Stalisme dodécaphonique*.

At some point in 1969, Charlebois invited Brian Barley, Daniel Lessard and Claude Ranger to a rehearsal with Jazz Libre as the first step toward enlarging his backing ensemble. The two bands spent a long day playing together with — from Lessard's perspective[15] — little to show for the effort. Aquarius Rising, even at its freest, never entirely abandoned structure, something that Jazz Libre only selectively embraced, preferring — as Guy Thouin explained to Eric Fillion years later — "to proceed without themes, without regular rhythms and without chords."[16]

Lessard advised Barley and Ranger that, as far he was concerned, one "rehearsal" with Jazz Libre was enough. Accordingly, the two bands never played together again, although Barley and Lessard worked individually with Charlebois — Barley before he left Montreal for Toronto in 1970 and Lessard a few years after Jazz Libre had parted company with Charlebois in order to follow its own, increasingly politicized path.

• • •

Aquarius Rising took two of its last engagements in Toronto at Meat and Potatoes, a small, unlicensed restaurant on Huron Street at the western edge of the University of Toronto campus. The club's location — which was three blocks due south of Rochdale College, the heart of Toronto's hippie community at the time — determined its clientele, which in turn defined its counter-cultural, *laissez-faire* ambiance.

"In this restaurant," Bob Levant, its owner, told Jack Batten of the *Toronto Star*, "the chef does his thing, the waiters do theirs, the physical space does its things, the musicians theirs, and we all just wait for all of them to come together."[17]

The musicians were young and generally venturesome — the pianist Ted Moses and the guitarists Sonny Greenwich and Michael (later Tisziji) Muñoz, for three, and the ensembles I Ching and Syrinx, all of them too progressive in one respect or another for the *other* restaurant in Toronto that was presenting local jazz musicians in 1970, George's Spaghetti House. Aquarius Rising would have seemed a natural booking at Meat and Potatoes if only for its descriptive name, although its music was, if anything, *more* venturesome — and certainly more visceral — than that of the local musicians on the restaurant's roster.

Rarely in this period did Montreal jazz musicians make the 500-kilometre trip west to perform in Toronto; nor did Toronto musicians often travel east to Montreal. The two cities had stronger connections to the New York jazz scene than with each other; musicians in Montreal and Toronto may have been aware of their counterparts, if only by reputation, but a fan in Toronto would have known of Barley and Ranger, if at all, only from *Jazz en liberté*, which was heard on the CBC's local French station, CJBC.

Aquarius Rising made the trip for the first time in September, its arrival in Toronto noted with some uncertainty by the *The Globe and Mail*: "Described as a new jazz trio from Montreal, Aquarius Rising features Brian Barley on tenor; Claude Rauger, drums; and Daniel Lasard, bass."[18]

The trio returned more eventfully in October, according to Greg Gallagher, who was travelling with the three musicians for the occasion. Montreal at the time was in the grip of the "October Crisis" precipitated by the criminal activities, including kidnapping and murder, undertaken by the Front de Libération du Québec in support of its campaign for Quebec sovereignty.

The Canadian army was patrolling the city's streets when the four musicians left for Toronto via the Décarie Expressway. "It was about 3 in the morning, after we had finished our various gigs," Gallagher recalls, "so we packed the instruments into the back of the station wagon. I guess somebody saw us in the car, four guys with long hair, and stuff in the back that looked nefarious. They pulled us over with machine guns drawn. It was serious. I was afraid for my life, because these guys were more scared than we were. They thought we had dynamite in the back of the car."[19]

In fact, all they had — in terms of explosive devices — were Ranger's drums.

The trauma of the trio's departure was offset by the warmth of its welcome in Toronto, culminating in an invitation at the end of one evening at Meat and Potatoes from Lilly Barnes, a writer and political activist, to repair to her home a short walk north.

"We spent the rest of the night," Barnes remembers, "talking, smoking and having a wonderful time. Because the band had been so great, and the music had been so exciting, we all had a kind of buzz. We sat around and talked and about 7 or 8 in the morning we went out for cigarettes and then sat around and talked some more.

"I remember that evening as being kind of a big discussion about Toronto versus Montreal and they were definitely excited about what they heard about was going on in Toronto and decided, I think, pretty well then and there, that they were going to come here.

"I think Brian decided that night that he wanted to move. That's how I remember it. I don't remember if Claude decided that night, but I think that it had a big influence on his decision. Things weren't going very well in Montreal."[20]

Chapter Five

La Misère

Claude Ranger smoked, although he suggested to friends that he did not inhale. He drank beer. He took "222s" washed down with Coca-Cola to relieve the pain of an injury that he had suffered as a boy to one of his arms — pain that remained with him throughout his career. At some point in the late 1960s, he had also become addicted to amphetamines, specifically to a small, pink diet pill marketed as Preludin.

"One day I was really fucked up," he admitted plainly, "so I took drugs for four years. Don't ask me about that. I did everything as crazy as possible, everything except shooting. Some guy came around and offered me some speed. I took it. And then he offered me a gig. So I took both. I started to play, and the speed started to do something, and I didn't stop for four years. It destroyed my family, destroyed everything."

Four years. Or five, as he told John Gilmore. Possibly fewer. Ranger's sense of time — as measured in months and years, rather than quarter and eighth notes — was approximate and may have reflected how long a given period *felt*, not how long it was in fact. Whatever its duration, he would be done with *la misère*, as he described it to Gilmore, by early 1972, at which point he began a new chapter in his career. For the time being, he found himself working less and less.

. . .

Ranger's vow at la Jazztek in 1967 that, henceforth, he would only play jazz, proved unrealistic. He returned to the world of showbands on at least two occasions, the first almost immediately with pianist Shirley Price at the Chez Paree that very summer and the second with Marcel Doré at the Casa Loma in 1970, backing *Touch of Venus*, a "Nude Musical Revue" starring the singer Marilyn Apollo, a pick-pocket comedian and 11 dancing girls.

The Doré band, by then reduced to a quartet with the leader moving from piano to organ, included Peter Leitch, who came to appreciate the way in which Ranger handled the various demands of the music that they were required to play. "He'd throw in a few surprises, but nothing that was vastly out of the context of the music that was happening," Leitch remembers. "I always got the impression that he was really just committed to music, *whatever* it was."

A show was still a show, of course, but some shows were more interesting than others in terms of the contributions that the musicians were allowed to make. According to Leitch, *Touch of Venus* was one. "It seems to me that there were sections of the music that opened up, where you could play a solo for 32 bars. Some shows, you couldn't. Particularly in theatres. In clubs, it was a little looser. That particular show had some space written into it, and that's why it was really fun to do it with Claude. When you *did* have a chance to play, you didn't want some hack back there."

. . .

One night after work at the Casa Loma, Ranger and Leitch adjourned to the Diana Restaurant, a musicians' haunt farther west on St. Catherine Street near Guy. There they ran into Guy Nadon, equally a legend and a character on the Montreal scene for his extraordinary skill and his colourful behaviour. As Leitch recalls it, the encounter was revealing of the complex dynamic that existed between the two drummers, and also — in passing — of Ranger's personal circumstances at the time.

"The conversation started and Claude said, 'Why are we paying for beer when I've got a case at my house?' Claude was living in Pointe-aux-Trembles at that time, and there was no sign of a wife, or girlfriend, or children. The apartment was very, very sparse. There was hardly any furniture as I remember.

"Sure enough, Claude had this big case of beer, and immediately he and Guy whipped out the drum sticks and started showing each other stuff, drumming on the kitchen chairs. As they got more and more drunk — I'm just sitting there sipping on a beer, because I wasn't into drinking at that point — they got more and more hostile, banging out these rhythms, paradiddles and stuff, trying to outdo each other, I guess. By the time I left, they were just screaming at each other."

Nadon, seven years older, was already well established when Ranger started his career in 1959. While the difference in their ages was relatively modest, it was enough to set them a generation apart in terms of their respective idiomatic allegiances. Nadon was the product of the Swing era; Ranger, of bebop and all that followed.

Nevertheless, Nadon's extraordinary level of musicianship — whatever its point of reference — could not help but have inspired Ranger, if only as a measure of what he himself could accomplish coming from the same, relatively isolated cultural milieu of east-end Montreal. Moreover, Nadon's resolute individuality offered Ranger a response to the conundrum as a jazz musician that he later expressed to John Gilmore: "I thought you had to be black to play." Nadon served as compelling evidence to the contrary, even if Ranger would come to look askance at the irrepressible showmanship that inevitably went with it.

"Claude didn't approve of Guy's showboating," suggests bassist Michael Morse, who worked with both men in the 1970s. "Like steering a cymbal on its stand as though he was driving a bus. For Claude, music was serious business."[1]

Morse found Ranger personally to be "a funny guy in a dry, droll sort of way." But, he notes, "one of the things you could possibly criticize about Claude's music is that it was humourless, in the same way that Coltrane's music was — Coltrane was many, many wonderful things, but humorous he wasn't."

Humorous, Guy Nadon was — in a frenetically inventive, theatrical manner born of his boyhood experience playing tins, cans and pie plates arrayed as a mock drum kit for spare change and tips in Montreal parks and nightclubs. He had learned how to entertain an audience even before he had come to own his first *real* set of drums.

In his way, however, Nadon was an even greater iconoclast than Ranger, idiomatically more conservative but conceptually more daring — "the quintessential Montreal jazz drummer," in the words of Lorne Nehring, a younger drummer on the scene in the late 1960s and early 1970s. "He was skilled, but he was also an artist — in the capital 'A' sense. He explored. He pushed the envelope. Claude was more focussed on playing jazz and devoting his energies to the tradition. He wasn't avant-garde in the same way Guy was; to me, Guy always represented the idea that if there's a different way to do it, let's give it a try."[2]

Thus Nadon tried, for example, to make his own drums — small drums, rectangular drums, masonite drums and drums that folded neatly together for ease of carrying. In a nod during the 1980s to his own mythology, he even assembled a new set of tins, cans and pie plates.

Nadon's audacity brought him an enthusiastic following once he finally formed his own band, la Pollution des Sons, in 1974. "In Quebec," Nehring observes, "that was an admired quality — the individual voice, the unique style. It was encouraged. It was cultivated.

It was promoted. It was appreciated."

Ranger himself later described Nadon in a single word. "Crazy." It was his highest accolade. "By 'crazy,'" he elaborated, "I mean, 'something else.' Rare. Played left-handed, right-handed. Very quick, very modern. When you're drumming in Montreal, it's easy to be scared by someone like that."

As indeed Ranger was at first, according to Michel Donato — perhaps in the same way that Ranger had been wary of Elvin Jones in 1965. "I remember that Claude was scared of Guy for a long time. I'd say, 'Let's go see Guy.' He'd say, 'No.' But then, of course, it changed."

Clearly it had changed by 1970, as it would with regard to Elvin Jones a year later. Ranger's own aesthetic was now firmly in place, both in terms of the music that he played and the uncompromising way in which he chose to play it. He was no longer susceptible in either respect to anyone else's influence.

• • •

Ranger and Peter Leitch moved on together in August 1970 from the Casa Loma to the Black Bottom, which had relocated in 1968 from St. Antoine in Little Burgundy to St. Paul Street East in Old Montreal. There, with bassist Freddie McHugh, they worked for several weeks backing Billy Robinson, an American tenor saxophonist new to Montreal from New York and recently a member of Charles Mingus' quintet.

Robinson, who was originally from Fort Worth, Texas, played in the voluble "Texas tenor" tradition introduced to jazz in the 1940s by Illinois Jacquet and Arnett Cobb. He was influenced in this period, however, by the more modern inclinations of Sonny Rollins, and in particular by Rollins' classic 1962 LP *The Bridge*, with guitarist Jim Hall. Robinson cast Leitch in Hall's role and added two standards from that recording, *Where Are You?* and *Without a Song*, to his own repertoire of rather freer original compositions.

"With Billy," Leitch wrote in his autobiography *Off the Books*, "the music was up on another level, more serious than anything I'd previously experienced."[3]

Ranger and McHugh evidently were an inspired team, and the quartet as a whole, known as Evolution's Blend, proved to be a revelation for some of the younger Montreal musicians who heard it at the Black Bottom. One of them, Michael Morse, was working that summer with Quest, a quartet led by drummer Richard Robinson at Jazz et Café in Val-David, north of Montreal, where Brian Barley, an occasional visitor, had spoken effusively of Ranger.

"It was like listening to a Russian soldier talking about The Great Stalin," Morse recalls. "Brian said, 'Claude can do this, Claude can do that...' Our eyes were popping!"

After hearing Ranger at the Black Bottom for themselves, Morse and another member of Quest, violinist Terry King, approached him to play a concert with them at Sir George Williams University. To their surprise, Ranger not only agreed but was willing to meet beforehand for a rehearsal, one that began with his composition *Le Pingouin*.

"The first couple of bars that I played with Claude were one of the most distinct memories of my life," Morse notes, of *Le Pingouin*'s descending bass vamp. "You have lobster-trap moments — you go through them and you can never go back to where you were before — and my understanding of 'jazz time,' of time, of music, of *everything*, just completely changed."

After the concert, Morse and King gave Ranger his share, and their own, of the money that the trio received — $20, maybe $30 altogether — by way of appreciation.[4]

Ranger was also receptive to a similar overture from two other Montreal musicians, younger still, tenor saxophonist Steve Hall and bassist Dave Gelfand, who coincidentally would work at Jazz et Café with Richard Robinson the year after Morse and King. Hall, still a teenager, had become friends with Brian Barley and was influenced, as Barley had been, by Archie Shepp.

"I was into a lot of 'out' stuff," Hall explains, "and Dave and I would play free. We got Claude to bring his drums, on his own dime, all the way out to Vanier College and spend a few hours playing with us. It was exciting at the time; now it seems amazing that he would do that. He was very giving, very open."

Indeed, even as Ranger was enjoying his first direct exposure to the African-American tradition represented by Billy Robinson, he was beginning to lay the foundation for a Canadian legacy of his own.

• • •

Ranger left Robinson in mid-September to travel with Aquarius Rising for the first time to Toronto. Robinson himself finished at the Black Bottom soon after. There would be other Evolution's Blend engagements, including appearances in Dorval, but Ranger otherwise spent the fall of 1970 and much of 1971 taking work when and where he could find it.

By then, Brian Barley had moved to Toronto, where he, too, struggled to make a living and also to control the increasing severity of the side-effects from the medication that he was taking for his seizures. For a time, he shared lodgings with Greg Gallagher in a Spadina Avenue rooming house not far from Meat and Potatoes, the one club where he was welcome to play.

In truth, Barley was as much at odds with Toronto musicians as he had been with their counterparts in Montreal. Again, the most modern of the city's other tenor saxophonists were looking no further than John Coltrane, and more distantly Sonny Rollins, for their lead. Alvin Pall had moved to Toronto from Montreal by then; Ron Park had moved back. Bob Brough, Glenn McDonald and John Tank were new to the scene, McDonald recently arrived from Vancouver, Tank home from studies at the Berklee College of Music in Boston and Brough just then emerging locally.

Perhaps in face of the city's relative conservatism, Barley summoned Ranger from Montreal for a reunion of sorts in March 1971 at Meat and Potatoes with Michel Donato, who was by then comfortably established in Toronto jazz and studio circles, having made the transition that was eluding Barley and in due course would prove problematic for Ranger.

"The trio worked hard to get the music happening," John Norris reported in *Coda* after the three-night stand, "but the small crowds were a disappointment and inspiration seemed to come only occasionally. Barley's extended solos were exploratory, rhythmically varied and always interesting while Ranger's percussion fulfilled a vital parallel commentary."

Evidently unaware of the trio's history in Montreal, Norris continued, "Lack of preparation prevented any real tightness [from] developing in such a short time but it is to be hoped that these musicians will be able to appear on a more regular basis where their obvious talents will have a better chance to coalesce."[5]

Barley returned to Meat and Potatoes at the end of April, by one account with Ranger and Donato again,[6] but by another with different musicians, including Ron Park on bass guitar, the instrument with which he made most of his living, despite his considerable skill as a saxophonist.[7] In a bizarre and tragic near-coincidence, Park died three weeks later of drug-related causes and Barley succumbed three weeks later still, on June 8, to a seizure. He was 28.

Greg Gallagher, who found Barley's body on the floor of his Spadina Avenue room, telephoned Ranger with the news. Ranger simply cursed.

● ● ●

Ranger spent much of 1971 alternating with tenor saxophonist Gerry Labelle as the nominal leader, according to circumstance, of a quartet usually completed by pianist Robert Bouthillier and bassist Claude Boucher. Labelle, Bouthillier and Boucher were all younger musicians, the first of many that Ranger effectively took under his wing.

The presence of a pianist in the quartet, notwithstanding Ranger's aversion to the piano, and the fact that Bouthillier and Boucher both played electric instruments, reflected a certain pragmatism in face of the need to make a living at a time when the Montreal jazz scene was in decline. Only the Café la Bohème and *Jazz en liberté* survived from the late 1960s; writing in the February 1971 issue of *Coda*, Len Dobbin suggested that, but for Nelson Symonds' presence at the café, he "would have to report jazz a dead issue in Montreal."[8]

The Ranger/Labelle quartet often took commercial work, most notably for several months at the Bar du Music Hall, a cabaret on St. Hubert, near *rue* Jean-Talon, where it backed a popular Italian-Canadian recording artist, singer Tony Massarelli, and — according to Terry King, who joined the band on occasion — accompanied participants in a weekly contest for Elvis Presley imitators.

"The same two guys always came," King remembers, capturing the *ambiance déclassée* of the club. "One was known as 'Elvis Presley Canadien' and the other was known as 'Elvis Presley Italien.' 'Elvis Presley Canadien' always won, and they always poured a bucket of water over 'Elvis Presley Italien.'"

On its own, the band was free to play what it wished, largely ignored by the bar's boisterous clientele, which — in King's recollection — preferred drinking to dancing. "The music we played wasn't designed for dancing. It wasn't designed for anything except for us to enjoy ourselves."

Ranger, with his years of showband experience, again responded to the demands of such situations conscientiously and — when dancers were indeed a consideration — with a surprising degree of sensitivity. "Regardless of how boring the music we played for dancers was," Labelle marvels, "Claude would always make magic with it. Always. He would say, 'You've never played a cha-cha like *this* before!'"[9]

Or a merengué — as Michael Morse discovered one night when he heard Ranger backing a singer and an organist at another east-end club. "The hook to the commercial merengué beat," Morse would write years later, "is four sixteenth-notes on the snare drum at the end of the second bar of the pattern, leading to the downbeat: 'ducka-ducka-DUM; ducka-ducka-DUM.' When the tune started my friends and I suddenly felt something utterly marvellous, and didn't know immediately what it was. We soon figured it out. Claude was playing all of the standard accents for the merengue, but was playing the principal figure on the ride cymbal instead of the snare. The first sixteenth-note, he left out altogether. The next was *piano-pianissimo*, the next *pianissimo*, the fourth and last *piano*, in a slight, incredibly controlled crescendo. The effect was magical, profoundly musical, and danceable, too!"[10]

There were, of course, opportunities to play jazz — at le Québécois in Laval, for example, including a week, possibly more, with the American bop pianist Sadik Hakim in Bouthillier's place. Hakim, who had recorded as Argonne Thornton in New York with Charlie Parker in 1945, lived for extended periods in Montreal on two occasions, the second beginning in 1966. He was struggling when Ranger brought him to Labelle's attention.

"Claude told me, 'Sadik is in town. He has no money, he has no place to go, he needs a job.' I wanted to help him, but I was scared. I knew I was not up to his level of playing. Claude said, 'Gerry, anything you can do...'"

Although not an ideal match — Hakim was naturally more comfortable with standards and bebop themes than with Ranger's decidedly contemporary compositions — the necessary accommodations were made. Hakim returned the favour by hiring Ranger for engagements in Dorval, where he replaced Tony Bazley, another American living in Montreal at the time.[11]

The quartet also opened for trumpeter Freddie Hubbard in late summer of 1971 at the Kiosque International of Man and His World on the old site of Expo 67, and, more significantly, shared the stage with Elvin Jones at the end of October at the Esquire Showbar on Stanley Street, below St. Catherine.

Jones was travelling with saxophonist Dave Liebman, bassist Gene Perla and a recent addition to the band, the Czech pianist Jan Hammer. "Piano players I'd heard before were all holding the music back," Jones told Dave Bist of the *Montreal Gazette*,[12] echoing Ranger's thoughts on the same subject. For the moment, though, both drummers had pianists in their bands.

Labelle remembers Jones sitting to one side of the stage and sizing Ranger up during his opening set. "The agreement that we had was that the music was to be non-stop. So they would play a blues and we would take over in mid-tune; they would walk off and we would finish the blues. So we started playing and Elvin wouldn't leave the stage. I could tell from the first night that Elvin just loved Claude."

• • •

It is not clear when, finally, Ranger addressed *la misère*. "I got out of it myself in Montreal," he later explained. "I didn't go out of the house for six months. Everything was scary. Outside, it was scary. It was scary every time a car went by. Anyway, I got out of that. I started to work a little bit, started to drink beer. Went out to see if I could still play. I couldn't. I couldn't play anymore. And then, one day, I said, 'Oh, I'm not feeling too bad.' So I got a gig. I got a gig to play for a singer, or a stripper. Again! Me!"

His account, in its vagueness, is difficult to correlate with any specific event, although he was playing for a singer, Tony Massarelli, at the Bar du Music Hall in 1971. Again, Ranger's sense of time may have been approximate; to that point in his career, there were no obvious periods of inactivity that lasted as long as six months. His conclusion, however, is unmistakeable. More than 10 years into his career, he was back where he had started.

"After doing all that," he continued, taking the story up to early 1972, "I said, 'OK, I'm packing my drums and I'm going to Toronto. Bye!' I left my family and just took the drums — went and lived with Alvin."

Chapter Six

"Thunder and lightning"

It was not an easy decision.

Gerry Labelle remembers driving Claude Ranger and his wife Denyse to the train station in downtown Montreal, there to send him off, alone, to Toronto. "Claude didn't want to leave. He was looking at his wife, and at me, and saying, 'Do I go?'"

His hesitance at that moment notwithstanding, Ranger later admitted that he had been thinking about the move — "getting ready," he said — as early as 1967. He had watched as the opportunities to play jazz in Montreal waned in the course of the next five years and as the other avenues to make a living inevitably led to a sense of *déja entendu*.

For a musician who always wanted to "go further," his encounter with Elvin Jones would have confirmed just how *much* further he could go. Equally, it would have reminded him that he had gone about as far as he could in Montreal.

On the other hand, he was leaving not only his family but his culture and his language; Michel Donato aside, the musicians who had preceded Ranger from Montreal to Toronto or were moving back and forth between the two cities — Brian Barley, Alvin Pall, Ron Park, and Herbie Spanier of late, Oscar Peterson, trumpeter Guido Basso and pianist Maury Kaye in years previous — were all anglophones.

Moreover, Barley and Park would soon die in Toronto; Ranger had worked with Park in Ron Proby's band in 1969 at the Black Bottom and on *Jazz en liberté*.

"*Câline*," he asked John Gilmore. "That's what happens in Toronto?"

In truth, Barley and Park died under circumstances that were specific to their own lives. But Toronto could be hard on a musician who was inclined to think for himself, as Barley did and as Ranger inevitably would. Ranger learned soon enough the difference between the exuberance of jazz in Montreal and the more temperate ethos of jazz in Toronto — the difference between the guitar styles of Nelson Symonds and Ed Bickert, for example, or the big bands of Vic Vogel and Rob McConnell.

"I find that guys in Montreal are more 'black,' less afraid," he himself suggested when asked by Gilmore to compare the two cities. "If they take more chances, they're not afraid. They *play*. Like Guy Nadon — like a madman. He's not afraid. He *plays*. In Toronto, guys take fewer chances. It's safer. That doesn't mean they're not as good. I find that guys in Toronto know much more — Bernie Senensky, Ted Moses, they *know*. Moe Koffman. They know how to play, these guys. But it's not free, not wild."

As much as he loved freedom and risk, Ranger also valued knowledge and discipline. What Montreal and Toronto offered in those various respects was almost conversely proportionate; what one lacked, the other had, and by 1972 Toronto had what Ranger wanted, if for no other reason than it was something different.

"I needed to hear other things, new things," he told John Gilmore, reducing his decision to its most fundamental level. And when he

encouraged Terry King to follow suit two years later, his justifica-
tion — as King recalls it — was effectively an affirmation of that
decision. "Claude said, basically, 'This is where the really great
musicians are. If you want to play this music seriously, you should
be here, not Montreal.'"

Still, Brian Barley's experience in Toronto would have been a
caution. "What happened to him here?" Ranger wondered years
later. "What did the guys do to him? Stop him from working? I
always thought Moe would never give him a chance. That, I'm
pretty sure of."

Of course, Ranger would scarcely have known on his arrival in
Toronto of the power that flutist and saxophonist Moe Koffman
exercised over the prospects of the city's jazz musicians as the
booking agent for George's Spaghetti House, 16 years in business on
the northwest corner of Dundas and Sherbourne streets and a haven
on his watch for many — though not all — of Toronto's modernists.

As it happened, and with little fanfare, Ranger found work fairly
quickly. By the summer of 1972 he was playing at George's with
Koffman's apparent blessing and once even with Koffman himself.
Some of his first engagements, however, were with Bernie Senensky,
both as a member of the pianist's quintet at Jazzland, an after-hours
club on College Street, and with a Senensky trio that accompanied
singer Salome Bey for an African Liberation Day event. He also
worked at Jazzland with Alvin Pall in this period and at another
short-lived after-hours spot, the Chameleon Club on Yonge Street,
with Lenny Breau.

The local press soon began to take notice. Ranger had been largely
ignored during his Montreal years, save for passing references in
Coda that culminated in Ron Sweetman's review of Aquarius Rising.
Now, one of that same publication's Toronto writers, Alan Offstein,
and *The Globe and Mail*'s jazz critic, Alastair Lawrie, were not only
taking note of his presence but attempting to capture something of
his drumming and its impact.

Offstein, who heard Ranger with both Senensky and Bey in

May, described the drummer as being "of the Ed Blackwell school, exploring all the territory of his surfaces in an unrelenting flow"[1] in the former instance, and complimented him for "a beautiful style on his instrument"[2] in the latter.

Lawrie was more ambivalent in his response to Ranger's work alongside Michel Donato at George's in July, first with Lenny Breau and then with Moe Koffman. His characterization of Ranger and Donato, with Koffman, as "the thunder-and-lightning kids from Montreal" was evidently not intended as a compliment, but it came with a favourable qualification. "Unhappy as I may have been with the volcanic nature of Ranger's drumming," Lawrie continued, "I have to admit that technically it is superb. He appears to be capable of almost infinite variation."[3]

Offstein, meanwhile, continued to follow Ranger's activities in Toronto through the summer, including his work at George's and his appearances at the Banana Factory, yet another after-hours club, midtown on Merton Street. Offstein was particularly impressed by the way in which Ranger accompanied the singer Dianne Brooks when he sat in with organist Terry Logan's band at the Banana Factory.

"Ranger demonstrated his incredible ability to swing popular songs," he wrote, "donating marvellous fills, dynamics and tone shadings to each number." But he also sounded a note of caution. "Somehow we got the feeling Ms. Brooks is not too keen on his style of playing."

That reaction, if true, appears to have been more the exception than the rule during his first months in Toronto. "Wherever Ranger plays," Offstein noted, "you can be sure to find a tight circle of musicians digging him, and such was the case at George's. He constitutes such a compelling musical force that he is compelling even establishment cats like Koffman to experiment with new modes of playing."[4]

Koffman was one, and Lenny Breau another, the latter caught in what Alastair Lawrie described as "a vice of sound"[5] when he worked with Ranger and Michel Donato at George's in July. The guitarist typically played in an impressionistic, technically and harmonically advanced style derived from an eclectic range of sources, country music through contemporary jazz. Ranger and Donato stiffened Breau's resolve; his solos on a CBC *Jazz Canadiana* broadcast from George's in 1972 show the distinct influence of his fellow Canadian guitarist Sonny Greenwich in their incisive linearity.

Ranger was in even more provocative form when he played on August 18 with Alvin Pall at the World Saxophone Congress, held in the Edward Johnson Building on the University of Toronto campus. Pall, who joined Moe Koffman, Jerry Toth and Bernie Piltch in the only jazz concert of a four-day event otherwise devoted to classical musicians, drew on the legacy of John Coltrane for his performance. Ranger concluded the final piece with a resounding rimshot that echoed defiantly through the hall.[6] Later that night at the Banana Factory he led his own band, a quintet, for the first time in Toronto.[7]

• • •

Woody Herman usually relied on the opinions of his musicians whenever he needed to find replacements for his Thundering Herd. In early September 1972, with his 16-piece band in residence for a week at the Savarin, a nightclub on Bay Street in the heart of Toronto's business district, the American clarinetist was looking for a new drummer. Joe LaBarbera, the most recent in a long, distinguished line dating back through the likes of Jake Hanna, Don Lamond and Dave Tough to the band's beginnings in 1936, had given notice.

LaBarbera, who had heard Ranger previously, encouraged Herman to arrange an audition during the Savarin's Saturday matinee. It was, as far as LaBarbera recalls, successful;[8] Ranger's experience with showbands in Montreal would certainly have served him well in handling the Herd's arrangements on the fly. Nevertheless, Ranger turned down Herman's invitation to join the band.

There were a few reasons, he later told John Gilmore. For one, he found big bands too limiting. For another, he felt that he was not strong enough, leaving unsaid whether he was referring to the power required to support 15 other musicians night in, night out, or to the stamina necessary in face of the rigours of life on the road. For a third, he admitted, he was afraid. This, too, went unexplained, but given his uncertainty about moving from Montreal to Toronto earlier in the year, the prospect of leaving Canada altogether would have been daunting, even with the example of Michel Donato, who had recently started to travel internationally with Oscar Peterson.

There was also another consideration, one that Ranger did not mention to Gilmore. By September of 1972, he was reunited with his wife Denyse and their daughters Danielle, Suzanne and Sylvie. The family grew to six with the birth of the Rangers' fourth daughter, Lani, the following summer.

* * *

The wisdom of Ranger's move to Toronto, evidently completed with the arrival of his family, was likely apparent when he, Alvin Pall, Bernie Senensky and Michel Donato travelled to Montreal in late October 1972 with Herbie Spanier for a Radio Canada International recording session that resulted in the trumpeter's LP *Forensic Perturbations*.

The local scene was, if anything, even quieter than when Ranger had left, with only the Esquire Showbar still presenting jazz; saxophonist Rahsaan Roland Kirk was visiting that week from New York.[9] Significantly, Nelson Symonds and his frequent partner, bassist Charles Biddle, who had always been able to find work *somewhere* in Montreal, left the city altogether for the first in a succession of engagements at resort towns in the Laurentians. They did not return until 1977.

Forensic Perturbations proved to be Spanier's only recording as a leader; two later compilations issued on CD, *Anthology/1962-93* and *Anthology Vol II — 1969-1994*, included pieces drawn from the LP and from older *Jazz en liberté* broadcasts, including two tracks from 1969 with Ranger and Brian Barley. Moreover, *Forensic Perturbations* was not, in the trumpeter's own estimation, a particular success.

Spanier had worked stateside in the mid-1950s with Paul Bley and Ornette Coleman at formative stages in their efforts — and his own — to move beyond bebop. Bley and Coleman would move further, but Spanier had moved far enough, and with a free-spirited sort of persona that became the stuff of legend, to put himself at odds with the Canadian jazz establishment on his return in 1959.

Forensic Perturbations captured only some of his mastery. "It's not really representative of the way I play," he complained some years later. "It's representative of a clichéd straight-jacket that you put people in: 'We are going to make a record. Count off the music and be creative!' But it wasn't just that. The musicians I hired were futzing about — it was like going on holiday. We were lucky to get anything down."[10]

Nor was it necessarily representative of the way Ranger played, poorly recorded as he was, and likely not at his own drums — circumstances that at times left him, for all of his skill and imagination, a disruptive presence. And although he and Spanier's other musicians do sound unsettled, they seem, if anything, to have been trying *too* hard, rather than not hard enough, as they worked through eight of the trumpeter's compositions. Ranger was featured on two, the title piece and *The Colonel's Mess*, and also engaged Pall in an intense dialogue on *On the Blue* that would have taken them back to Stanley Street and the Café Pascale six years earlier.

. . .

Clubs in Toronto, as in Montreal, came and went. The Savarin, where Woody Herman had appeared, was not long for jazz. Nor were the Banana Factory and Meat and Potatoes. On the other hand, touring American bands still stopped at the Colonial Tavern on Yonge Street, sustaining a tradition that had started in 1950. And the owner of George's Spaghetti House, Doug Cole, had recently transformed another of his restaurants, George's Italian Cafe — on Queen Street West, near University Avenue — into Bourbon Street, where American soloists appeared with Toronto rhythm sections for a week or two at a time.

Ranger would work on and off at Bourbon Street throughout the 1970s, but not before a false start in early November 1972 when he and Michel Donato were hired with Maury Kaye, a bop stylist, to accompany Kenny Davern, a rather idiosyncratic dixieland clarinetist and soprano saxophonist from New York. Alastair Lawrie, a rather idiosyncratic dixieland clarinetist in his own right when not working for *The Globe and Mail*, was naturally sympathetic to Davern's plight.

"The rhythm section, however admirable it might be in its own line of work," Lawrie observed, "was hopelessly incompatible with the straightforward style of jazz that was clearly Davern's objective." So it was that Kaye, Donato and Ranger, "by a large measure of mutual consent," in Lawrie's words, withdrew after the first night in favour of other musicians more suited to Davern's *métier*.[11]

Kaye and Ranger returned with bassist Richard Homme three weeks later in support of another New York musician, the robust, hard-bop tenor saxophonist George Coleman. This time, Ranger would seem to have been an ideal choice — Coleman, after all, had worked for Max Roach and Elvin Jones in the past — but he again met with some disfavour from Alastair Lawrie, who reported, "Claude Ranger, slightly restrained — but not enough — was doing his customary elaborate thing."[12]

* * *

The drum chair at Bourbon Street and, for that matter, at George's Spaghetti House, was more often taken by either Terry Clarke or Jerry Fuller. Clarke, three years younger than Ranger, had left

Vancouver in 1965 at the age of 20 to work in the United States alongside Don Thompson, who was playing bass, with the San Francisco alto saxophonist John Handy. Clarke appeared later that year with Thompson on Handy's LP *Live at Monterey*, which proved to be one of the most popular jazz recordings of the 1960s and brought the young Canadian 21st place — between Jo Jones and Milford Graves — in the drum category of *Down Beat*'s 1966 Readers Poll, which was won by Elvin Jones.[13]

Just months after Ranger had chosen not even to *hear* John Coltrane at Jazz Hot in January 1965, Clarke would accept an invitation from the same Elvin Jones to *play* with the saxophonist at the Jazz Workshop in San Francisco. Clarke's vivid recollection of the incident, its significance and his response to it puts Ranger's diffidence further in perspective.

"All of a sudden — and I've never *seen* this band before, and this is the band I've been *listening* to for the last four years, this and Miles [Davis], that's all — I'm behind this drum set that I've been *hearing* on records, and there's Coltrane, there's McCoy [Tyner] and there's Jimmy [Garrison]. They just started playing 'free.' And I thought, 'What the *fuck* am I doing here? This is ridiculous!' In a sheer panic from not having played much 'free' music, I grabbed a tempo and in about a milli-second Trane was right there with me, and the whole thing went thundering down the runway and we took off."

As Clarke suggests, he and Ranger shared similar touchstones as drummers in the early 1960s, in particular Elvin Jones and Tony Williams. And they reacted in much the same way to finding themselves in an unfamiliar and challenging situation, Clarke's "What the *fuck* am I doing here" at the Jazz Workshop echoing Ranger's "What *is* this *shit*?" at the Café Pascale.

But Clarke was undaunted by Coltrane's presence only a few feet away, much less a flight of stairs up. "I just played for my life," he remembers, "and it was the most wonderful feeling, the most intense thing. Here I am, thrust into a situation I'd only dreamed about *hearing*... And after, Trane came over and thanked me for playing with him. And Elvin came up, with his baseball hat, and said, 'Keep up the good work...'"[14]

Clarke remained with John Handy until 1967, then travelled with a very successful Los Angeles pop group, the Fifth Dimension, before returning to Canada and settling in Toronto in 1970. His experience stateside with both jazz and pop music at such a high level quickly brought him first-call status — previously held by Jerry Fuller — in the city's jazz clubs and recording studios.

Fuller, a few years older than both Clarke and Ranger, played in a vigorous style influenced by Philly Joe Jones, Jimmy Cobb and the other drummers of the 1950s who followed Max Roach and Kenny Clarke stylistically but preceded Elvin Jones and Tony Williams. He was adaptable to the range of jazz played by visiting musicians at Bourbon Street, but less comfortable with the pop and rock styles that were increasingly prevalent in jingles, radio and television assignments and film scores.

Just as Fuller had displaced Archie Alleyne, Ron Rully and others when he moved to Toronto from Vancouver, via Montreal, in 1963, he was supplanted by Clarke, who was in turn challenged by Ranger. Tenor saxophonist Michael Stuart, new himself to Toronto in 1969 from Kingston, Jamaica, recalls the sequence of events leading up to and immediately following Ranger's arrival in 1972.

"Terry Clarke rolled in and started taking a lot of work, and then Claude came from Montreal and brought this whole other thing. I don't think anyone looked at him and thought, 'Man, this guy's going to get a lot of studio work,' or whatever. It was more an artistic thing. 'Here's an individual, he's got his own sound, he's got his own personality, and he *wears* it when he plays. It comes through his instrument.' Everyone was amazed."[15]

Everyone, including Terry Clarke. "All of a sudden, Claude literally popped up on the scene and blew everyone away. 'Where the fuck did *he* come from?' Who *is* this guy?"[16]

CHAPTER SEVEN

"It had to be something real"

Claude Ranger remembered his first year in Toronto only too well.

"Right away, I was at George's sometimes three weeks in a row. They used to try me out. Then it all stopped. Everything stopped. I was starving. Why did it stop? I don't know. For a long time I only had *Music Machine* with Doug Riley. That's all I had. Almost no jazz gigs. It just happened that I was not doing them."

Ranger's association with pianist Doug Riley led to several interesting projects in the mid-1970s, but *Music Machine* — a weekly CBC-TV show that went on-air in September 1973 with singer Keith Hampshire as its host and Riley's vocal and instrumental ensemble, Dr. Music, as its house band — would not have been one of them.

"Maybe I was hard to play with," Ranger mused five years later, still wondering about the turn of events that found him in the city's studios but not its jazz clubs. "I don't know. But I think it's just part of learning. I had to learn. Now I'm much better. Now I can talk. Before, I couldn't speak English; it was pretty rough. Some days, I would wake up and forget it all. 'No words in English today!'"

Language aside, Ranger could indeed be difficult to play with, especially when he was unhappy about the motivation, or lack thereof, behind the music at hand. His disdain precluded the sort of casual work — business events, weddings and other private functions — that was essential to a jazz musician's livelihood, were a jazz musician agreeably adaptable. By and large, Ranger was not.

"I tried to get Claude in on that in Toronto so he would make a bit of money," Michel Donato notes. "But I guess he didn't like it, and from the second tune on, nobody knew where '1' was!"

• • •

Ranger's second year in Toronto passed largely without event, save for a brief flurry of activity in the summer when he participated in a music camp organized by Humber College at Geneva Park on Lake Couchiching north of Toronto[1] and returned to Montreal for a recording session with Dave Liebman, pianist Richie Beirach and bassist Frank Tusa under Gerry Labelle's leadership.[2]

As suddenly as his prospects had stalled in 1973, however, they began to rise in January 1974, when he was booked for two weeks at Bourbon Street with the American saxophonist James Moody. The engagement marked the start of one of the best years of Ranger's career.

Moody, known to that point for his work with Dizzy Gillespie, was an early and expressive bebopper who had remained open to later developments in jazz, including the assertive hard-bop style of John Coltrane. He nevertheless surprised John Norris of *Coda* with the "highly volatile, intensely energetic" nature of his playing; Norris was similarly impressed by the work of Moody's Toronto rhythm section — Ranger, Richard Homme and, at the piano, Don Thompson.

The three musicians, Norris wrote, "were light years ahead of the regular occupiers of the Bourbon Street stage and they assisted greatly in giving Moody the high level energy so necessary for the success of his playing methods. Claude Ranger, in particular, constantly provoked the saxophonist with his unexpected accents and very open time. He was like a whirlwind — constantly changing the shading and direction of his rhythmic pulsations yet always coinciding with Moody's lines."[3]

Ranger in turn was clearly inspired by Moody, pushing himself — as Thompson recalls — to the point of injury. "I remember one night he came in and I noticed that he was playing left-handed. You couldn't tell; I just happened to glance over and I could see that he was playing that way. It didn't *sound* any different, but he was playing the ride cymbal with his left hand, because he'd split his right thumb open the night before and he couldn't hold the stick. We were playing *Cherokee* at a really fast tempo and it didn't make *any* difference."

Norris returned several times to hear Moody and was especially impressed on one of those occasions by the saxophonist's version of the Sonny Rollins blues *Sonnymoon for Two,* played "in great style, building chorus after chorus over the driving support of bass and drums" — much as Rollins, Wilbur Ware and Elvin Jones had first recorded it at New York's fabled Village Vanguard in late 1957.

Seven weeks after Moody had left town, Ranger and Michel Donato were playing in the same trio setting with Rollins himself. The encounter, which Ranger later identified as one of the main professional achievements of his career,[4] came during a benefit organized in Toronto at Mackenzie's Corner House, Charles Street East and Church, by Alan Offstein and others on behalf of the American drummer Ed Blackwell, who was battling kidney disease. Rollins travelled from New York City on his own for the occasion and played two sets in a 12-hour program divided between afternoon and evening shows that also featured the German vibraphonist Karl Berger and his wife, the singer Ingrid Sertso, up from the Creative Music Studio in Woodstock, New York, and pianist Sadik Hakim, who had recently moved to Toronto from Montreal. Several Toronto musicians completed the bill, including Salome Bey, Terry Logan,

Ted Moses, Alvin Pall, Bernie Senensky, pianist Stuart Broomer and tenor saxophonist Gary Morgan.

The city's drummers were properly represented in the Toronto bands — Terry Clarke with Moses and Senensky, Jerry Fuller with Bey, Bob McLaren with Logan and Morgan, and George Reed with Hakim — but the honour of playing with Berger and Rollins went to Ranger. His playing in support of the vibraphonist immediately caught the ear of Barry Tepperman, who suggested in *Coda* that his "astute percussion fit the group as if he'd been working with them for years, and was in many respects the key to this performance."

Noting the rather amorphous nature of Berger's integration of composition and improvisation, Tepperman added that it "seemed to dissolve into nothingness during interludes when Ranger sat out. The group's phrasings and sound placements seemed aimless and stilted without the kind of drive that Ranger had to inject."[5]

Enter Rollins, in effect "walking the bar" in reverse as he emerged from the back of the darkened room and played his way through the audience toward Ranger and Michel Donato, who were accompanying him from the stage. Tepperman, clearly enthralled by what followed, would describe the two Canadians as "unequivocally the finest rhythm section in the world."

Kieran Overs, a younger musician in attendance that day, put their presence in a more immediate context. "They had a sort of 'star' status when they came here from Montreal and the place where that really came to the fore was when they did the gig with Sonny Rollins. I was there for the full 12 hours. It was obvious: who else was going to do that gig, that way? They were the guys."

Who else? Certainly Terry Clarke and Don Thompson — with Thompson playing bass — had a comparably long history together, first during the 1960s in Vancouver and with John Handy in the United States, and latterly in Toronto clubs and studios. Theirs, however, was a more discreet sensibility — less appropriate to Rollins, for example, than to the New York guitarist Jim Hall, with whom they would record so notably at Bourbon Street in 1975.[6]

Ranger and Donato, on the other hand, immediately took Rollins back to his Village Vanguard recordings in late 1957, and to *The Freedom Suite* with Oscar Pettiford and Max Roach in early 1958, while drawing on their own experience in the same trio setting with Brian Barley during the late 1960s.

Donato recalls that he and Ranger in fact suggested to Rollins that they should play *The Freedom Suite*. "He flipped! He said, 'Really?' We could have named five hundred standards, but we said *Freedom Suite*." In the event, the trio's two sets included three other classic Rollins compositions, *St. Thomas*, *Oleo* and *Alfie's Theme*, as well as Oscar Pettiford's *Blues in the Closet* and the Benny Carter ballad *When Lights Are Low*.

"I've already noted Claude Ranger's singular drumming talents," Barry Tepperman wrote afterwards. "Apart from the diversity and power of the drive he generates, he seems to to be able to play well and stay on his own terms with just about anyone." Jack Batten, in a review of the afternoon show for *The Globe and Mail*, acknowledged that Ranger and Donato were "both in superb form."[7] Peter Goddard, assessing Rollins' "rambling" evening set for the *Toronto Star*, went further, suggesting that the saxophonist was "clearly outplayed" by his accompanists.[8]

Not that there was anything competitive about the performance. Steve Wallace — another younger musician in attendance, indeed still a teenager — watched from the edge of the stage as Ranger and Donato, "flying blind" without a rehearsal, rose to the occasion. "I was so impressed," Wallace later wrote, "by how they really played together [and] presented a united front behind Sonny, who really liked them, turning around to them at one point and bellowing 'Yeahhhhh!'"[9]

• • •

Ranger participated in a postscript of sorts to the Blackwell benefit when he opened for Karl Berger, Ingrid Sertso and bassist Dave Holland in early May at the Masonic Temple on Yonge Street. This time, Berger brought his own drummer, Steve Haas, while Ranger called on Michel Donato and three saxophonists, Glenn McDonald, Alvin Pall and John Tank.

Tank remembers Ranger in general as being rather taciturn. "I found it very hard to talk to him, because I never knew what to say. You couldn't talk about the weather. You couldn't do small talk with Claude. It had to be something real or he wasn't interested."

On this occasion in particular, Ranger was even more inscrutable than ever in his reluctance to offer his musicians anything other than figurative direction. "We didn't know what we were going to play before the gig," Tank explains. "Claude just wouldn't call any tunes. He wouldn't let us know. We had a rehearsal, and he said, 'Play like a waterfall.' Whatever *that* meant..."

McDonald evidently thought he knew, or was willing to guess, and took it upon himself to give the performance some shape with a variety of nods, waves, shouts and melodic prompts.[10] Despite McDonald's initiative, the result — in Tank's memory — was little more than a jam session.[11]

• • •

Doug Riley continued to call. With CBC-TV's *Music Machine* winding up its first season, he had turned his attention in February and March 1974 to a new LP with Dr. Music, bringing Ranger in for several tunes. "Doug liked being pushed," explains the band's trumpeter, Bruce Cassidy, "and that's why, I think, he had Claude. He wanted to have the very best people he could possibly have around him, just to push the envelope."[12]

By the measure of Dr. Music's two previous recordings, which featured pop songs with a gospel flavour that reflected the band's origins as a vocal and instrumental ensemble in Toronto's studios, the third LP, *Bedtime Story*, did indeed push the envelope, venturing rather boldly into contemporary jazz.

It ventured furthest with Ranger's composition *Tickle*, a four-bar flourish repeated three times to frame what would be the longest of the LP's six tracks at 11-1/2 minutes and substantially the freest, with Cassidy, Riley, Don Thompson, on bass, and the composer himself featured in turn as soloists.

Riley effectively compromised Ranger's presence on *Bedtime Story*, however, by pairing him with a rock drummer, Dave Brown, for the LP's three other jazz tracks, his own *Take That Rollo*, Thompson's *Gandalf*, and the Herbie Hancock composition, *Tell Me a Bedtime Story*, that gave the album its title. The concept of a band with two drummers was enjoying some currency in jazz and rock music at the time, whether the precedent was John Coltrane's 1965 sextet — with Elvin Jones and Rashied Ali — or, more recently, the Allman Brothers. Of course, Jones soon left Coltrane in frustration; Ranger was similarly unhappy.

"I don't think Claude liked that too much," Thompson suggests. "He couldn't figure out why Doug had two drummers. He couldn't see the point."

At the very least, the result was cumbersome. But Ranger had been in this situation before, playing on occasion alongside Terry Clarke in the bands of Bruce Cassidy and Ted Moses. And he would find himself in the same setting again, working with Dave Brown when Dr. Music appeared at the Colonial Tavern and recording with Clarke on Riley's next major project, *Solar Explorations* by Moe Koffman.

Riley, a widely and remarkably accomplished musician, had served variously as producer, arranger and keyboard player on several of Koffman's instrumental albums — less jazz recordings, typically, than simply *jazzy* recordings, if even that — and would do so for several more. He was as adept at showcasing Koffman in the classical repertoire of *Moe Koffman Plays Bach* from 1971 as in the disco setting of *Jungle Man* from 1976.

Solar Explorations from 1974 and a live recording from George's the following year were notable exceptions to Koffman's commercial ventures during this period; *Solar Explorations* in particular stands as an ambitious and ultimately important contribution to the Canadian jazz discography for the range of musicians involved — both establishment figures and freer spirits — and for the imagination with which they were deployed.

Based programmatically on the planets in the Earth's solar system, it featured compositions by Koffman, Riley, Don Thompson, Ron Collier, Freddie Stone and Rick Wilkins performed over two LPs by ensembles of six to 14 musicians, with Koffman and guitarist Sonny Greenwich — a surprising and inspired choice — as the primary soloists.

Ranger played drums on six of the compositions, Terry Clarke on two. Ranger and Clarke also collaborated on Riley's *Earth*, which proved in the studio to be a revelation with respect to a facet of Ranger's skill that had been lost in the commotion over his arrival in Toronto two years earlier.

"The melody was all over the place, really tricky and fast and Claude was doubling Moe and Doug," Thompson remembers from his vantage point of playing both bass and piano on the session. "We ran it down once *at tempo* and Claude just played it perfectly. When it was over, I said, 'Claude, I didn't know you could read like *that*.' Terry didn't know either. *Nobody* did. And Claude — I remember his exact words — said, 'The day I can't read my music is the day I give away my drums.'"

Ranger handled the album's larger compositions no less comfortably — Stone's orchestral *Uranus*, a bolero of sorts, as well as Collier's *Jupiter*, a more conventional big band piece — and was featured in a long, ruminative solo on Thompson's *Mercury*, which concluded *Solar Explorations*.

If the project signalled a change in the relationship between Ranger and the Toronto jazz establishment, largely through Riley's intercession, that relationship nevertheless remained on uneasy terms for the rest of the decade in face of the chafing conformity it demanded of him. It was clear now, if it had not been already, that there were no limits on what he was able to do — only on what he was willing to do.

. . .

Ranger would surely have been willing to work with Phil Woods, the American alto saxophonist who played bebop with startling virtuosity and, at times, almost overwhelming intensity. Woods had followed James Moody into Bourbon Street by a matter of weeks in March 1974, but without the benefit of the musicians who had made up Moody's rhythm section.

On that occasion, according to Peter Goddard of the *Toronto Star*, he was "simply all too much for his backing trio to handle." Woods' accompanists, Goddard wrote, "seem more interested in staying out of his way than in trying to keep up with him."[13]

Woods was far better served by Ranger, Bernie Senensky and Richard Homme when he made a quick return to Bourbon Street in late August. "Woods and Ranger really got off on each other," John Norris reported in *Coda*, "and only the conventional thinking of the other musicians prevented Woods from soaring outside..."[14]

Jack Batten, reviewing for *The Globe and Mail*, was similarly, if more generally impressed by Woods and his bandmates. But he also made much of Woods' "walrus mustache" and, in the same spirit of descriptive journalism, seemed more taken with Ranger's cigarettes than with his drumming. "Ranger apparently stops chain-smoking only when he sleeps," Batten speculated, "and even that is open to question."[15]

. . .

Ranger took other jobs in the course of 1974, including weeks at George's with Bruce Cassidy, Alvin Pall, Don Thompson and, finally in late November, a quartet of his own. This last engagement fell during an especially busy period of seven days in which he also appeared in concert with Sonny Greenwich and participated in an evening of classical music and jazz with Moe Koffman and the Toronto chamber sextet Camerata.

Ranger and Greenwich had played together in passing during the late 1960s in Montreal. "It never worked," Ranger later declared, without elaboration, "It *couldn't* work. *Impossible* to play together." According to Greenwich, Ranger had made no secret of his frustration at the time. "I don't remember if it was a jam session, or what, but right on the bandstand Claude threw down his sticks, stood up and said, 'I can't play with this guy!'"[16]

By 1974, however, Ranger had changed, at least to the degree that he could begin what would become an eight-year association with the guitarist. Where he had been, in Greenwich's words, "high strung" in Montreal, he was comparatively calmer in Toronto, although still temperamental enough to make his feelings known on the bandstand.

Greenwich in his day was as singular a figure among Canada's jazz musicians as Ranger. He emerged in the early 1960s under the apparent influence of the American guitarist Grant Green. His touchstones, like Green's, were horn players, notably Sonny Rollins, John Coltrane and Miles Davis, and his concept by choice — like theirs of necessity — was determinedly linear. Greenwich simply did not play chords. This, in a city where his fellow guitarists Ed Bickert and Lenny Breau would take harmony to new levels of colour and sophistication.

Greenwich was further influenced by Coltrane's spiritual quest, as documented by the album *A Love Supreme*, to follow a similar path of his own, both in music and in life, to the point where a *career* in music was at best a secondary concern. He had worked stateside with John Handy in 1966 — Don Thompson and Terry Clarke were still in the band at that point — and he recorded in New York with tenor saxophonist Hank Mobley in 1967, but once back in Canada, and settled in Boucherville on Montreal's South Shore, he periodically withdrew from performance altogether in order to pursue other interests.

Greenwich continued at first to work with Toronto musicians, notably Thompson and Clarke, both of whom — together with Richard Homme and percussionist Clayton Johnston — played in February 1974 on his classic Radio Canada International LP *Sun Song*. Thompson, in fact, served Greenwich as something of a music director and was responsible for choosing the musicians who would accompany the guitarist on his visits to Toronto and his engagements locally in Montreal.

In the wake of the *Solar Explorations* sessions, Greenwich and Thompson introduced a new sextet, retaining Homme, replacing Clarke with Ranger and adding Michael Stuart and Doug Riley. Stuart's presence affirmed Greenwich's loyalty to the legacy of John Coltrane; Riley, playing electric piano, brought that same legacy into the 1970s.

The band made its debut without Stuart at George's at the end of October 1974, then appeared at the St. Paul's Annex Theatre in late November. Writing in *Coda* of the latter engagement, Barry Tepperman attributed the "ongoing metamorphosis" of Greenwich's music in part to the guitarist's "ever-questing maturity" and in part to "the advent of Claude Ranger, indisputably the best drummer on the Canadian scene, a fiery dancer of stick and skin whose dynamic subtlety and rhythmic diversity opened a new set of driving alternatives to the old quartet..."[17]

For his own band, which opened at George's the following night, Ranger looked not to the members of his quintet at the Masonic Temple in May — Michel Donato, Glenn McDonald, Alvin Pall and John Tank — but instead summoned Terry King and Gerry Labelle from Montreal and added Dave Field, a young bass player who had moved to Toronto from Vancouver earlier in the year.

Not only was the instrumentation unusual — violin, saxophone, bass and drums — but King and Labelle, as Montreal musicians, were rather impolitic choices for Ranger's first engagement as a leader at George's, one that was at least a challenge and at most a snub to the status quo that the club, and that Moe Koffman as its booking agent, represented on the local scene.

Ironically, Ranger had to take time off from one of his evenings at George's for two concerts with Koffman and Camerata at the Art Gallery of Ontario. The theme was Mozart and improvisation; Koffman and his musicians were heard at length in Mozart's *Flute*

Quartet in D Major, with Ranger doing some "superb work" behind Don Thompson, "absolutely faithful to the pianist's ideas," according to Jack Batten, writing in *The Globe and Mail*.[18]

Batten had already visited George's that week. "[I]f you've never quite appreciated [Ranger's] energy and inventiveness before, this is a splendid opportunity to make up for lost time," he advised, before returning to, and developing, a favoured refrain. "Ranger lights fires when he plays — not just with the cigaret that's constantly in his mouth — and at George's the night I dropped by, he was in incandescent form."[19]

Terry King describes Ranger's impact that week in different terms. "I think Claude wanted to say to the Toronto establishment, 'Look you guys, you think you've got everything happening here, and all the best music is going on here, but I'll knock your socks off with something you've never heard before.' He wanted something really different from the standard George's offerings. Which he got. Musicians in Toronto either loved it or hated it. They really lined up on one side or the other. All the relatively conservative musicians hated it, Moe in particular."

As predictable as Koffman's response might have been, Ranger looked back on the experience rather ruefully a few years later. "I prefer not to be a leader," he admitted. "I'd rather just go and play. Maybe I don't like the responsibility. That might change."

As indeed it did.

"The thing is," he continued, "I had a gig at George's, but it never happened again. I guess it was not wise to get people from Montreal, but I didn't know about those things. I didn't know Toronto was like that. I understand that now."

Chapter Eight

"All feel"

Whatever Claude Ranger's relationship with the Toronto establish-ment — however complex, however contrarian — he cut a compelling figure in the city's jazz community more generally.

The cigarettes, certainly, and those bottles of beer — the classic iconographic details of a rebel — would have been especially attrac-tive to the younger Toronto musicians who were confronting for themselves the prim conservatism of a scene still largely defined by the values of the 1950s.

And the drums — so small and yet so powerful, a set, probably made by Gretsch, that Ranger had customized to his own preferences. Bill Smith, writing for *Coda*, could only marvel at "the incredible Ranger, Canada's master of percussion dynamics sitting there at his tiny drums providing dialogue at every level necessary,"[1] in a review of a band led by the American tenor saxophonist Junior Cook at Bourbon Street in December 1974.

Ranger's bass drum was a mere 16 inches in diameter — 18 and 20 inches were more common sizes in jazz — and his toms, 12 and 14. In fact, his bass drum was a floor tom that he had turned on its side and refitted at one end with a wooden rim wide enough to support the clamp of his kick pedal.

"A small bass drum moves very quickly," he once explained, emphasizing implicitly the importance of sustaining an uninterrupted flow in his drumming. "It doesn't *stop* the sound. It's like another tom-tom. That's why I have it. If the bass drum sounds that way, like a tom-tom, it always keeps the sound moving. It's pretty hard to follow, it's all over the place, it's not definite, but it's a lot of fun to play that way."

Not for Ranger the "bombs" of bop drumming, although his playing was certainly explosive in other ways. And as if his drums were not already small enough, they seemed smaller still in the shadow of his ride and crash cymbals, mounted rakishly high at an angle almost perpendicular to the floor.

The cigarette, the beer, the drums and the cymbals created a striking tableau in the half light onstage at George's and Bourbon Street. They were also rather subversive. If, as Ranger's example seemed to suggest, there was *another* way of doing things in face of the conformity that characterized modern jazz in Toronto, then perhaps there could be *many* other ways. And even though Ranger was simply attending to his own priorities in a typically self-absorbed way, he had fans and followers — impressionable younger drummers especially — tracking his every move.

"I remember going down to George's," Terry Clarke recalls, "and this one kid, who was a follower, told me, 'Claude's upper tom is tuned a little sharp tonight.' I said, 'Oh, *really*? Compared to *what*?'"

The boldest of those younger drummers asked to study with him; he did not always say yes. Others just watched. "In a sense," comments Bob McLaren, one of those who just watched, albeit very closely, "*everybody* studied with him."

Not just drumming, but commitment — and the cost of that commitment. "He lived dangerously," McLaren continues. "He completely sacrificed everything for the muse. So in terms of all of us in the community, we looked up to him. He was an attractive person. And he had the talent to back it up. He was a bit exotic — the cigarette, the French accent, the Quebec flair — and he only talked about music. People wanted to get next to that, to see what it was like to sacrifice yourself and not aspire to the middle class like the rest of us did."[2]

Barry Elmes, who did approach Ranger for lessons in the mid-1970s but found him unwilling to oblige, admired his creativity, adventurousness and fearlessness. "And the fearlessness," Elmes adds, "could translate into, 'I don't need this gig.' In other words, to me Claude was an artist. He'd rather not eat — he'd rather quit a gig and not eat — because he didn't feel it was right, where the rest of us would have thought, 'Well, I've got to make the rent...'"[3]

• • •

Ranger had given lessons in Montreal — Jacques Masson was a student at 15 — both *chez lui* and at Bel-Air Musique on de la Salle Avenue. His willingness to teach, or his unwillingness as would often be the case, was at least in part a function of financial considerations. "When I was not working," he explained in 1978, "I taught more."

He was certainly well placed to take students, if only because he had written for his own use a series of exercises in eighth notes designed to develop the sort of independence — hand from hand, foot from foot and hands from feet, all in relation to a constant cymbal ride — that came to characterize his own drumming. There were eventually enough exercises for a "book," albeit one seen in its entirety during the 1970s by only a few of his students, who remember it running to hundreds of pages.

"It's just exercises for myself," he noted. "That's why I've never published it. Anyone can sit down and write it. I don't wish to have a drum book like everybody else has. All the drum books are the same, so I don't want to have my name out there as having a regular drum book, even if it is not *that* regular."

Far be it from Ranger to have created something "like everyone else has," his reluctance in that regard reflecting the same resistance on principle that he expressed toward musicians who played "the way everyone does it on record."

He described the "book" to John Gilmore. "There are no words, just music. It's written mostly in the genre of Max Roach — how to play the cymbals, the snare, the bass drum, the hi-hat. How to play with two hands on the snare and make music, play solos, play bebop. It's a book for that. Anyone with a little imagination could write it; any competent drummer could write it... It's all in 4/4, all improvised against the cymbal. It's for teaching a drummer how to play the cymbal 'straight,' and the other things he can do around it."

Indeed, Ranger had used it — or at least had drawn on the process of developing it — to teach himself. "It has always been my impression that Claude was a product of his own educational process," suggests Lorne Nehring, who studied with Ranger in Toronto during this period. "Where most of us learn skills and then use those skills to generate performances that have some relevant creative value, Claude heard what he wanted to play and created a system to learn the skill required to play it. The basic skills are the basic skills. He was skilled enough, and smart enough, and talented enough, and worked hard enough, that he understood what it was to be a working drummer — your time, your feel, your sound. He understood that everything he would want to do had to be set in that context. But from there, he just kind of created a system for himself — reams of exercises to deal with this issue, or that issue. What you heard in him as player was a product of that. It wasn't, 'Now I've gone to five different great teachers, and I've learned everything there is to know about playing drums, and now I'm going to play the way *I* think.'"

Ranger evidently destroyed his "book" in a moment of frustration with music at some point before 1980, or so he told John Gilmore, but his exercises remained "in his head" and he continued to write them out — for himself, for his students and even at times in lieu of agreeing to a lesson.

"At George's," Don Thompson recalls, "we'd take a break and he'd go and sit on the stairs that went up to the second floor. He'd sit there, all by himself, for the whole break, and write drum exercises — pages and pages of them. He showed them to me. I didn't have any idea what they were. They weren't random; they were organized, one led to the next. And night after night, for the whole week, he'd sit out there. I couldn't tell you how many he did."

Inevitably, copies proliferated, handed down over the years from one drummer to another. "I got a lot of material from him that I'm still passing out to my students," Bob McLaren admits. "All the drummers in town have it. I'm sure it's pretty much all over the country."

• • •

Ranger's students often came to know him better than the musicians with whom he worked, if only by virtue of visiting him at home and seeing him in an informal setting. His aesthetic principles, moreover, were evident in the lessons he gave and the things that he is remembered to have said and done.

Vito Rezza was one of his first students in Toronto, if not his first — just 16 when he heard Ranger at George's with Lenny Breau in 1972. Rezza and his friend Mario Romano, an aspiring pianist, returned often to the club, relying on the good will of its maître d', Leo Mascarin, who indulged their love of jazz and allowed them to stay.

"We didn't have any money," Rezza explains, "so Leo used to let us sit at the back where the coffee was. He'd say, 'You guys don't make trouble, eh?'"[4]

Soon enough, they introduced themselves to Ranger. He was not entirely approachable, Rezza recalls, "but he was gentle with us because he knew we were kids." Ranger at first refused Rezza's request for lessons, but eventually relented, inviting him to the semi-detached house in which he lived with his family on Ellsworth Avenue, midtown near St. Clair and Bathurst.

"He'd have practice pads facing the walls," Rezza remembers, "and that big 22-inch cymbal that he would grind with almost like the stones you use to sharpen skates. He wanted to get all of the overtone series out of it, to get the gloss off. He wanted it *ugly*. 'Like Tony,' he'd say. That cymbal had to be clear.

"He would just have his ride and crash cymbals, and the pads with towels on them. He'd put up exercises that he'd written. He'd be doing puzzles — 1000-piece jigsaw puzzles — or he'd melt crayons while I was practicing. He'd build stuff, like castles, out of crayon. He wouldn't say much, just 'Do it again.' 'Too 'ard.' 'It doesn't swing.' An hour later, 'It doesn't swing, keep going.' Those were my lessons.

"I don't know how many I had. They were never 'official' lessons. Sometimes we'd be out walking with his bike — I held the seat, he had the handle bars — and he'd stop and talk to me about drums. He'd say, 'Vito, when you play the high-hat on 2 and 4, it's bullshit. The hi-hat have to be free.' And I'm thinking, 'What? We're in the middle of a park here!' We'd walk some more, and then he'd stop again. 'No, Vito, that swing, it's "de-ding, de-de-ding." It's not "ding-dinga-ding." *That's* like a machine, there's no *flow*.'"

Inevitably, they also talked about jazz more generally, and about the Toronto scene in particular. Ranger was candid. "He'd say, 'It's all bullshit. What Moe's playing is bullshit, it's not jazz.' He'd really had it with Moe. And Peter Appleyard. All of those guys."

Of course, all of "those guys" were the elite musicians who spent their days at the CBC and CTV, or at Toronto Sound, Eastern Sound, Manta Sound and other studios, playing for radio and television shows, jingles and film scores, work that demanded great skill and versatility and yet could often be mindless.

"That bothered Claude," Rezza insists, "the guys who were doing four or five sessions a day, making five, six hundred dollars, then going out and playing jazz — slumming — at night. He hated that. What I loved about Claude was his attitude: 'If you're going to be true to your art, cut the bullshit.'"

Of course, Ranger himself worked in some of those same studios with Doug Riley and had also taken similar calls from other bandleaders, including Jimmy Dale, the music director for Bob McLean's

CBC-TV talk show in the mid-1970s.

"Claude would sub in lots of times on that," notes Don Thompson, who played bass in the Dale band. "Jimmy really liked him. So Claude would come in and it was perfect. No matter what we played, and we played everything — country music and everything else — it was perfect."

If Ranger's years in Montreal showbands had prepared him well for "country music and everything else," his values nevertheless lay elsewhere, as Rezza, who occasionally drove him around town, witnessed one night at a suburban banquet hall.

"I saw him hanging out with the Italian musicians who played there on Saturdays and Sundays. And he was jamming with them until 1 o'clock in the morning. He was almost like Jaco Pastorius in that respect. He would find shit to get into. He wanted to be with the blue collar guys."

Ranger also revelled in another scenario no less worthy of the notorious American bassist when he met Master Park Chu Sam, a 7th Degree Black Belt in Tae Kwon-Do, with whom Rezza had started to study. "Claude loved him," Rezza remembers. "He always grabbed Master Park's hands; he had blunt, scarred hands. Claude said, 'These hands are power!'"

No less than the power, and the evident physical sacrifice, Ranger would have related to and respected the discipline that took Master Park to such a high level of skill as a martial artist. The respect was apparently mutual: Master Park and some of his other followers occasionally joined Rezza at George's, culminating in an extraordinary scene out on Dundas Street at the end of the night.

"Sometimes after a gig we'd all surround Claude. I was *here*, a couple of other guys who were master fighters, quiet guys but tough guys, they were over *there*. Master Park would walk beside us. So we were like Claude's entourage. He'd have his bag with his 222s and his beers, along with his sticks. He loved it! I could see it in his eyes.

"Can you imagine? Claude leaving with *this* crew? And he would tell us about the bandleader he was playing with. 'He drives me crazy,' he'd say. 'This guy won't let me play the way I can play.'

"Master Park would say, 'Claude, you want me to take care of him?' Of course, Master Park would never hurt a fly!"

• • •

Greg Pilo, like Vito Rezza, made Ranger's acquaintance at George's. Originally from Sault Ste. Marie in Northern Ontario, Pilo, still in his teens, had moved to Toronto in 1973 after studying drums at the Berklee College of Music in Boston and with Tony Williams in New York.

"We hit it off right away," Pilo remembers, of that first evening in 1974 at George's, where Ranger was working with Bruce Cassidy. "I was telling him about Tony Williams and I did this sort of flam on the table. Leo had to throw us out of the restaurant because we were still pounding on the table at, like, three in the morning!"[5]

Pilo's personal connection with Williams, and his experience stateside of hearing Elvin Jones, Roy Haynes and other great drummers of the day, gave him several points of reference when he studied with Ranger — a unique perspective reflected in his various recollections of the way Ranger played and taught.

"Tony was a rudimental drummer," Pilo observes. "He had the flam thing going. He had beautiful snare drum technique. Claude, on the other hand, was all feel — *all* feel. He wasn't like any of those guys. He really wasn't. He was just as unique as Elvin or Roy Haynes.

"We used to listen to Tony together, and Claude was amazed by him. He thought Tony had so much guts. Tony wasn't afraid to make mistakes. That's one thing Claude said to me, 'Look, man, don't be afraid to make a mistake, or you'll go nowhere.'

"I found with Claude and Tony, they weren't great teachers, man. It was more a master/apprentice kind of thing, not a teacher/student thing. You couldn't ask dumb questions. They didn't like teaching guys who asked dumb questions. They didn't want to waste their time with 'Show me this paradiddle pattern.'

"I'd have a lesson with Claude about once every two weeks. I would go and *see* him three or four nights a week, and *then* I'd have a lesson, and he'd have to tell me about certain things he'd done. I'd go and see him three or four times to make sure I asked the right questions. That was big with Tony, and it was big with Claude: 'Ask me the right question and I'll answer it.'

"Claude's concept was about improvising and jazz playing, not about drumming. If you weren't going to be a jazz player, if that wasn't your calling, if you were just going to be a drummer, he wasn't going to help you much. But if you wanted to know about the cymbal, if you wanted to know how to swing, if you were really committed to that genre of music, then he was your guy.

"The cymbal — that's your voice. If you're not centred on that being your voice, you're not going to get the cymbal thing. And Claude knew that's where his music was, the cymbal. Everything else was colour."

Pilo was neither the first nor the last young musician to find Ranger generous with both his time and his knowledge. "A lesson with Claude would be over three days at his apartment," he remembers of their initial meetings, which began after Ranger had moved his family uptown to North York. "He used to charge me a pack of Export 'A's and a six-pack of Molson 'Ex.' That was it. That's all he ever wanted from me."

Pilo, however, was troubled by what he saw on his visits. He often found it necessary to supplement Ranger's fee of cigarettes and beer with groceries for his daughters.

"I loved the guy, and I loved studying with him," he admits, prefacing a rare and revealing glimpse into Ranger's family life. "But, oh my god, his kids would be hungry. He'd have a case of beer and they're eating baloney sandwiches for dinner. '*C'mon*, man!' He made me angry. He frustrated me. He wasn't father of the year."

* * *

There were other teachers in Toronto, most notably Jim Blackley, a championship pipe band drummer who emigrated in 1952 from Scotland to Canada and served as an instructor for the Royal Canadian Mounted Police in Ottawa before turning to jazz on hearing Max Roach at the Colonial Tavern during a visit to Toronto. He opened his own store and studio in Vancouver in 1957.

Blackley moved back east in 1967 to New York and on in 1973 to Toronto, where several of his former Vancouver students, notably Terry Clarke and Jerry Fuller, held sway over the local scene; other Blackley students remained significant figures in Vancouver, among them Duris Maxwell, Gregg Simpson, Al Wiertz and Blaine Wikjord.

Blackley's Toronto roster was already full by 1974, when Lorne Nehring, newly arrived from Montreal, inquired about lessons. He looked instead to Ranger; he would study with Blackley in due course and describes Ranger's approach to teaching in comparative terms.

"It was never a formal thing the way Jim's was. It was very much, 'Show up, and I'll show you what I'm working on at the moment.' He would pick an independence thing that was just what was in his head at the time. So that would be the lesson: 'Play this. Play this. Play this.' Much of it I couldn't play, but I could figure it out."

Nehring describes it as an "unfocussed process," not least the result of Ranger's divided attention, subject to the same distractions that Vito Rezza had encountered. "I must admit," Nehring continues, "that I probably needed to be better prepared to deal with him as a teacher. Often when I'd leave there it was like I'd fallen into this black hole of music. 'What just happened?'"

Studying with Blackley, on the other hand, "was all about structure. It was about hard work. It was about detail. It was very professional."

Ranger and Blackley were nevertheless in some philosophical accord, both about music and about teaching. "The most destructive value musicians can embrace is the desire for acceptance," Blackley told Adele Freedman of *The Globe and Mail* in 1977, words that Ranger could certainly have lived by. "Society teaches us that the key to life is winning," Blackley added, "but there's no race to be won in music."[6]

The two men also shared a similar goal as teachers, according to Barry Elmes, who had been rebuffed as a student by Ranger but accepted by Blackley. "Claude was very big on the individual. He didn't want to show you how to play the drums, he wanted *you* to figure out how *you* were going to play them. But it's like all roads lead to Rome: I think Jim felt the same way to a certain extent, but that's not the route he would take you down to get you to your own thing. He was very much hands-on, one-on-one, tailored to you."

. . .

The act of playing drums is ultimately a mechanical issue, but the art of playing drums is an entirely musical matter. One can be taught far more readily than the other.

Buff Allen, a young drummer who moved to Toronto from Vancouver in 1976, approached Ranger for lessons and found him unwilling. Allen chose instead simply to listen to Ranger when and wherever he could. He soon realized the limits of what he might have learned had Ranger been agreeable.

"What Claude did was quite easy for me to imitate, but it would sound horrible when I played it. If *he* played it, it was pure magic. It wasn't a special style, or a technical style, it was his emotional power. That's something that you can't learn. It's innate."[7]

Barry Elmes heard something similar when he first encountered Ranger. "It was like, 'What the hell is that?' I mean, I liked it, but I didn't have any idea what it was. All I know is that it was incredibly powerful, incredibly musical. I think it was the dynamic range of his playing that I wasn't used to. This would be a matter of one beat to the next — all of a sudden, there'd be this power, and at times in the music when I wasn't used to hearing it. And then, afterward, I thought, 'Well, that actually made a lot of sense.'"

It — that power, that timing — was not, however, something that Ranger's hundreds of exercises could either capture or impart. They were clinical — by some measure, mathematical — in their systematic review of the independence of movement that a drummer might develop; they captured nothing of the intangible quality that made his own playing so compelling.

"Whatever it was," Allen suggests, "he couldn't teach it. He could only teach what he knew. That raw, emotional power wouldn't transfer, because it was just *him*."

Such was the dichotomy inherent in Ranger's own artistry, so disciplined in its conception and so impulsive — *all* feel, as Greg Pilo puts it — in its execution.

Allen characterizes Ranger's technique as "loose and sparse," not an entirely flattering description. "There were bursts that really shocked me in terms of how technically wonderful they were, but most of the time, I felt, he had a kind of rough and tumble technique. As opposed to Terry Clarke, who's perfect, right? Terry's almost the perfect drummer; Claude would be almost the opposite. And yet they're both fantastic for different reasons."

Indeed, Ranger and Clarke were at least foils, if not opposites, on the Toronto scene. "Claude was always a bit of a ghost," Bruce Cassidy observes. "That was his vibe. And he had a bit of a wicked sense of humour. I remember once, we were playing 'fours' and he took a four-bar break and he came in a beat early — he turned the time around — and then just watched to see if anyone picked up on it. It's kind of a cruel thing to do. Claude could be edgy like that. Unlike Terry. If you turned the beat around with Terry, he'd go right with you and you'd never know you had done it."

At a personal level, the two drummers had a guarded relationship, neither quite rivals nor quite friends in view of the challenge, musically and professionally, that they posed one another.

"It was very tentative," Clarke explains, "because Claude was tentative with *everybody*. It was always a matter of, 'Am I going to understand what he's saying? Can I make out what he's saying?' He would say things to me that I didn't quite understand; I didn't know what direction they were coming from, whether they were malicious or complimentary. It was that indeterminate.

"I remember him once saying, 'How can you do that?' when I

came off the bandstand on some gig. *'How can you do that?'* I could take that in one of two ways, either 'How'd you *do* that — I'd love to be able to do that,' or 'What the fuck are you *doing?*' Right there — is that a matter of the tenses between French and English? Is that something to do with grammar? As a result, everything was kind of two-sided. I'd wonder, 'What did he mean by that?' I'd say, 'Okay, thank you... I think.'

"With me, I felt there was an animosity at times, but then I saw that same animosity with other people. So it wasn't just me; I'd find somebody else who'd say, 'Yeah, did you get a funny vibe about that too?'"

Clarke, of course, was central to the studio world that Ranger regarded with some disdain, even as he skirted it himself at Doug Riley's behest. But that, too, came to an end at some point around 1975, curtailed not by Riley — who, for the better part of two years, had indulged Ranger's idiosyncrasies as the price of his brilliance — but by Ranger himself.

"Doug offered him the world," Greg Pilo remembers. "Claude just said, 'I don't want to do this anymore.' Doug couldn't understand. He told me, 'I could have made that cat a millionaire. I offered him anything he wanted; he could have done anything of mine that he wanted.'"

Chapter Nine

"Not nice, not a lot of fun"

Claude Ranger returned briefly to Montreal in mid-March 1975 with Sonny Greenwich's new sextet for two concerts in the parish hall of Notre Dame de la Salette, a Catholic church on Park Avenue. He found himself paired in the rhythm section for the occasion with the conga drummer and percussionist known simply as Dido, a popular figure locally.

If the combination was at all awkward, as the presence of a second drummer had been for Ranger with Dr. Music the year before, it did not keep the Montreal writer and broadcaster Nighthawk — Claude Rachou — from lauding both men in her review for the *Montreal Gazette*. She described Ranger as "one of the most dynamic, versatile and melodic drummers on the music scene," by way of introducing a perceptive summary of his apparent contradictions as a musician. "The man is a mixture of the poet and the stampeder. He drives with a fury, and is a master of the most delicate touches."[1]

Ranger was back in Toronto by month's end to join Bernie Senensky and Dave Field in support of the American clarinetist Buddy DeFranco for two weeks at Bourbon Street; Jack Batten noted in *The Globe and Mail* only that Ranger was "newly slimmed down but still smoking up a storm."[2] Other drummers prevailed at Bourbon Street during the spring and summer of 1975, however, including the American Marty Morell, who had recently moved to Toronto after six years on the road with pianist Bill Evans. He joined Terry Clarke, Jerry Fuller and Stan Perry in the club's usual rotation.

What little work that did come Ranger's way in this period was not always to his liking, notably — it would seem — a concert in late June at the St. Paul's Annex Theatre with Michael Craden's Poke-A-Dope, which featured not one other percussionist, but two, Craden and Russell Hartenburger. Ranger's performance, as Barry Tepperman reviewed it in *Coda*, was consistent with his reaction to circumstances in which he was unhappy.

"Ranger seemed to be having an off day; even when allowed to play his head, Canada's finest drummer was simplistic and plain loud."[3]

Tepperman added parenthetically, and rather gratuitously, "(Perhaps all the bread gigs are finally getting to him)," as if to suggest that engagements offering a musician financial compensation — to wit, "bread" — commensurate with his skills might be a threat to the skills themselves, not an uncommon view held by critics, and in truth perhaps by Ranger himself, with respect to the dulling effect of studio work on those members of the jazz community who took it.

By then, however, Ranger had forsaken "the bread gigs." He would soon forsake Toronto.

• • •

Ranger returned to Montreal with his drums and his daughters for at least six months, spanning the latter half of 1975 and the first months of 1976. Denyse Ranger remained in Toronto.

Ranger and the children, now ranging in age from two to 12, stayed with Jacques Masson and his wife, Manon, and Ranger himself joined Masson, Con Murphy and Tommy Léveillée at the drum studio that they had established on the former premises of Bel-Air Musique on *avenue* de la Salle, the same street where he and Denyse had lived a dozen years earlier. Once again he had come full circle.

At first, he set himself the goal of getting back in shape, both physically — he told John Gilmore that his weight had soared to 185 pounds by that time — and at the drums. For once, he could dispense with practice pads in favour of a full kit; there were other drum sets at the studio as well, allowing his students to play *with* him, as Greg Pilo did during a visit of several weeks' duration.

Ranger returned briefly to Toronto in October at the behest of Doug Riley to participate in a live recording at George's. The result, *Dreams*, was one of several Canadian LPs issued in the mid-1970s by P.M. Records, an American label run by bassist Gene Perla, who had taken an active interest in Toronto musicians — Bernie Senensky first, followed in turn by Riley, Don Thompson, saxophonist Pat LaBarbera and guitarist Ed Bickert.

Dreams was the most adventurous of the initial P.M. releases, a consequence of being recorded live and a product of Riley's interest on one hand in the electronic effects and the rhythms current at the time in jazz-rock, and his openness on the other to the influence of late-period Coltrane that his saxophonist, Michael Stuart, brought to the bandstand.

Dreams was not an entirely coherent album, however, in part due to its range of directions, which also included the gospel stylings of Riley's solo piano *Blue Dream*, and in part due to some questionable editing, not least the reduction of Frank Zappa's *Chunga's Revenge* to a short drum solo and closing theme, less than three minutes of what had clearly been a longer performance. But *Dreams* was notable for its reprise of *Earth*, Riley's composition from Moe Koffman's *Solar Explorations*, played even more precipitously this second time than the first, with sharp shifts from funk to swing and back, catching

Ranger, a drummer possessed, in one of his most inspired performances on record.

Back in Montreal for the winter, he formed a band of his own with, variously, soprano saxophonist Jane Fair, alto saxophonist Maurice Bouchard, tenor saxophonist Steve Hall, pianist Geoff Lapp and bassist Brian Hurley. Fair, Hall, Lapp and Hurley were members of a small cohort of English-Canadian musicians whose number also included Terry King, Michael Morse and guitarists Burke Mahoney and Ted Quinlan. Some of them shared a house on Bleury Street, the site of many a jam session, including one of some legend in which Ranger had alternated with the American drummer Billy Hart, who was in town at the time with tenor saxophonist Stan Getz.

Maurice Bouchard, meanwhile, lived in Quebec City, where a small but venturesome jazz community flourished in some isolation in the bars and boîtes on and near *rue* St-Jean, cut off from the rest of the country, and indeed the continent, largely by its French unilingualism, as formidable a barrier in its way as the 18th-century ramparts that surrounded the old part of town.

Ranger had visited Quebec City in the late 1960s with Lee Gagnon and Herbie Spanier and in 1970 with Aquarius Rising. His presence there again during the winter of 1975-6 — at l'Harmonique with his own band and elsewhere — inevitably attracted the attention of the younger drummers on the scene, Raynald Drouin, Yves Jacques and Pierre Tanguay among them.

Accounts differ as to the nature of the music that the Ranger quintet played in this period. Fair and Hall, between them, recall a post-bop repertoire that included Herbie Hancock's *Dolphin Dance*, Wayne Shorter's *Wildflower* and Joe Henderson's *Gazelle*. Hurley remembers an element of fusion, rhythmically[4] — Ranger had explored rock rhythms with Doug Riley on *Dreams* — but Fair speaks of Ranger's own compositions as being rather less obviously grounded.

"Claude's music was really mysterious to me, very abstract, very open. The blowing sections would be open, sometimes no changes, or maybe one. There'd be these short melodic themes, and that's all you had. The themes were generally dark, and I just couldn't get next to that. So it was really challenging."[5]

In addition to its appearance at l'Harmonique, the Ranger quintet also worked locally in Montreal at the Rainbow Bar and Grill on Stanley Street and took its final engagement, four nights in early March 1976, at the Rising Sun, a second-floor room on St. Catherine Street West, near Bleury. There, as part of a late-winter lineup that also included Stan Getz, Bill Evans, Archie Shepp and bluesmen Willie Dixon and Muddy Waters, it was billed under Fair's name — and only Fair's name — as Women in Jazz.[6] Steve Hall wore a dress for the occasion. Ranger left town soon after.

In truth, he had overstayed his welcome with the Massons by then. "He never paid his part of the rent," Jacques Masson explains, citing the terms of their arrangement at the studio on de la Salle. "The way I was seeing it, I was learning a lot just by having Claude around, listening to him practice and talking about music. To me that was worth paying for his rent and putting up with the bullshit — for a time. But when it got to the point where he would buy beer and he wouldn't feed his children, I got on his case. *'C'mon*, man, *c'mon*. Get your act together, this doesn't make sense.'"

Ranger's irresponsibility evidently came to a head after he became involved with a woman in Quebec City and left his daughters entirely, and apparently without prior arrangement, in the Massons' care. When, in due course, Ranger followed his daughters back to Toronto, he stayed for a time with Greg Pilo's family before finding a room of his own on the top floor of a house on Chicora Avenue.

• • •

Ranger had returned to Toronto by late March 1976, when he appeared with Sonny Greenwich at a St. Nicholas Street gallery known as A Space. He also played in mid-April for the American singer Chris Connor at Basin Street, upstairs in the same building that housed Bourbon Street. His prospects were otherwise no more promising than they had been before he left Toronto in 1975.

He worked occasionally at a new club, the Mother Necessity Jazz Workshop, which Ted Moses had opened in January in a second floor space on Queen Street a few doors east of Yonge above what was once the Town Tavern, a fabled Toronto jazz room in the 1950s and 1960s. Moses, a pianist, composer and teacher from Oklahoma City, had been challenging the status quo in Toronto ever since he arrived in 1967 with his wife Kathryn, a flutist, not least by playing his own compositions, which had a decidedly contemporary flavour, rather than drawing on the standard jazz repertoire favoured by so many of the musicians who appeared at George's Spaghetti House.

Moses described Mother Necessity to Jack Batten as "a pure jazz room," an idea that he suggested was "kind of frightening in a way." His explanation was pointed and damning. "I think a lot of musicians have hidden behind the spaghetti scene and told themselves the pressure wasn't on them because people were there to eat their dinner. But in our place, it's entirely up to the musicians to produce."[7]

Equally, it was up to their music, and only their music, to draw listeners in sufficient number to provide those musicians with a reasonable financial return on an evening's work. Often it did not, as Barry Elmes learned one night when he gave Ranger a ride home from the club.

"Claude announced that he didn't have his rent. Could I loan him some money? I can't remember the amount. I said, 'Well, I think I've got forty dollars.' So I gave him my forty dollars, and he insisted on giving me his ride cymbal. It was probably not the one that he always played, but it was an old Zildjian 'K.' I still have it. I tried for years to give it back to him. He would have none of it. He said no, I'd saved his ass that day."

● ● ●

In time, Ranger's straitened circumstances forced him to take a steady job with a trio led by pianist George McFetridge in support of Vic

Franklyn, a Welsh pop singer who worked a circuit of Toronto restaurants and lounges, most notably in 1977 the Hacienda, near the city's international airport.

"When I was with Vic," Ranger explained, "I did nothing but make money for a year. There was nothing wrong with that, except I had to learn."

He "had to learn" — the very same words he used when discussing his marginalization in Toronto four years earlier, as if he were being taught a lesson, the way a child might be punished.

"It was my first gig in Toronto working steady," he continued. "The last time was over 10 years ago in Montreal. So I'd never worked steady in all that time. But I was not doing anything for a year and a half, and I had a chance to make some money every week, so I did it. Not nice, not a lot of fun, no, but..."

Franklyn had been enjoying some success as a recording artist during this period and was host in 1976 and 1977 for his own show on CHCH-TV in Hamilton. His nightclub act, which brought him comparisons to Frank Sinatra, mixed standards with newer pop material, some of it with Latin or reggae rhythms.

"As these things go," comments Steve Wallace, McFetridge's bass player for much of the time that Ranger was in the trio, "it was pretty jazzy."[8]

Pretty jazzy, of course, would not have been jazzy enough to keep Ranger happy, although he played Franklyn's music as creatively as he could under the circumstances. Frank Falco, who filled in at the piano for McFetridge on an engagement at another suburban spot, the Hotel Triumph, marvelled at Ranger's attention to detail, much as Michael Morse described his handling of a *merengue* on a meaningless night in an east-end Montreal bar years earlier.

"Without attitude or histrionics, and quite effortlessly," Falco later wrote, "Claude would come up with some intriguing two and sometimes four bar pattern, when just a one bar pattern would do, that lifted the song off the ground. These two or four bar patterns would then be slightly varied on the bridge or the last section. I realize now this was almost an encyclopedia of all the tone possibilities that a drum kit can produce. He could get at least three or four sounds from the cymbal, two or three from the snare, four or five from the high hat... all incorporated into his accompanying pattern. I would involuntarily look over to see just how many people were actually playing the drums. Even if the material wasn't inspired, his playing was."[9]

Wallace, however, recalls that Franklyn had other ideas. "He used to tell Claude, 'You gotta *lean* on it.' He told Claude that he wanted a *Count Basie Live at the Sands* kind of feel." Franklyn was referring, of course, to the classic 1966 recordings that the Basie band made in Las Vegas both on its own and — more to the point — with Frank Sinatra. "'You gotta *lean* on it,' he'd say. That used to bug Claude."

As did, no doubt, many other aspects of working with someone as demanding as Franklyn, whose engagements generally ran six nights a week and sometimes several weeks in a row, offering Ranger little time for reflection — had he been so inclined. There were tensions as well between Ranger and McFetridge.

"Whatever it was," Wallace suggests, speaking of his various experiences at Ranger's side more broadly, not just with Franklyn, "he'd get dragged whenever things didn't feel right. And sometimes it didn't feel right because of *him*. Claude wasn't the most consistent player, either. He's one of those guys who plays how he feels. And if he didn't feel good, you could tell.

"When I played with him at his best, he was as good as anyone I ever heard or played with. But there was nothing functional about it. He wasn't able to turn himself off, size up what a gig was supposed to be about and just *do* it. Whereas some guys, by dint of their personality, can do that. With Claude, a lot of people thought it was the drinking, but if he was bugged, or not inspired by what was going on around him, he just wouldn't play. He'd almost play *not* well on purpose. Or, he'd stop. I remember that. He did that on gigs I was on. He'd stop."

With Franklyn, Ranger was at the very least bored, as Wallace realized during the time that they spent together on their breaks each evening. "There were certain things he liked to do. He loved to play dominos. And he was always drawing. I forget how the dominos started, but it really helped because it was a mindless thing to do. He used to move them around and make designs — aside from actually playing the game."

Ranger, in character, took the younger Wallace — 21 that summer — under his wing. Wallace in turn invited Ranger to his family's Christmas dinner; Ranger's girlfriend at the time, a woman from Rimouski, had gone back to Quebec.

"I didn't think he should be alone," Wallace remembers. "*He* probably didn't care. But I invited him. It was strange because it was like the Wallace family — my brother and sister, my parents and my Irish grandmother, who was about 85 — and this guy from Quebec. I went out and got two cases of beer. Claude didn't say much, smoked like a chimney and ate like a bird. My dad loved him, he thought Claude was great. But it was a little uncomfortable. Claude tried to be as nice as he could, but I think he was really shy about the whole thing."

Seven weeks later, in February 1978, Franklyn, McFetridge, Wallace and Ranger moved downtown to reopen the Victoria Room, newly refurbished, in the venerable King Edward Hotel. Ranger did not complete the engagement.

• • •

"When I quit I was scared," Ranger admitted a few months later. "I thought I was not able to play any more. Everything was new." This, despite the fact that he had continued to play jazz all along, at least intermittently, including a week with the American alto saxophonist Charles McPherson at Bourbon Street in February 1977 and shorter engagements through the year with various Toronto musicians at Yellowfingers, a new basement club at the corner of Bay Street and Yorkville Avenue. He had also travelled to Edmonton for a record date with alto saxophonist P.J. Perry in July and to the Netherlands for a jazz festival in Laren with Don Thompson in August.

Perry and Ranger shared similar musical values in at least a general sense, a commitment to immediacy and risk — to going further. Perry's chosen style was bebop in a very pure form, an idiom that Ranger had moved beyond but could, and did, revisit quite comfortably when required.

"He had wonderful capacity to play with relaxed intensity," Perry notes. "That was what I dug — his time was always dead on, with a big, wide groove to play over."[10]

Perry assembled a quintet from across Canada for *Sessions*, his first recording as a leader, employing Ranger and George McFetridge from Toronto and bassist Torben Oxbol from Vancouver, as well as a bright young Edmonton trumpeter, Bob Tildesley. Ranger's playing in particular was notable for its efficiency; for once, *his* was generally the even hand in the band, so passionate were Perry's solos and, equally, so inspired by Perry's example were McFetridge and Tildesley. Only when Ranger traded fours with the three of them on McFetridge's *Nameless Blues* did he draw on all of his resources with all of his customary urgency.

As deftly as Ranger played for Perry, he was rather more directly in his element with the quartet that Don Thompson took a few weeks later to Holland and then in September to McMaster University in Hamilton. The latter concert was recorded by the CBC for its Radio Canada International transcription series, capturing Thompson — at the piano — with Ranger, Michael Stuart and Richard Homme in a program pervasively influenced by John Coltrane. Indeed, the most substantial piece on the RCI LP, *Don Thompson Quartet*, is Thompson's *Lament for John Coltrane*.

Ranger's drumming in Hamilton was tumultuous in its dynamic range and its detail — too tumultuous, apparently, for a reviewer from the *Hamilton Spectator* who described Ranger as "a two-fisted performer who likes to hammer a little too loud, a little too long,"[11] an estimation that was one fist too many with respect to the drum solo on Thompson's *Full Nelson*.

Thompson still wonders at the memory. "I looked over and

Claude's reaching down with one hand and rooting in his bag for a cigarette. He gets it out, and somehow gets it lit, and he's still playing the solo. You can't tell on the record, because he's still playing so much stuff with his other hand and his foot."

Ranger's trip with Thompson to the Netherlands would prove to be his only European venture. He was not, in any event, entirely suited to the demands and quick decisions of travel, although he participated in several tours later on, including trips with Thompson and Torben Oxbol in 1979 to Halifax, where they played at Pepe's, and to Victoria, where they were recorded for the CBC show *Jazz Radio-Canada*.

"I had to stick with him at the airport," Thompson comments, "because he would get confused. Like going from one terminal to another, or finding gates — he wasn't very good at that. I had to be with him. And I knew that, so it wasn't a problem, I just stuck with him all the time. That's okay, a lot of guys are like that. Lenny Breau couldn't find his way home at night. I'd have to take the subway with him, because otherwise he'd get off at the wrong stop."

Ranger did, however, make his way in this same period to Nyack, north of New York City, for a record date with the guitarist Muñoz, who had been a regular performer at Meat and Potatoes in Toronto earlier in the 1970s. The result, released as *Rendezvous with Now* under the India Navigation label, was not particularly to Ranger's liking. He was uncomfortable, he said at the time, with the "big, big" drums that were provided for him to play, as well as with the bass player on the date, Cecil McBee, and with what he described as the "religious feeling" of Muñoz's music.

He would make only a few other trips stateside during the next 20 years.

CHAPTER TEN

"Cynical"

His timing was excellent. No sooner had Claude Ranger left Vic Franklyn in February 1978 than Sonny Greenwich, off the scene since 1976, returned for two shows in March at the Colonial Tavern, followed by full weeks in April and May at Yellowfingers. Ranger, Don Thompson and Gene Perla completed the guitarist's latest band; Perla had the second Yellowfingers engagement recorded and released in part on his P.M. label as *Evol-ution, Love's Reverse*, an LP that proved to be something less than the classic of the Canadian jazz discography it might have been as the only substantial document of Greenwich and Ranger together. Ranger is once again poorly recorded — his drums have little resonance, as if cardboard boxes — and the music is extensively edited in ways that, title track aside, vastly diminish Greenwich's transcendent power.

Ranger also slipped back into the rotation at Bourbon Street with two Americans, flutist Sam Most in April and trumpeter Lew Soloff in June. He was not entirely happy there, but he tried to be philosophical.

"It's too much work playing drums in a rhythm section like that," he remarked of his bandmates with Most. "Even if you get strong, the rhythm slows down, gets heavy. So I don't like it. But I go and have a beer, go back, try to relax, and then it works — for a song or two."

At the same time, he had started to update some of his old compositions with a view to forming a new band of his own. "It will be eight pieces now," he advised, harking back to his septet 10 years earlier in Montreal, "because I'll be using Don on piano."

In July 1978, however, his career took a much different direction when he accepted an invitation to replace Marty Morell in the Moe Koffman Quintet. Canada's most successful jazz group in the 1970s promised reasonably steady employment, including a week every month at George's, concerts throughout Southern Ontario and regional tours elsewhere in Canada.

"People couldn't understand why Claude would be with Moe," Greg Pilo admits. "Well, Claude was like anybody else. When he was down, when he wasn't working, and when people said, 'I really want to play with you,' he could be talked into it. He certainly didn't volunteer for it."

Ranger joined the quintet at the same time as Neil Swainson took over from Richard Homme as its bassist; Bernie Senensky soon succeeded Don Thompson at the piano and subsequently added electric keyboards, while Ed Bickert, midway through an association of more than 40 years with Koffman, remained constant on guitar.

Twenty-one years earlier, Koffman, with Bickert and others, had recorded a rather catchy flute instrumental, *Swinging Shepherd Blues*, and watched as it became an international hit. Koffman adopted the tune as his theme song and took its success as something of a portent, continuing throughout his career to pursue wider popularity, or at least directions that showed some potential in that regard, be they lightly jazzy renditions of classical favourites, disco or the music of Andrew Lloyd Webber.

Ranger thus found himself a member of one of the most commercial jazz bands in the country, while working during the same period, if far less frequently, with one of the least, the Greenwich quartet.

For good measure, he also played on occasion in 1978 with vibra-phonist Peter Appleyard on CHCH-TV's *Peter Appleyard Presents*, whose host characterized himself well when he told Frank Rasky of the *Toronto Star*, "If you want to cut the mustard like a pro on TV today, it's not enough to be a good musician. You must sell yourself and your music to the customers, you've got to prance and dance a little and deliver some of that old showbiz razzmatazz."[1]

Ranger, certainly not one for prancing, dancing or razzmatazz, understandably showed little evident enthusiasm when he backed three veteran Americans — tenor saxophonist Zoot Sims, pianist Hank Jones and bassist Slam Stewart — on one of the Appleyard shows, and Koffman, Guido Basso and trombonist Ian McDougall, Toronto studio stalwarts in the unlikely guise of a dixieland frontline, on another. His drumming in each instance was nevertheless the model of discretion.

"I don't think you can be more cynical than me," he declared at the time, with reference neither to Koffman nor to Appleyard specifically, but to the incongruity of such situations in general. "Sometimes I'm playing and I'm laughing at the guys. It's crazy. 'What am I doing here?' I have to wonder. Being responsible, I said, 'Yes, I'll be there,' and now I'm suffering. 'What *is* this shit?'"

• • •

Ranger spent much of the first half of 1979 on the road, travelling in the Maritimes and around Ontario with Moe Koffman, recording stateside with Lenny Breau, appearing at the Rising Sun in Montreal with Sonny Greenwich and then relaxing for a month or so — mid-April into May — in Quebec City on his own.

Ranger and Breau had not played together in at least five years, a period in which the guitarist attempted to address his drug and alcohol addictions and, in the process, had returned to the United States, the country of his birth, after more than 20 years in Canada. He was living in Nashville when he summoned Ranger and Don Thompson to par-ticipate in a "direct-to-disc" session that required the three musicians to complete one side of an LP in a single, uninterrupted take of 15 minutes' duration or longer with no significant miscues.

Between the challenges presented by this relatively new technology on one hand, and the effects of an ill-advised gesture of hospitality on the other, the session did not — in Thompson's memory — go well. "We showed up early in the afternoon, and the producer had brought in cases and cases of beer. So right away, Claude and Lenny start drinking. And we'd do take after take, because we'd have to do the whole side. Well, by the time the sound was right, neither one of them could basically play anymore. It was just too late."

The resulting LP, released simply as *Lenny Breau*, was nevertheless notable for an inspired version of the Bob Dylan song *Don't Think Twice (It's All Right)*, driven in part by Ranger's deft brush work, something rarely heard on record. The trio played John Coltrane's *Mr. Knight* and Breau's own *Neptune* in sometimes unsteady haste, then ventured into *Claude (Free Song)*, credited as another Breau composition but, as performed, a barely disguised rumination on *The Shadow of Your Smile*.

Ranger's reunion with his friends in Quebec City was by all accounts a happier affair. He stayed for a time with Maurice Bouchard and more briefly with drummer Pierre Tanguay, spending many of his days, as the weather warmed, cycling in the country. He appeared with Bouchard on a *Jazz en liberté* broadcast — the series was nearing its end by then — and accepted an invitation to be the featured artist for a week at the Café Rimbaud, where drummer Yves Jacques, long a Ranger fan, was the bandleader.

Ranger also encountered a free and kindred spirit at l'Ostradamus in tenor saxophonist Claude Béland, whose affinity for the exultant music of Albert Ayler — an avant-garde influence otherwise scarcely heard in Canada save from Jazz Libre in Montreal — was a far and bracing cry from anything that Ranger had been doing of late with Moe Koffman or even, for that matter, Sonny Greenwich.

• • •

Ranger's working relationship with Koffman was, in Neil Swainson's words, "cordial at first." Koffman even added Ranger's ballad *Freedom for the Child* to the quintet's repertoire. Inevitably, though, there was conflict. "Claude was pretty uncompromising by nature," Swainson observes, "but this was a fairly compromising gig, so he was looking at it as a chance for financial security — you know, a steady job, make some money — and still play artistically within its confines. And he was magnificent when he felt like playing. But sometimes he didn't, and when he didn't, it was pretty awful, because there was a vibe attached to that scenario — he was obviously pissed off at somebody or something.

"It was pretty good most of the time, then it got to be about fifty-fifty. The gig was pretty much the same every night, the same tunes in the same order. Moe wasn't very spontaneous about mixing it up; it was like a show. We all thought, 'Oh well, it is what it is.' But Claude wasn't as philosophical."[2]

Quite so, according to Greg Pilo. "When Claude played with guys who played the same all the time, no matter how good they were, that would enrage him, absolutely enrage him."

Ranger's response to this and other aggravations would escalate with his level of frustration. "One thing Claude used to do," Don Thompson explains, "he'd just start playing free, right in the middle of a straight-ahead tune. He'd be playing 'time' and the bass would be pushing it little. So instead of going with the bass, he'd just start playing free, he'd go out of tempo. And everybody would think that he was just being weird. He did that with Moe's band and it drove everybody nuts.

"He told me once, 'Everybody says I don't like to play time. I like to play time, I just don't like to *have* to play time.' And he really *could* play time. He had a groove that was unbelievable. But if the bass player was pushing, he couldn't deal with it. He'd get really angry and he'd stop playing, or he'd play free. Sometimes he'd get up and walk away. He just couldn't stand it."

Even Sonny Greenwich felt his displeasure. The two musicians had started off badly years earlier when Ranger abandoned the guitarist onstage in Montreal. And there were still issues, at least in passing, when they worked together during the late 1970s and early 1980s.

"I was playing at the Rising Sun," Greenwich remembers, without apparent malice, "and his sticks came flying over my head. I looked back, and he was just sitting there, cigarette in his mouth, smiling away. We never talked about that — whether he did it purposely or not."

On another occasion, Greenwich called *As Time Goes By*, made famous by the movie *Casablanca*, as the last tune of the evening. It was, he acknowledges, "an unusual song to be playing," one that apparently did not meet with Ranger's approval. "He was playing kind of funny behind me. You would hear some some stray bashes on the cymbal where you wouldn't expect them and you would look around and wonder, 'What was *that*?'"

Indeed, it was a tribute of sorts to Ranger that Koffman, Greenwich and other bandleaders were prepared to cope with him at his worst in the perpetual hope that he might be at his best. "When it was obvious that Claude didn't feel like playing," Neil Swainson notes, "Moe was pretty good at smoothing things over and being philosophical. 'Next time it'll be better.'"

After a tour of Australia in March 1980, however, there was no more next time. Ranger had travelled with the Koffman quintet across Canada and in September 1979 to the Artpark and Monterey jazz festivals in Lewiston, in upstate New York, and Monterey, California, respectively. But the trip to Australia was a far more ambitious proposition, 21 days altogether, including eight nights at the Adelaide Festival Jazz Club followed by stops in Melbourne, Canberra, Brisbane and Sydney.

By then, Ranger had been in the band for almost 20 months. "He was ready to leave that gig long before he left," Swainson suggests. "He was probably there a year longer than he wanted to be." The story of his departure has become the stuff of legend and, as legend so often is, subject to considerable exaggeration: how he stormed off the stage, expletives flying, in the middle of a concert at the Adelaide Festival with television cameras rolling and Koffman's guest, the distinguished Irish classical flutist James Galway, looking on.

In the event, the surviving members of the Koffman quintet — Bickert, Senensky and Swainson — recall a rather less dramatic, and certainly less public, confrontation in the presence neither of television cameras nor of James Galway. At that, even *their* versions of events differ from one another. There had been irritants, they agree, including an issue with money; Ranger had either already spent his allotted *per diem* before leaving Canada or simply had nothing left over in Australia, after cigarettes and beer, for food.

At the same time, though, the trip was not without its pleasures. Ranger cycled when he could and was sufficiently taken with Australia and its natural beauty that he talked openly, and made inquiries during the tour, about moving there. He later described his experience to Peter Goddard of the *Toronto Star*.

"During the days," Goddard summarized, "he'd laze around on the beaches, soaking in the sun. He felt he had so much energy by the time it'd come to play that he just wanted to bust loose. But busting loose was exactly what wasn't wanted."[3]

Instead, as heard and seen in the CBC-TV production *Moe Koffman in Australia* — in equal parts jazz concert, variety show and Adelaide travelogue, with a big band version of *Waltzing Matilda* as its closing theme — Ranger was on his very best behaviour, even to the extent of not smoking on camera. His drumming, moreover, was remarkably restrained — appropriately so, given Koffman's cautiously contemporary style.

Tensions between the two men nevertheless came out in the open on a club date toward the end of the tour — likely at the Cellar in Brisbane — during either an afternoon sound check or the evening show. A relatively minor incident led to a standoff that, as Senensky describes it, was resolved only when Koffman suggested, in so many words, that Ranger could quit the band if he was unhappy. Ranger duly agreed, although he completed the tour.

"We had one more night," Senensky recalls. "I think it was in

Sydney, at a nice club. Claude played better than he'd played the whole tour, and I remember thinking, 'What a drag, he's leaving, and he's really playing great.'"[4]

If, as Steve Wallace suggests, Ranger could "almost play *not* well on purpose," he could also play *very* well indeed on purpose, if only to make a point. Or an exit.

Chapter Eleven

"Fifty minutes of pure joy"

Claude Ranger returned to Toronto, and to an uncertain future, at the end of March 1980. His response to the precariousness of his new circumstances was simply to withdraw — or so he told Peter Goddard.

"I just quit. I didn't want music. And except for two weeks with James Moody at Bourbon [Street] I was completely out of jazz."

While his rationale rings true, his timeframe once again does not. "I spent a year-and-a-half doing nothing, nothing at all," he continued. "Day after day, I was sitting in my apartment. I was crazy, but I felt I had no other choice. I was getting near 40 and I'd spent most of my life playing this style, that style, but not expressing myself. I was losing myself, and once you've done that, you've lost everything."

He was indeed reunited with James Moody at Bourbon Street in late April, but far from being otherwise "completely out of jazz," he was also working during this period with tenor and soprano saxophonist Ron Allen. Their trio, completed by bassist Kieran Overs, had made its debut in late January 1980, while Ranger was still with the Koffman band, and continued with either Overs or Dave Field well into the summer.

Allen was just the latest of Ranger's discoveries in his perpetual search for "one good horn player" — at 20 already an intensely expressive soloist in the tradition of John Coltrane as personalized by two other saxophonists in the same lineage, the Norwegian Jan Garbarek and the Argentinian Gato Barbieri. He was playing at one or another of the secondary rooms that presented jazz in Toronto at the end of the 1970s — possibly the Soho Cabaret on Queen Street West or Danielle's at Chartwells on Yonge Street north of Davisville Avenue — when Ranger first approached him.

"Claude came up in the middle of a song, after a solo," Allen recalls, "and just basically said, 'I've got to have you. You've got to play with me. I will show you the world.'"

Ranger was dismissive of the other musicians with whom Allen was playing that night. "'You can't fool around with these guys. They'll ruin you. I can show you how to play.' He might even have been talking into the microphone a bit, but he wasn't aware of it. And he gave me his phone number, or someone gave me his phone number — maybe the girl who was with him — and they left immediately after that. I called him the next day; I think I was *over* there the next day."

Ranger was living at the time above a store on Bathurst Street just north of Bloor. Kieran Overs remembers it as "basically an empty apartment with a set of drums, a mattress and a fridge full of Coca-Cola and 222s." Another friend from this period adds a small television, a radio and some house plants to the furnishings, and carrots to the contents of the fridge. For a time, there was also an upright piano, which Ranger was forced to sell when money ran low, as they often did, even while he had been with the Koffman quintet.

His apartment did not have a buzzer. Visitors called in advance from a pay phone at the Bathurst subway station down the street or a donut shop nearby; Ranger would meet them at the front door downstairs. Allen, who stopped by frequently to rehearse, likens the exercise to a "covert operation," but suggests that Ranger's quarters otherwise had their advantages.

"Claude was an icon where he lived. He probably knew that. The other tenants were very supportive; as long as it wasn't late at night, it seemed that he could play."

At home (Bathurst Street), with Kieran Overs, Toronto, 1980.
Photograph by Mark Miller.

Although it was Ranger who had initiated this new collaboration — and who was, in Allen's words, "really directing it" — the trio carried Allen's name alone when it appeared for the first time publicly at Danielle's. "Either the music had to sound the way Claude wanted it to sound or we wouldn't play it," Allen explains. "But even when a club wanted to use both of our names, he'd say, 'It's not time yet.' Eventually there came a point when it was."

Prodigiously creative, Allen was turning ideas over very quickly and moving in and out of the jazz tradition. Typically, one of his most dynamic compositions for the trio, *March of the Dead*, was inspired by hearing Ranger play military snare patterns as practice exercises. But not all of Allen's notions appealed to Ranger, who referred to the most unconventional of them as "Chinese music," the same characterization famously employed by Cab Calloway 40 years earlier to dismiss Dizzy Gillespie's nascent bebop style.

"Claude told me he wanted to understand what my 'Chinese music' was all about, because it was different, but at the same time he wanted *me* to understand and have the feel of jazz. He didn't want me to be a naive kid from Mississauga. He was very concerned, *very* concerned, that I hadn't lived, that I was too preppy. He wanted me to be authentic."

Allen remembers writing a piece that involved a rhythmic pattern of five beats against four, prefiguring his eventual move away from jazz into World Music. "Claude got it right away. He even added a three on the high-hat. But he just looked at me and said, 'Ron, that's for the next guys. I can't make it swing. You go and try to make it work, but not with me.'"

Ranger and Allen inevitably parted ways, but not before completing a short tour that took the trio — by then billed under both of their names — to CW's in Ottawa, l'Air du Temps in Montreal and the Drugstore in Quebec City. "The Quebec thing was to show his buddies at home what he had," Allen suggests. "He was proud of it in a very French-like way, very proud of it. He said, 'I want to show my people what we're doing.'"

There were also concerts in June and July, the former incongruously as an opening act for the American guitarist Ralph Towner, who performed a solo, acoustic concert at the NWDT Theatre, and the latter no less improbably over the supper hour in the food court of the Village by the Grange. Each in its way demonstrated the difficulty that the trio had in finding a place — any place — for itself on the local scene.

Ranger later played fairly circumspectly in October 1980 on three quartet pieces recorded at Danielle's for Allen's debut LP, *Leftovers*, and contributed a personal endorsement to the album's back cover. "For a young man to become strong and powerful in his early life, to be able to master the instrument so quickly," he wrote, "shows great talent. It gives me great pleasure to participate in his effort to produce this beautiful music."

Ranger was no less supportive privately, if rather darker, offering Allen some practical advice clearly based on his understanding of his own experience in Toronto since 1972. "Claude was never harsh with me, but what *was* harsh, sometimes, was the truth. 'You have to live more,' he'd say. 'You have to get away from here. Don't do what I did and stay here. People here will stab you in the back. If you're good, watch out, you're a target.'"

Allen in turn drew his own conclusions — more philosophical than practical — from Ranger's example. He offers them in a series of subordinate clauses: "That art is sacred, that you can't destroy it on its own, but that you can mismanage it as a person. That if you're carrying it around as a gift, then it is a gift that is a blessing and a curse. That it's a shame to mismanage it or ignore it. That it's — I was going to say 'a crime,' which is probably what Claude would have said — if you don't honour the art or honour the gift. That music has to come directly from the heart, and if it doesn't, then there's no point."

• • •

It was at Danielle's one Sunday early in 1980 that Ranger's life took a favourable turn. It began with an unexpected apology. He and Kieran Overs were not in step rhythmically in support of Ron Allen that evening, and Overs was prepared to hear about it in no uncertain terms, mindful of Ranger's remark a couple of years earlier to a young bassist with whom he had been unhappy, a remark that had already entered the annals of jazz in Toronto.

"Man," Ranger had complained, "you're ruining my life!"

Overs expected something similar. "I thought I was in for it, because we were playing and it's getting worse and worse, and I feel like I can't put two beats together with him, and I'm thinking, 'Okay, here it comes. He's going to figure out a way of making me regret ever picking up the bass and starting to play music.'

"Claude pulls at me, says, 'C'mere.'

"I asked, 'Is everything okay?'

"He said, 'Sorry for my playing.'

"'*What*?'

Ranger explained that he was distracted by a woman in the audience. "'Sorry man, she's driving me crazy. I can't focus.'"

The woman was Ali Karnick, with whom Ranger would live for the next four years.

Karnick, an American, worked in Toronto film and television circles as a casting director, a position that demanded a degree of empathy for artistic temperaments and an understanding of the entertainment business. She provided Ranger with both the personal stability — not least a comfortable home on Silverbirch Avenue in the east-end Beach neighbourhood of the city — and the practical support that allowed him to leave the nightly grind of the jazz world behind. As he told John Gilmore, "She saved my life."

Ranger worked almost exclusively with his own bands during this period. On the rare occasions when he took other engagements — with Lenny Breau at Bourbon Street in March 1981, for example, and with Sonny Greenwich variously at the Ontario Science Centre, the Stratford Jazz Festival, Bourbon Street and Pears Restaurant into early 1982 — they often ended badly. He was fired by Breau after two evenings and quit Greenwich's band at the end of the Pears engagement.

"If that's all you do, playing what others want," he advised Peter Goddard, "then somewhere along the way you can't play what you want. You lose yourself."

Ranger would find himself again, and play what he wanted, with two successive and evolving bands of his own. The first, a quintet, made its debut at The Edge on March 29, 1981, the evening before the ill-fated Breau engagement began; Ranger's preoccupation with his own music might well have accounted for his apparent distraction, and his drinking, at Bourbon Street, where his drumming over the course of opening night, as noted in a *Globe and Mail* review, "became less adroit than usual and less sensitive to Breau than the guitarist's music requires."[1]

His new quintet had its origins in a call made by cornetist Roland Bourgeois for a recording session in late 1980 with saxophonist Chris Chahley, pianist Mark Eisenman and bassist Marty Melanson. "'Sure,'" Bourgeois recalls Ranger saying in French. "'Buy me a case of beer, and I'll be there.'"[2]

Bourgeois and Melanson worked together during the mid-1970s in Moncton, New Brunswick; they had played more recently alongside Chahley in a jazz ensemble at Mohawk College in Hamilton. All three, as well as Eisenman, agreed to Ranger's suggestion early in 1981 that he take them on as his own band. By their third engagement together, in late May again at The Edge, he had reverted to his old format of horns, bass and drums — no piano — and had added a second saxophonist and third Maritimer, Kirk MacDonald, originally from Nova Scotia. Bourgeois at 27 was the eldest of Ranger's musicians, MacDonald at 21 the youngest.

At first, Ranger proceeded cautiously, aware of the general conservatism of Toronto audiences and of the backgrounds of his musicians. Rather than reviving his old compositions from *Jazz en liberté* or from his association with Brian Barley, he looked to jazz standards of similar or older vintage, including Bill Evans' *Blue in Green*, Benny

Golson's *I Remember Clifford*, Herbie Hancock's *One Finger Snap*, Freddie Hubbard's *The Intrepid Fox*, Lee Konitz's *Subconscious Lee* and Charles Lloyd's *Sweet Georgia Bright*. He also transcribed an arrangement of *Stella by Starlight*, as recorded in 1958 by one of his early influences, Max Roach, on the LP *Max on the Chicago Scene*.

His retrospection did not, however, extend to his performances, which were remarkably immediate in their hard-boppish energy and urgency, with every tune — ballads aside — played a shade faster than discretion might advise. At the same time, his own arrangements were carefully wrought, often quite intricate thematically and invariably subject to refinement as his musicians worked through them in rehearsal; Bourgeois, in the role of straw boss, would bring the band together twice a week in Ali Karnick's basement as schedules allowed.

"Claude would always have a stack of new music," MacDonald remembers. "We'd play through things and he'd hear stuff, and he's kind of thinking, 'So, I had *this* in mind, but it doesn't quite sound right.' We'd go back three days later and most of that time for him would have been spent rewriting everything. The stack of music would be much smaller, but it would be the same music and it would be reworked."[3]

Ranger's meticulousness extended to the actual appearance of the music on the page. "He'd have it hand written, looking perfect on paper," Bourgeois marvels. "His penmanship was amazing. He'd bring it to a rehearsal and if there was one little thing that was wrong with his arrangement, he'd pull all the pages back and rewrite everything. He wouldn't scratch stuff out. His charts were *clean*."

As such, Ranger's scores were just one more manifestation of the visual creativity that was also apparent in his wax sculptures, his drawings and, new in this period, his interest in photography and his decision, unaccountably, to cut patterns into his cymbals — classic Zildjian "K"s — with metal snips, much to the horror of his fellow drummers.

"Every drummer in town," MacDonald recalls, "was saying, 'Oh, my god, *no*!' Any one of them would have killed to have those cymbals.

They sounded so great and basically Claude just destroyed them. He played them for a while and took them on a few gigs. I suppose they looked good, but the sound was like *'pish, pish.'"*

Poster by Claude Ranger, 1982.
Author's collection.

With Ali Karnick providing Ranger with moral and business support, and likely his new set of Paiste cymbals, the band continued as a quintet with Chris Chahley until March 1982, appearing at Pears Restaurant and in various rooms along Queen Street West including the Mother Necessity Jazz Workshop, which Ted Moses had revived briefly in the basement of the Drake Hotel, and the Music Gallery, a performance space operated by members of the CCMC, musicians devoted to improvisation even freer than was Ranger's wont.[4]

The quintet also performed in early February 1982 for CJRT-FM's *Sound of Toronto Jazz* concert series at the Ontario Science Centre and made a studio recording — never released — later in the same week. By then, Ranger had gradually replaced the band's early repertoire of modern jazz standards with new compositions of his own — *East 14th*, *Le Jouet magique*, *Wood Nymph* and *Boxing* for the CJRT-FM broadcast — and while he maintained the elements of closely rehearsed melodic intricacy and counter movement in his themes, quite unlike the quick, angular jab of *Challenge* and *Showbar* from the 1960s, he loosened the structural constraints on his musicians' improvisations.

"Initially, Claude was writing some modal things and he was writing some things with changes that were quite difficult for the quintet," MacDonald explains. "When the band changed to a quartet — when it became two horns — his writing became much more open, and typically there were no changes. With some things, there might have been a tonality, or a scale to start from, but for the most part it was pretty free."

• • •

Ranger's accomplishments in this period were variously recognized. Ali Karnick had prepared a Canada Council application on his behalf and, in March 1982, he was one of 46 recipients of an Arts Grant "A," valued at up to $19,000 plus expenses. Only three of the other 45 successful applicants were musicians — Ian McDougall, the Quebec classical composer Claude Vivier and the Vancouver harpsichord builder Edward Turner.[5]

In April, Ranger took Bourgeois, MacDonald and Melanson to l'Air du Temps in Montreal; in May he augmented them with a second trumpet, two trombones and baritone saxophone for a concert at the Music Gallery. Came July, the quartet returned to Montreal for two outdoor shows at Vieux Port as part of the Festival International de Jazz de Montréal; it was during this trip that Ranger was interviewed by John Gilmore. The band also appeared in August at the Jazz City International Jazz Festival in Edmonton, sharing a bill before an audience of 500 at the Shoctor Theatre with Hugh Fraser's Vancouver Ensemble for Jazz Improvisation on a night headlined by Max Roach.[6]

The significance of playing on the same stage as Roach, if only earlier in the same evening, was not lost on Ranger. "When Claude would be nervous and scared," Bourgeois remembers, "*we* would all be, too. And that night he was. But he really played well."

Festival International de Jazz de Montréal, July 1982.
Photograph by Mark Miller.

Ranger himself, looking ahead from Montreal to the evening with Roach in Edmonton, told John Gilmore, "It's an honour, after all this time." In the event, he may or may not have stayed for Roach's show — recollections vary — but he turned up later that night at the festival's after-hours jam session at the Four Seasons Hotel, where he agreed to sit in despite feeling, and inevitably showing, the full effect of an evening's drinking.

The Montreal and Edmonton festivals, both in their third years, were formative to the development of a national summer circuit that offered a broader representation of contemporary jazz — American and European — than was typically heard at Bourbon Street, the Rising Sun and other clubs across the country. As the festivals grew in number and size over the next 30 years, many would eventually sacrifice the historical and creative integrity of the jazz tradition by booking pop, rock, blues, rhythm and blues and World Music as well. For the moment, however, Ranger's quartet, in its fervour and relative freedom, fit comfortably with the festivals' comparatively enlightened aesthetic, and his performances were favourably received at both events.

Peter Danson, writing in *Coda* from Montreal, described the quartet as "without a doubt the hottest new group on the Canadian scene," and added, "someone had better record this band, and quick."[7] Hal Hill, in the same publication, referred to Ranger's set in Edmonton as "fifty minutes of pure joy" and commented on "a high energy level not met too often throughout the festival."[8]

Ranger was also reunited at the Montreal festival with Michel Donato in support of the vociferous young baritone saxophonist Charles Papasoff, and similarly did double duty in Edmonton, where he appeared with two ad hoc groups of festival all-stars, one led by trumpeter Kenny Wheeler and the other by alto saxophonist Phil Woods, in place of an American headliner who had been turned back at the Canadian border.

Even as his quartet's fortunes were rising, however, Ranger's interest was starting to wane. "He was very patient," MacDonald suggests, reviewing Ranger's relationship with his young bandmates. "And I'm sure with his later bands it was the same thing — he was very patient in giving the music, and the musicians, a chance to realize what was there. Particularly with the quartet, there was enough room in the music for us to accept the challenge of growing with him, and with the music."

The challenge of growing with Ranger proved to be the challenge of moving from hard-bop, a style with which Bourgeois, MacDonald and Melanson were more than comfortable, to something approaching free jazz, an idiom with which they were less familiar. "Let's see how far we can go with this," he would suggest to his musicians. In time, they apparently could not go far enough.

Bourgeois, like MacDonald, remembers Ranger's cordiality. "When you were in his band, he would take good care of you, make you feel good, make you feel part of it." But Bourgeois also caught glimpses of frustration. "Sometimes the alcohol would take over and you'd get a call at 2 in the morning. He'd say, 'OK, the band's done.' Then you'd hear Ali pick up the other phone and say, 'Don't listen to him!' And you'd think, 'Man, this is screwed up.' But the next day it would be, 'OK, Roland, organize a rehearsal.'"

After 19 months of performances, however, Ranger decided that the band had truly run its course. The explanation that he offered to his musicians on what would be their last appearance together — a concert in October 1982 at the Music Gallery — was not a little disingenuous.

"My first son was born on October 7," Bourgeois remembers, "and on October 10 Claude announced that the band was finished. He said, 'Roland won't have time anymore.' He meant I wouldn't have time to do the same duties as before — to be his driver, to organize rehearsals."

Ranger may well have been projecting his own rather jaundiced view of parental responsibility on to his cornetist's immediate future, but Bourgeois understood his words for what they were. "I think it was just his way of saying that he was tired of playing with us."

CHAPTER TWELVE

Feu vert

Within weeks of bidding Roland Bourgeois, Kirk MacDonald and Marty Melanson *adieu*, Claude Ranger started to organize his next band — one that proved to be bigger, by and large younger and certainly freer.

His new tenor saxophonist, Perry White, not quite 21, had arrived from Vancouver in September 1982, only weeks after he had played with the Vancouver Ensemble for Jazz Improvisation on a bill with the Ranger quartet at Jazz City in Edmonton. Once in Toronto, White busked on Yonge Street with a teenaged drummer, Graeme Kirkland, until winter set in.

"We'd been playing on the street quite a bit," he recalls, "and sometimes we'd meet interesting people. One time we were playing Jimmy Forrest's *Night Train* and his wife came by and said, 'My husband wrote that song!' That was cool."

On another occasion Ranger stopped to listen and, according to legend, sat in. "To see Claude there was really exciting. And it was neat just to be around him. He was kind of coy at first. He was taking photos because he was into photography at the time — just taking some shots of us playing. He talked to us for a while, asked us some questions. And then the next day he called me up and asked me to play in his band."[1]

One by one, other horn players followed. White's brother Michael, 22, also a veteran of the Vancouver Ensemble for Jazz Improvisation, was studying trumpet at the University of Toronto. Rikk Villa, a precocious soprano and tenor saxophonist, just 17 and still in high school, took lessons privately with Ron Allen and was influenced, as Allen had been, by Jan Garbarek. Steve Donald, 24, a trombonist in the music program at York University, had previously played with Ranger in a clinic there.

And so the rehearsals in Ali Karnick's airless basement began anew, with Dick Felix, a little older than the others, playing bass. "Claude would be chain-smoking," Perry White remembers, "and we'd be choking to death. It was brutal. You couldn't breathe. But you'd never say anything. Sometimes you'd cough and wave the air a bit."

Of course it would be unrealistic to expect Ranger, in his self-absorption, not to smoke — or for that matter to drink — when the band got together. "He used to drink when we rehearsed," Donald admits, "and I always had the sense that the rehearsal was over when he felt that his drinking was affecting his playing. It wouldn't necessarily stop him from drinking, but it would stop the rehearsal."

Ranger was otherwise quite solicitous of his musicians. "He really cared about the guys in the band," Donald adds, echoing Roland Bourgeois' remarks about Ranger's relationship with his young charges. "He wanted everyone to feel good about playing. He was always asking, 'How's so and so doing?' He always wanted to know what we were doing. Did we have girlfriends? Did we have nice, happy relationships?"[2]

Moreover, he revealed a hidden side both of himself and of his music one evening when, after a year or so with the new lineup, he invited Villa to visit on his own and asked that he bring his soprano saxophone. "I was in the dark regarding his plans," Villa later wrote, "and when I arrived he took me upstairs to a room where I saw his

Fender Rhodes for the first time. Its music stand was thick with staff paper, all filled with songs that I would have never attributed to him had I not known his notational style.

"He put one in front of me and sat down at the keyboard and played the intro, and I followed with the melody. It was a sweet, clear and poignant song, almost a lament, and he played the Rhodes with an innocence and delicacy that was the polar opposite of his drumming. It was immediately obvious to me that I was in Claude's private realm; a place of longing and love, of hope and loss, a place of immense emotional complexity.

"We played the song to its conclusion and he was silent for a few moments with his head down. He then got up and came to me with glistening eyes and we just held on to each other for a while. I felt like a father and a son at the same time."[3]

. . .

That the early 1980s were the years of the Young Lions in jazz was, with respect to Ranger's bands, merely a coincidence. Not for him this or any other trend; his interest in working with younger musicians had predated the emergence of the New Orleans trumpeter Wynton Marsalis, 21 in the fall of 1982, whose success opened the door for those of his contemporaries who, like him, played in a "neo-traditional" style based on modern jazz of the 1950s and 1960s.

To the contrary, Perry White suggests, "Claude was always looking for something fresh, something breaking out of the box a bit. He wasn't happy with something that had happened before. He was always trying to find new sounds. So I guess when he came by and heard us playing on the street he heard something he liked — something that suggested something different to him."

Michael White describes Ranger's quest in much the same terms. "He was searching all the time. If *you* were searching, and even if something wasn't quite right, but it was different, he'd say, '*Go*, man. Let's see what we can do with that!'"[4]

The new Ranger sextet made its debut in January 1983 at the Arbor Room in Hart House on the University of Toronto campus and subsequently appeared later in the winter at the Cabana Room of the Spadina Hotel and at the Rivoli, clubs that were part of the "Queen Street scene" of the day — even though the Spadina Hotel was three short blocks south on King Street.

The Queen Street scene was largely known for its rock, punk and reggae groups but in 1983 was also home to a modest jazz subculture, represented on one hand by the CCMC at the Music Gallery and free-improvisational ensembles led by saxophonists Maury Coles and Bill Smith, and on the other hand by such bands as Nic Gotham's Gotham City, Bill Grove's Whitenoise, Gerald Berg's Malcolm Tent and Tom Walsh's Thin Men, whose predominant influence was Ornette Coleman's Prime Time, with its rock and funk rhythms and its electric guitars.

Ranger's music did not fit either ideologically or idiomatically into either camp, but was similarly at odds with the Toronto jazz mainstream as represented, still, by the musicians heard at George's Spaghetti House. Moreover, his band's size was problematic, and if a sextet was not difficult enough for Ali Karnick to book, Ranger impulsively added a seventh member in mid-1983, alto saxophonist Jonnie Bakan, who was sharing a house on Bertmount Avenue in east-end Leslieville with the Whites, Donald and Graeme Kirkland.

"I was downstairs practicing and Perry was talking to Claude on the phone," Bakan remembers. "Perry came down and said Claude asked him to bring 'the guy in the basement' to the next rehearsal."[5]

• • •

Steve Donald, Jonnie Bakan and the Whites were also — or would soon be — involved with Freddie Stone, who was a force parallel to Ranger in terms of his personal impact on the development of many of Toronto's most creative younger musicians in the early 1980s.

Stone, five-and-a-half years Ranger's senior, had followed a much different career path to a similar position of influence. Although he too had started in showbands — in fact with his father, Archie, who was the orchestra leader at the Casino — he became a first-call trumpet and flugelhorn player in Toronto studios and a featured soloist with big bands and, on occasion, symphony orchestras during the 1960s. For all of his obvious discipline as a musician, though, he was the freest of spirits and the most idiosyncratic of improvisers, a flugelhorn player whose fancifully melodic, mercurially emotional solos were unique in modern jazz.

No less than Duke Ellington, who prized individuality in a musician, famously remarked on hearing Stone for the first time, "I don't know what he's doing, but he sure is good at it!" Ellington was sufficiently captivated to take the Canadian into his orchestra in March 1970; Stone, only the second Canadian — after bassist Al Lucas — to be so honoured, returned home five months later a changed man.

Having spent years matching tones with Guido Basso, Arnie Chycoski, Erich Traugott and other Toronto trumpeters to create the polished, uniform section work that defined the sound of the city's studio and jazz orchestras, he found himself playing alongside Ellington legends Cat Anderson, Cootie Williams and — apparently on at least one occasion — Ray Nance in a band whose aesthetic was rather different.[6]

"I was having trouble phrasing a 'shot' in Duke's band," he later told Bruce Cassidy, "so I said to Ray one night, 'Ray, how should I play that A-flat?' Ray said, 'It's *your* A-flat, play it any way you want!' The penny dropped. I realized that there was a whole other world out there."

Stone took some of that world and its possibilities back to Toronto and, instead of picking up where he had left off in the studios, turned to teaching. In time he began performing with ensembles made up of his students, several of whom also played during the mid-1980s with Ranger's bands.

Stone had not been long off the road with Ellington, nor Ranger long in Toronto from Montreal, when they worked together for the first time under Stone's leadership at a concert in London, Ontario.

According to the pianist in the band, Don Thompson, Stone and Ranger met just moments before the start of the performance.

"I introduced them, and then we went out to play. Claude had no idea what Freddie was about, and Freddie had no idea what Claude was about. There was no music, there was no discussion of what we were going to do, there was no set list. We just went out onstage. The place was full of people.

"Freddie had this little plastic toy canary. He wound it up, put it on the stage, and it started to tweet. And then he took his flugelhorn and played a theme from *The Rite of Spring*. You can imagine what Claude must have thought, coming from Montreal and playing with someone he had never met before. The first thing he sees is this canary on the floor, and then he's playing Stravinsky!"

Whatever Ranger's initial reaction, he and Stone continued to work together occasionally in the years following, notably on the recording session in 1974 for Moe Koffman's *Solar Explorations*, where Ranger played on Stone's big band composition *Uranus*. But each was on a mission of his own; their concerns were similar, but their methods were different.

Stone liked to talk about the "uniqueness" of a musician's "state-ment,"[7] words that echoed Ranger's imperative that his bandmates "improvise their own way, not the way everyone does it on record." But Stone's music — particularly with Freddie's Band, the large improvising ensemble that he led publicly from 1984 to 1986 as an outgrowth of the workshops that he ran privately — was at once more directed and more spontaneous. In its immediacy, and its blurring of improvisation and composition, it paralleled in both functional and philosophical terms the work that Butch Morris and Gil Evans were doing in the same period with their orchestras in New York.

Ranger's compositions, on the other hand, were carefully, if briefly conceived, closely rehearsed and at least implicit in terms of their form, no matter how unrestrained the improvisations that he expected from his musicians when he wrote "Free Atonal" or, more colloquially, "Freak Out" as solo cues on his charts — or that he left to be inferred from the title of one of his new themes in this period, *Feu vert* (Green Light), a scrambling four-bar start to a race of indefinite length.

Stone, who once described his strategy rather grandly as "enhanced communicative sensitivities directed toward unified compositional objectivity,"[8] preferred to shape a piece of music in its entirety, from beginning to end, both structure and content, on the spot. He typically started with the briefest of notated ideas — a folk melody, perhaps, or a classical motif — and developed them organically, designating tasks to his musicians individually, or in ad hoc groupings, with physical gestures and by singing or playing what he wished them to do.

"Freddie's approach to music was completely different to Claude's," Steve Donald explains. "Freddie was the ringleader, the master of ceremonies. He was the guy who would put some music on the stand, usually something we had played around with before, and every time would be different. He'd say, 'OK, drums and bass and sax, play around with this. You guys over there, do this background. And *you* — you solo.' There was always this directing-traffic approach."

Procedural differences aside, however, Ranger and Stone did share certain philosophical values. "If there was a commonality between Claude and Freddie," Jonnie Bakan notes, "it was their complete and utter commitment to the sound that's happening *right now*, as though their lives depended on it."

That commitment extended to the integrity of their respective visions at a time when — and in a city where — such idealism inevitably came at a cost. "What connects Claude and Freddie," Perry White observes, "is their point in history and their uncompromising vision to find something new and to take it somewhere else — to find new sounds, change things, follow their intuition and let it lead them rather than thinking, 'How are we going to make money out of this?' They were totally concerned about making their artistic decisions for their own, purely artistic reasons."

. . .

Jonnie Bakan had joined the Ranger band by the time it appeared for three nights in August 1983 at le Grand Café on *rue* St. Denis in Montreal; Charles Papasoff sat in there and was invited to make the band an octet for two nights at Basin Street in Toronto in October.

Engagements otherwise remained sporadic, and Ranger worked as a sideman on at least two occasions, one a big band concert under Ron Collier's direction as part of CJRT-FM's *Sound of Toronto Jazz* series in October and the other a four-night run with a Papasoff quartet at l'Air du Temps in Montreal the following February.

There would be a few other septet appearances — at the Music Gallery in February and November 1984, for example, and at Bourbon Street in April — but when Ranger travelled to the Festival International de Jazz de Montréal in July, he took only Perry White, Steve Donald and Dick Felix.

Ironically, his relatively low profile in this period coincided with his first appearance in *Down Beat* magazine's International Critics Poll, where he tied for eighth among drummers with Andrew Cyrille and Marvin (Smitty) Smith in the "Talent deserving wider recognition" category won by Ronald Shannon Jackson.[9] He tied the following year for 13th with Milford Graves in the same category, this time won by Smith.[10] In 1986, *Down Beat* introduced a higher cutoff point for the results that it published; Ranger did not appear in the poll again.

• • •

Phil Dwyer was 18 when he arrived in Toronto during the summer of 1984 and found his way to the house on Bertmount Avenue where the Whites *et al.* lived. He was on his first extended trip away from home on Vancouver Island and had already spent 10 months in New York City, studying and sitting in around town, a bold first step in what would be an uncommonly accomplished career as a saxophonist, pianist, composer and arranger that brought him an appointment to the Order of Canada at the remarkably young age of 48.

Dwyer and Ranger played together in the basement of the

Bertmount house, just tenor and drums. Ranger, understandably impressed by the skill and spirit of so young a musician, started to talk about putting together a new band, a plan dashed — for the time being — by Dwyer's return to Vancouver in the fall.

Dwyer had nevertheless been in Toronto long enough to appreciate Ranger's significance to the scene, and particularly to the young musicians with whom he chose to work. "Claude was unique in that the level of respect that he was able to summon from my peers was incredibly high relative to how they felt about other musicians on the Toronto scene. There was a large group of people who really gravitated to the Claude Ranger/Freddie Stone axis. I don't know how much Claude and Freddie had to do with each other, but there was definitely a really deep loyalty to those guys.

"With Claude, the fact that all of the young guys, like Perry, really loved him, and that someone like Don Thompson had the same respect for him as well, put him on a level footing with almost anybody that I'd met anywhere. And deservedly so — the way he played drums was worthy of that respect.

"He was welcoming to younger musicians but also he was rebellious. Even though he was involved in the mainstream scene, he was never *of* it. He was never a guy who seemed to be beholden to anybody. He was never a clock puncher. Thinking back, the way the young guys — the people who were part of my generation, approximately, at the time — felt about a Jerry Fuller or a Terry Clarke, compared to the way they felt about a Claude Ranger, was really different. But given the benefit of hindsight, it's obvious that *all* those guys deserved a lot of respect.

"Claude was not a conformist. He could *try* to be a conformist, but I never really felt that he was a *good* conformist. I've seen a video of him with Ed Bickert. He's not *really* playing, he's just sort of doing his thing. Whereas Terry Clarke would show up on a gig like that and do whatever was appropriate to make the situation work. But, generally speaking, the adaptable people have not been the ones who leave the most profound legacy. There's a raw purity to musicians who aren't adaptable that makes them appealing, especially to young people."[11]

Despite Ranger's expressed interest in forming a band with Dwyer, he continued into and through 1985 with Perry White, Jonnie Bakan, Steve Donald and a new bassist, Mike Milligan. For a time in 1984 and early 1985, Ranger also ran a series of workshops in Ali Karnick's basement, some for drummers and at least one on a weekly basis in which the participants — saxophonist Daniel Miles Kane, guitarist Nilan Perera, clarinetist Jeff Reilly and trumpeter Kevin Turcotte variously among them — paid a nominal sum to play his compositions with him.

"It basically was a band, but that's not how it was broached," notes Turcotte, who was 21 at the time and new to Toronto from Sudbury. One such ensemble appeared publicly at the Toronto Percussion Centre, but the workshop was clearly subordinate to Ranger's formal quintet. "I was OK with that," Turcotte admits. "It was cool; I was just happy to be there and to get my butt kicked on a regular basis."[12]

The Ranger quintet itself appeared in June 1985 at the Art Gallery of Ontario as part of Toronto's first du Maurier International Jazz Festival,[13] and performed in July at two other significant events, Toronto's Great Jazz on the Lake at Harbourfront and at the Ottawa International Jazz Festival on the grounds of the National Arts Centre.

Ranger also played during the du Maurier festival at Basin Street with Dave Liebman, renewing an acquaintance first made in 1970 when the saxophonist was working with Elvin Jones at the Esquire Showbar in Montreal. This latest encounter followed the release of Liebman's LP *Sweet Fury*, which he had recorded in Toronto with Ranger, Don Thompson and the New York bassist Steve LaSpina at Thompson's basement studio, Puget Sound, 15 months earlier.

Art Gallery of Ontario (l-r): Claude Ranger, Steve Donald, Jonnie Bakan,
Mike Milligan, Perry White, Toronto, June 1985.
Photograph by Mark Miller.

"Whenever you said 'Canada,' you said 'Claude,'" Liebman
remarks, from his perspective as an American musician who often
travelled internationally and found himself working with local
musicians along the way. "It's like when you go to France, you get
Daniel Humair. In those days there was only one drummer in each
country, if that. And that was always a big 'if.' So when you went to
another country, be it Denmark, France or Canada, you'd be told,
'Well... there is... *one*... guy.' Now, of course, there are a million guys."

Indeed, even in the 1980s, there was more than one guy just in
Toronto, but Liebman had established a particularly productive
relationship with Ranger, one that found Ranger consistently on
his best behaviour, as Liebman's inventory of his playing would
suggest. "He was a very exciting drummer. He was strong. He *played*,
which I liked coming from the guys *I'd* been playing with. He was
enthusiastic. He learned the music. He *enjoyed* playing. He had a
joie de vivre."[14]

Their rapport is apparent on two of the pieces that they played for *Sweet Fury*, a new version of Don Thompson's *Full Nelson*, which Thompson and Ranger had recorded in Hamilton seven years earlier, and the only version on record of Ranger's own *Feu vert*. Both were assertively free, set further awash by Ranger's drumming at its most inventive.

Thus the "fury." The rest of the recording — the "sweet," as it were — was also relatively open in its execution, but generally more reflective, breaking the quartet into smaller units and taking advantage of Thompson's skills on piano, bass and vibes. One of the tracks without Ranger would prove to be incidentally prophetic. Liebman called it *Missing Person*.

CHAPTER THIRTEEN

"When I play, I own the world!"

Claude Ranger's life and career took a new turn in the summer of 1985 when he met Lili Wheatley, a young artist whose work was inspired by jazz. "I'd go and listen to jazz," she explains, "and then I'd paint it."[1]

After hearing Ranger at Bourbon Street, Wheatley found his phone number and spoke to Ali Karnick about getting a recording of his music. Ranger, listening in on an extension, was drawn to the sound of her voice. They met in person when he and Karnick dropped off a tape of solo drumming that he had put together for her.

Within a few weeks — not long after the festival season was over — he moved from Karnick's house in the Beach to Wheatley's studio apartment downtown on Mutual Street.

Once again, after four years of Karnick's support, he needed to make a living. To that end he returned to the role of sideman, beginning in September first with Sonny Greenwich at le Grand Café in

Montreal and then with the American guitarist Larry Coryell at East 85th and Front, a small room in the basement of a 19th-century warehouse in the oldest part of Toronto.

His reappearance on the club scene was roughly coincident with Terry Clarke's decision to move to New York. Although Jerry Fuller played for most of the American visitors at East 85th, and was also still active at Bourbon Street, other drummers slipped into the rotation at both clubs, including Ranger, Archie Alleyne and Barry Elmes; Ranger backed saxophonist Gerry Niewood, trombonist Curtis Fuller and, in early 1986, trumpeter Woody Shaw at East 85th.

He also accompanied an aging Swing-era star, tenor saxophonist Georgie Auld, for a week at Bourbon Street and joined the ad hoc Composers' Co-Op Jazz Orchestra, led by guitarist Tim Brady, for a concert in November 1985 at the Music Gallery featuring the influential trumpeter and composer Kenny Wheeler. Auld and Wheeler were both born in Toronto and had taken their careers abroad, Auld to New York in the early 1930s and Wheeler to London in 1952.

Ranger was better suited to playing with some of these visitors — Wheeler and Woody Shaw in particular — than to others, and they in turn to playing with him. Inevitably, there were frustrations that Ranger did not always handle well. His drinking, moreover, was increasingly an issue, prompting one of the Americans at East 85th to marvel, in conversation with Greg Pilo, "On the first set I played with him, he was one of the best drummers, if not the best, I'd ever worked with. By the third set, he was probably the worst."

• • •

Ranger's own band was largely inactive through this period, although he himself did a solo concert in November at the Parasol Arts Centre, a performance space established by Freddie Stone in an old Victorian mansion on Jarvis Street. For a time Ranger and Wheatley lived in an apartment upstairs, an arrangement that brought Ranger into accidental contact with the next tenor saxophonist to capture his imagination.

Rob Frayne, who was a tradesman as well as a musician, stopped by the centre to do some repairs. "I happened to have my horn with me. Claude said, 'Hey, do you want to play?' So we played. Afterwards, he said, 'I didn't know.' He knew me — I'd been to his gigs and we'd say hello — but he didn't know that I could play."[2]

Frayne, who had studied with Freddie Stone and played in Freddie's Band, took Jonnie Bakan's place in the Ranger quintet with Perry White, Steve Donald and Mike Milligan just before it appeared in July 1986 at the Festival International de Jazz de Montréal, the third time that a Ranger band had appeared there in five years. On this occasion, however, it was as an entrant in the festival's Concours de Jazz de Montréal, whose prizes included the opportunity to record an LP for the CBC's Jazzimage label and an invitation to perform at the Paris Jazz Festival later in the year.

The competition was open nationally in 1986 for the first time; it had been limited in its first four years only to musicians based in Quebec, with Ranger's old friend Michel Donato the inaugural laureate, followed in turn by the band Quartz and two young pianists, Lorraine Desmarais and François Bourassa.

Ranger was chosen to represent the "Centre Region" of the country in a juried competition with four other Toronto bands — Time Warp, co-led by Barry Elmes and bassist Al Henderson, saxophonist John Johnson's Paan Logo with former Ranger pupil Vito Rezza, and the quintets of pianist Brian Dickinson and drummer Keith Blackley. Each played a single, hour-long set at George's Spaghetti House; Ranger's appearance there was his first with a band of his own in 12 years.

The process was repeated during the Montreal festival proper, where Ranger, Mr. Toad's Wild Ride from Vancouver, pianist Jon Ballantyne from Saskatoon, pianist Louise Beauchesne's Latin Band from Montreal and the Halifax Jazz Connection all performed at the Théâtre St-Denis II. Ranger played three original pieces in the allotted hour, *Stars in Tears*, *Feu vert* and *Gefilte Fish*, as well as the competition's test piece, Dizzy Gillespie's *A Night in Tunisia;* Gillespie himself was scheduled to close the festival on a bill that would also feature the

Concours' eventual winner, whose identity was evidently a foregone conclusion as far as Ranger and his musicians were concerned.

"I remember playing, and thinking that we had it in the bag," Steve Donald admits. Frayne was similarly encouraged. "The reaction of everyone who heard the band was, 'Yeah, this is by far the best thing.' Unofficially, Claude was, hands down, the best."

Festival International de Jazz de Montréal, July 1986.
Photograph by Mark Miller.

They were not alone in their assessment. Alain Brunet, writing in *La Presse*, described the quintet as "the most mature [*mure*] band of the competition," and although he questioned the length of some of Ranger's pieces, deemed its performance "very difficult to outclass."[3]

Ranger went as far as to hold a celebration in his hotel room the night before the winner was announced. Indeed, he went even further by inviting his parents; it would be one of the last times that Aurèle and Lucille saw their eldest son, who was by then well into a career that they evidently did not understand, much less appreciate. Mike

Milligan suggested to them that they must have been very proud; he recalls that they responded, blankly, "Of what?"

Their skepticism would only have been confirmed the following day by the news that the Concours had been won by Jon Ballantyne; Ranger received the consolation of a "special jury mention" for his drumming. While Ballantyne had played with an assurance and sensitivity beyond his 22 years and would go on to a modest career stateside, his trio in the Concours — completed by two older musicians — was no match for the Ranger quintet.

There followed speculation that Ranger's age had worked against him in a competition implicitly — and in later years explicitly — intended for younger musicians. Moreover, even though he had been living outside of Quebec for the better part of 14 years, he would have been seen as yet another French Canadian winner in the very year that the Concours was trying to establish itself on a national basis.

However the jury arrived at its decision, Ranger was despondent. "He couldn't believe it," Frayne remembers. "To me, it was disappointing, but just one of those things. To Claude, it was a really big deal."

Milligan puts Ranger's reaction in even stronger terms. "He was absolutely slaughtered that he didn't win." But Milligan also recalls Ranger's immediate resolve. "I remember him saying something to the effect of 'I'm going to go home and start lifting weights,' which was actually him saying that he needed to get stronger."

Instead, the quintet rarely performed again, if at all, after its return from Montreal. And although Ranger was reunited with Ron Allen in the company of another young tenor saxophonist, Ralph Bowen, for a tribute to John Coltrane at Harbourfront's Great Jazz on the Lake just days later in July, he, too, was otherwise largely inactive during the rest of the year and for much of 1987.

Both East 85th and Bourbon Street would falter and then close in the course of 1986, leaving George's and a basement room on Wellington Street East, the Café des Copains, as the only clubs booking jazz on a regular basis. At that, the music policy at George's remained under Moe Koffman's control, and the café limited its bookings to solo pianists. Ranger's prospects dimmed accordingly.

He and Lili Wheatley supplemented their limited income in part by starting a business refinishing drums. "We advertised in the paper," she explains, "and ended up with three or so customers whose kits we completely transformed." One of their clients was Ranger's friend from Montreal, Norman Marshall Villeneuve, who had moved to Toronto in 1974 and in later years exerted his own influence, in both the spirit and the hard bop style of Art Blakey, by purposely associating with the city's younger musicians.

"Claude did all the sanding by hand," Wheatley continues, "and he seemed to know exactly how much wood to take off in order to make the sound resonate. He loved working with wood. And then we both would do the staining and afterwards brush on many thin coats of urethane."

That, of course, had a predictable effect. "Claude would be buzzed on polyurethane a lot," recalls Rob Frayne, whose association with Ranger continued into the 1990s. "He'd have been finishing drums, and he'd be a bit wobbly."

• • •

Ranger took Frayne and Mike Milligan into the Music Gallery in October 1986 for an evening in which he and Milligan also played in a quartet led by Michael Stuart. When asked, in wonder, where he found the energy that he put into the two bands that night, Ranger simply replied, "I *have* to play; who knows if I'll be alive tomorrow?"[4]

His response, as melodramatic as it may have seemed, accounted in both practical and philosophical terms for the immediacy of his approach to music, no less than to life. It may also have reflected his sense of his own mortality more generally, a sense that would have been shaken by the early deaths of Brian Barley, Lenny Breau — murdered in Los Angeles during the summer of 1984 at the age of 43 — and Freddie Stone, victim of a heart attack in December 1986 at the age of 51.

Ranger had previously broached the subject of age and death quite specifically with Milligan. "At some point in my time with Claude, he called me up and said, 'Mike, I'm really broke, could you lend me some money?' So we met on the subway and went for a ride together. He wanted to talk as well.

"He was exactly 20 years older than me, so he'd have been 45 or 46 when he said, 'Mike, I think I've got about 20 years left.'

"I said, 'Claude! That's really young, man. That's like 65, 66! Why would you think that?'

"He said, 'I'm going to be getting out of shape, and I don't want to be out of shape.'

"I said, 'People get wiser as they get old. Keep playing the drums. You'll stay in shape. Look at Roy Haynes!'

"But it was one of those things Claude had his mind set on. He just had a very negative conception of being old."

He also had a very casual conception of money and possessions. He dismissed the loan that Milligan gave him that day as "history," when reminded of it some months later. Milligan, who could scarcely afford to lose the money, a sum of fifty dollars, was nevertheless forgiving.

"Claude was kind of The Guy in terms of being non-materialistic. He told me, 'Ah, when I get money, I get rid of it as soon as I can.' Just the opposite of what nearly anyone else would do. This 'living in the moment' thing was a big part of his personality."

So it was, Milligan recalled, that when Ranger once acknowledged the success that his brother Jacques had enjoyed in his career, he added, triumphantly, "He may make a hundred thousand dollars a year, but when I play, I own the world!"

• • •

During the summer of 1986 Jane Bunnett and Larry Cramer were invited to do a concert in CJRT-FM's *Sound of Toronto Jazz* series for the 1986-7 season. Bunnett, who played flute and soprano saxophone, and Cramer, a trumpeter who had studied with Freddie Stone, were just at the outset of careers that would take them, strategically under Bunnett's name alone, to the world — international tours, Grammy Award nominations — on the basis of their embrace of Cuban music and, in a humanitarian sense, Cuban musicians.

For the moment, however, they needed a band, and before even a band, they needed a direction. In search of inspiration, they made a trip to New York — not their first and far from their last — where they heard Tony Williams at the Village Vanguard.

"We sat in the front row," Cramer recalls, "and it just hit us. *That's* the thing, the *rhythm*. It seems obvious now, but that's when we realized it had to be the focus of what we do musically."[5] As indeed it would be in their exploration, beginning in the 1990s, of Cuba's various traditions, whose very essence was rhythm.

"It was like a lightning strike," Cramer continues. "And back in Toronto, Claude saved our asses, because that rhythm thing just wasn't important in Canadian jazz. If he hadn't been here, I don't know what we would have done."

Or, if Ranger had not been interested.

They could only ask, a task that fell to Bunnett. "I remember getting up the nerve to call him. He had this reputation of being fiery and crazy and a pain in the ass and everyone was saying, 'Don't call him, *forget* it!' But we were adamant. He was the greatest drummer here.

"So I was laying in bed, telling myself, 'I'm going to call him, I'm going to call him. Alright, *here I go...*' I called him. And he was so nice! He just said, 'What kind of music is it?'

"I said, 'It's my tunes and one of Larry's.'

"He said, 'Can we rehearse?'

"That was what was so great about him, he *wanted* to rehearse. I got off the phone, and it was like, '*Yeah*, he's *into* it!'"

The new Bunnett quintet, completed by Brian Dickinson and Kieran Overs, made its debut in late November 1986 at Phillip's, a club in London, Ontario, before appearing a few days later at the Ontario Science Centre.

Bunnett subsequently approached Moe Koffman about a booking

at George's Spaghetti House.

"Moe said, 'Is Claude Ranger your drummer?'

"I said, 'Yes.'

"He said, 'Well, get another drummer. It's up to you. You want to play here? *He's* not playing here. Get another drummer and maybe I'll consider it.'"

Bunnett received a much warmer reception from some of the country's jazz festivals, where Ranger's presence would have actually been a selling point, if not *the* selling point. It was certainly a factor in Ken Pickering's willingness, as artistic director of the du Maurier International Jazz Festival in Vancouver, to present Bunnett at such an early point in her career.

"When Jane told me that she would have Claude Ranger," Pickering explains, "I pretty much said, 'I'd love to give you a gig if he's in the band.' I really wanted to get him out here for the festival."[6]

With no more than a tape of the CJRT-FM concert and copies of a review from *The Globe and Mail*,[7] she was able to arrange festival appearances in the summer of 1987 in Montreal, Edmonton and Vancouver, although not in Toronto, where she and Cramer played instead with Ranger under *his* name at Harbourfront's du Maurier Theatre Centre.

Ranger and Lili Wheatley, meanwhile, realized that the tour presented them with an opportunity to leave Toronto altogether. Work remained scarce in 1987, interesting work especially — other than two successive days in February when Ranger recorded with Michael Stuart in Hamilton, and then played for one last time with Sonny Greenwich at the Premiere Dance Theatre in Toronto; Stuart's LP, *The Blessing*, paid compelling tribute to the spiritual legacy of John Coltrane in both its serenity and its savagery, the latter aspect — in *The Call* and *Celebration* especially — alternately braced and buffeted by Ranger at his most resolute.

As summer approached, Ranger and Wheatley, by then living in the Beach, sold most of their possessions, including two expensive road bikes, and held a farewell party, fully intending to stay out west once Bunnett's festival tour was over. Their ultimate destination was Victoria, which Ranger had visited with Moe Koffman in 1978 and Don Thompson in 1979. After his concert with Thompson, he was approached by a young Victoria drummer, Bill (later William) Stewart for a lesson. Ranger not only agreed but postponed his flight home and stayed on for a week at Stewart's basement studio in the north end of the city.

Ranger's impromptu layover left a lasting impression and, according to Stewart, inspired his decision to move to Victoria in 1987. Ranger had been thinking about leaving Toronto at least as early as 1980, when Australia beckoned; asked by John Gilmore two years later whether he would ever consider returning to live in Montreal, he replied, "If I leave Toronto, I'll move to the sun, where it's warm all the time."

Among Canada's major cities, Victoria came closest to meeting that stipulation; Ranger, moreover, was attracted to the natural beauty of the west coast with its ocean, its mountains and its forests — much as he had been drawn to the scenic wonders of Australia.

Bunnett's tour took Ranger and Wheatley as far as Vancouver, where the quintet played a free concert on the former site of Expo 86. "We were all staying at the Sylvia Hotel, right on Stanley Park," remembers Dave Field, Bunnett's bassist for the tour, "and we were getting ready to go back to the airport. Claude was there standing beside the bus.

"I said, 'OK, Claude, time to go.'

"He said, 'Well, I'm staying.'

"'Really?'

"'Yeah, I like it here.'

"So we shook hands and said goodbye. He walked around the corner of the Sylvia Hotel and that's the last time I ever saw him."[8]

Chapter Fourteen

"There was a buzz"

They had not counted on the crows.

Claude Ranger and Lili Wheatley rented a one-room apartment, complete with Murphy bed, when they arrived in Victoria, a city where the murder rate, as it were, was notably high.

"Neither of us knew about the crows," Wheatley admits. "And in the back alley there were crows, and they kept up this racket all the time. Claude was really sensitive to sound, so that was tough — those crows, always cawing."

Work for both Ranger and Wheatley, moreover, was scarce in Victoria, and their money — little as it was to begin with, and some of it spent on collapsible bicycles once they arrived — quickly ran out. After two months, they moved over to Vancouver and initially found lodging with trumpeter Kevin Elaschuk and alto saxophonist Roy Styffe, who were sharing an apartment on the city's east side. Ranger had met Elaschuk in Edmonton five years earlier and knew Styffe from Toronto.

In due course, he and Wheatley rented a four-room flat upstairs in a frame house on Union Street, an address in Strathcona popular with musicians. Saxophonist Graham Ord, pianist Paul Plimley and bassist Clyde Reed all lived within a block or so to the west, and singer k.d. lang was right across the street.

Ranger and Wheatley each took a room in the flat as a studio; Wheatley also worked outside the house in the office of a forestry company. They filled their respective rooms with plants — Ranger's of the green leaf variety; Wheatley's, cacti and succulents — and over the next several years opened their home to several stray cats.

Soon enough, word that Ranger was living in Vancouver began to circulate. "It started as kind of a rumour, not entirely substantiated," remembers guitarist Ron Samworth, who would work frequently with Ranger over the next eight years. "It was like, 'You've got to be kidding! Claude's in town?' I'd revered the guy from his recordings. We've always felt so isolated from the Toronto-Montreal nexus, so it was a thrill to have a guy like him immigrate out here. It usually flowed the other way, right?"[1]

While Ranger had moved to Toronto from Montreal unannounced and all but unknown 15 years earlier, he arrived in Vancouver preceded by his name and, to the extent that word-of-mouth among musicians carried across the country, his reputation — further supported by the commercial LPs that he had made in the 1970s with Doug Riley, P.J. Perry and Sonny Greenwich, and his chapter with Guy Nadon in the book *Jazz in Canada: Fourteen Lives*.[2] He was considered important enough by Ken Pickering to merit his own billing in 1987 on the du Maurier International Jazz Festival flyer even though he was simply playing there with Jane Bunnett.

Once the rumours of Ranger's presence in the city were confirmed later in the fall of that year, his impact was immediate. "There was a buzz," Pickering notes. "I'm sure not everybody knew who Claude was, but most jazz musicians — if they didn't know — figured it out pretty quickly."

The element of surprise that had greeted him in Toronto was replaced by a degree of wonder in Vancouver. "It was very rare for anybody of Claude's stature to move *to* Vancouver," suggests Phil Dwyer, echoing Ron Samworth; Dwyer himself had returned to the city in the summer of 1985 after his second sojourn in New York at 19. "It was common for people there to get really good and then *leave*. So a musician who moved there without any caveats attached — and Claude was certifiably good; famous musicians loved him — had a big impact."

Ranger was in fact ideally suited to a scene where the freer aspects of contemporary jazz were honoured in ways that they had not been in Toronto. The Vancouver festival, then in its second year, reflected — and would continue for the next 30 years under Ken Pickering's direction to reflect — a vision of jazz firmly rooted in the present, not the past. Vancouver musicians of like mind had a central rather than peripheral place in its programming, and in the concert series that the festival's organizing body, the Coastal Jazz and Blues Society, presented each fall under the banner TIME*flies*.

"A guy like Claude could move to a new scene," Dwyer continues, "but that doesn't necessarily mean there's a place for him. But in his case, everybody tried to create a spot for him to do his thing. The Clyde Reed/Paul Plimley crowd created some space for him. So did the crowd I was in; I was working a lot in those days with [bassist] Chris Nelson and [pianist] Bob Murphy. Chris was very conscientious; he wanted to take advantage of Claude being there. So when Claude arrived, it created this kind of energy to go out and make stuff happen, stuff that wasn't there before — stuff that would involve him."

The "Clyde Reed/Paul Plimley crowd," with its avant-garde leanings, was known more formally as the New Orchestra Workshop (NOW),[3] then a year into its second incarnation with Reed, Plimley, Ron Samworth, Gregg Simpson and saxophonists Coat Cooke and Bruce Freedman as its principals.[4] Ranger made two of his earliest Vancouver appearances as a leader at NOW events at the French Cultural Centre in late November of that year and in March 1988, playing on the latter occasion with Rob Frayne, lately arrived from Toronto, and bassist Scott White.

Chris Nelson, meanwhile, was booking some of the city's modernists at Studio 19, a basement space of some legend on Water Street in Gastown. Ranger worked there — and at the nearby Classical Joint, a small coffeehouse on Carrall Street — quite frequently during his first year in Vancouver, often in Dwyer's company. He and Dwyer also appeared on New Year's Eve 1987 with the American bassist Charlie Haden in a "First Night" concert at the Law Courts by Robson Square; Haden had played on the early Ornette Coleman recordings that were a formative influence on Ranger's thinking in the 1960s.

The concert was sufficiently to Haden's liking that he called Dwyer on New Year's Day to suggest that they find another engagement before he — Haden — had to leave town. Dwyer persuaded Andreas Nothiger, owner of the Classical Joint, to open on the following Monday, a night that was usually dark. Haden in turn agreed to play for whatever was collected at the door, as long as the house was "turned over" for a second show, thus doubling the proceeds — something, Dwyer remembers, that was "never done in Vancouver." With Bob Murphy added on electric piano, the evening was a success.

"I ended up giving Charlie about eight hundred dollars," Dwyer marvels. "We made about two hundred each. That was a banner night for the Joint. Usually you'd get forty dollars or something."

Ranger and Dwyer worked together again just days later at the Western Front, the East 8th Avenue gallery and concert hall that has served Vancouver as an important home to the experimental arts, appearing there in a quartet co-led by Dwyer and Don Thompson — the latter back briefly from Toronto — and completed by bassist Rene Worst. Their performance brought Ranger his first local notice, one that set the generally negative tone that the Vancouver media adopted on the rare occasions that they commented on his work during the next several years.

Gary Pogrow, writing in the Vancouver *Sun*, thought well of the contributions that Thompson, Dwyer and Worst made to what he called the "conversation" that characterizes jazz. "On the other hand," he continued, "Ranger on drums distorted the 'conversation.' His sound was intrusive. It sprawled out across the symbols [sic], over drum rolls and at times drowned out the fine work of the others."[5]

By contrast, another reviewer, James Adams of the *Edmonton Journal*, was quite taken with Ranger when the same quartet appeared at the

Yardbird Suite three months later. Adams described Ranger as a "head-snapping drummer" and the "most arresting" member of the band.

"With heavy-lidded eyes," Adams continued, "an omnipresent cigarette dangling insolently from the left corner of his mouth, a gravity-defying arc of ash extending from butt's end, this Montreal native is the epitome of rumpled Gallic cool. If you're needing a Jean-Paul Belmondo fix, Ranger is the next best thing. And he's a ferocious, unflagging drummer to boot."[6]

• • •

There were, of course, other drummers in Vancouver capable of the intensity that had so disconcerted Gary Pogrow and impressed James Adams, notably Al Wiertz and Gregg Simpson. Wiertz, just two months younger than Ranger, was already a local legend — "the only guy in Vancouver who could come close to matching Claude's power," according to Dwyer. "But Al was a lot louder," Dwyer adds. "Claude had power, but he was never super loud. And Al wasn't as steady; he was a beat dropper. But he was great, he was a lot of fun to play with."

As warmly as Wiertz himself has been remembered in the years since his death in 1997, his drumming inevitably inspires qualified praise. "Al could sit in for a tune," Clyde Reed explains, "and all of a sudden he'd raise the whole vibration of the room, not just the band." But if he played for much longer, Reed adds, he could quickly overstay his welcome. "He loved getting kicked off the bandstand."[7]

While Wiertz could be domineering to a fault — a fault often compounded by his impulsive nature — Gregg Simpson, six years younger still, was instinctively and assertively responsive, a drummer whose power was as much a function of velocity as of volume.

"Gregg and Claude shared one thing," Reed observes. "Big concert or rehearsal, it was all the same: you played the very best you possibly could. There were no throwaway situations for those guys. They were the same no matter what the gig was."

It was ultimately Ranger's range — his unparalleled ability to swing, in particular — that set him apart from Wiertz, Simpson and a third venturesome Vancouver drummer, Roger Baird, who had participated in the fabled New York loft scene of the 1970s. It also brought Ranger calls to play in more conventional settings that would otherwise have been the domain of Buff Allen, by then back from Toronto, Blaine Wikjord, George Ursan, and the younger Bruce Nielsen and Stan Taylor. So it was, for example, that Ranger came to renew acquaintances with James Moody one night at the Vancouver East Cultural Centre in February 1988.

The fullest measure of his skill, however, was on display the following summer at the du Maurier International Jazz Festival, where he played with seven different bands in ten days, a total of 13 appearances altogether, foremost among them a set opening for Charlie Haden's Quartet West at the Vancouver East Cultural Centre with a quintet of his own — Dwyer, Rob Frayne, Perry White and Rene Worst.

With White home just for the festival, Ranger organized the quintet on the fly, forgoing the careful preparation that had typically gone into his concerts in Toronto. White recalls a single rehearsal; Frayne suggests that Ranger's strategy in this period was generally even more informal.

"Claude would throw down charts and we just played them. I don't remember rehearsing even once. He'd say, 'Play like the bomb will fall at midnight.' He meant the nuclear bomb. 'Play like these are your last moments on earth.' That was his approach, and he took it very, very seriously."

Duly instructed, Ranger's three saxophonists presented Quartet West with a formidable challenge to its temperate and lyrically elegant renderings of pop standards and bop classics. "Most of the people who were at that concert," Worst notes, "said that Claude's set blew away Charlie's set."

Ranger and Worst also worked together in support of two New York musicians, trumpeter Jack Walrath and tenor saxophonist Carter Jefferson, at the Landmark Jazz Bar in the Sheraton Landmark Hotel on Robson Street. While Walrath would remember Ranger very favourably more than 25 years later,[8] Alex Varty, writing at the time in the *Georgia*

Straight, was dismissive. He suggested that Worst and Ranger "captured the spirit of the melodic hard-bop music," but that the band "lacked the necessary punch to make the back rows stand up in silence." Varty went on to fault "squinty-eyed Ranger," observing that he "seemed more interested in keeping his ever-present cigarette going (the festival's sponsor must have loved it!) than in communicating with the other men."[9]

Ranger and Worst worked together for two more nights at Hot Jazz on Main Street as part of an "all-star" Canadian band nominally co-led by alto saxophonist Dave Turner from Montreal and Ranger's rival at the 1986 Concours de Jazz de Montréal, pianist Jon Ballantyne from Saskatoon. The Danish saxophonist John Tchicai, who had played with Archie Shepp and appeared on John Coltrane's conflagratory album *Ascension* in the mid-1960s, asked to sit in on one of the evenings but was initially turned away; once festival organizers had intervened on his behalf, he and Ranger engaged in a heated musical exchange that entered the annals of festival lore.

If Jon Ballantyne's presence at Hot Jazz was not reminder enough of the Concours two years earlier, Ranger had just been caught up again in its machinations, finding himself disqualified on the basis of his age — this time explicitly — from playing in the Pacific Region's semi-finals as a member of Turnaround, Rob Frayne's new vocal/instrumental quintet with Vancouver's most daring jazz singer, Kate Hammett-Vaughan.

"It was like salt in the wound of 1986," Frayne notes, having been witness to Ranger's disappointment in Montreal. "We were mad," Hammett-Vaughan recalls, "and Claude was mad."[10]

Ranger was nevertheless back with Turnaround at the festival; his schedule also included a second performance under his own name with Frayne, Dwyer, White and Worst, this time on the old Expo 86 site, as well as other appearances at the same location in ad hoc groups led by Frayne and by the Montreal alto saxophonist Robert Leriche. One such band, a sextet under Leriche's name, included Frayne, Dwyer and White, as well as Clyde Reed.

For Reed, it was one of his first of many performances with Ranger. For White, it was his last. Frayne, meanwhile, remained in Vancouver for another few months before returning east to Ottawa; he was reunited with Ranger and Mike Milligan at the Sound Symposium in St. John's, Newfoundland, in 1990. Dwyer moved back to Toronto in 1989 but worked again on occasion with Ranger in Vancouver and Victoria as late as 1995.

For Ranger, his prominence in the festival served as an affirmation, if any was necessary, of his decision to leave Toronto. "Vancouver is the kind of place that's in keeping with Claude's artistic vibe," observes White from the perspective of living and working in both cities himself. "He always wanted to do something that was fresh, where there was less history and more *now*. You can just do whatever you want in Vancouver, you don't have to be tied down to what's come before."

• • •

Toronto continued to beckon. Ranger returned at least three times in the months following his arrival in Vancouver, most notably in late February 1988 to play on Jane Bunnett's first LP, *In Dew Time*.

The initiative that Bunnett and Larry Cramer had taken in asking Ranger to join their band in 1986 became the pattern of many of their projects in the years that followed. Encouraged by his response, they continued to call on the services of jazz musicians more established than themselves and benefitted from both the experience and the exposure that these new alliances offered.

Accordingly, *In Dew Time* featured three noted Americans — pianist Don Pullen, tenor saxophonist Dewey Redman and French horn player Vincent Chancey — as well as Ranger and the Toronto bassist Scott Alexander. Pullen had worked with Charles Mingus, as had Redman with Ornette Coleman and Keith Jarrett; their presence on *In Dew Time* brought Ranger as close as he would come — just a single degree of separation — to two of the musicians, Mingus and Coleman, who had been among his guiding influences in the 1960s.

In Dew Time recording session (l-r): Vincent Chancey, Jane Bunnett, Scott
Alexander, Don Pullen, Dewey Redman, Larry Cramer, Claude Ranger,
Toronto, February 1988.
Photograph by Bill Smith.

He was entirely in sympathy with Pullen and Redman, no less than with Bunnett and Cramer, when it came to the general view that they all shared regarding the importance of freedom in jazz. When he engaged the Americans — mixing it up with the combative Pullen on Bunnett's *Limbo*, for example, and swinging at a gallop beneath Redman on Cramer's *In Dew Time* — he did so directly, with neither hesitation nor concession. And even as *In Dew Time* brought Bunnett the early international attention that she and Cramer sought, it also — by virtue of its success in that respect — carried Ranger's name farther afield than any of the other recordings on which he had appeared or, for that matter, would appear.

• • •

If Ranger's move to Vancouver offered a fresh start, it was nevertheless one that he embraced entirely on his own terms as he began to move around on the local scene.

"The first couple of times I played with Claude," Ron Samworth remembers of evenings at the Classical Joint, "you'd be playing along — you could be in the middle of somebody's solo — and he'd drop out. And you'd think, 'Oh, shit, he's really unhappy. He doesn't like it. He doesn't want to participate.' If you were the soloist, it would psyche you right out. It took me a while to find the courage to look back. And it was like, 'Oh, he's just lighting a cigarette and opening a beer!'"

Kate Hammett-Vaughan, meanwhile, quickly found herself caught up with Ranger in something of a contest of wills. Turnaround aside, she had been working of late without a drummer; her trio Garbo's Hat, new as of early 1988, was completed by one of Ranger's Union Street neighbours, saxophonist Graham Ord, and bassist Paul Blaney. By the end of the year, however, she had also started to sing in settings that included Ranger.

"It was such an overwhelming sensation to be standing right in front of Claude's drum kit. I say this jokingly, but I think it's really true: I think my back hurt for two days after because of the ferocity of the energy. He created such a swirl of sound, such a vortex, that it really felt physical — as well as emotional — to me.

"I remember one gig pretty early on in my time with him when he kept picking up the tempo. The way he felt it was edgier, and a little more on top of what I wanted, so I felt in the first set that everything was speeding up.

"I remember going to him and saying, 'It's a little faster than I'm setting it up.'

"He said, 'Where I come from, it's the drummer who sets the pace.' Ranger may well have been referring to the bass drummer in the marching band that had so inspired him as a cadet in Montreal some 40 years earlier.

"And I thought," Hammett-Vaughan continues, "'Well, this *is* Claude Ranger, so I'm not going to mess with him, because I'm honoured just to play with him.' So I would count everything in a little bit slower than where I felt it and wait for him to bring the tempo up. He didn't know that I was doing that. It was my way of negotiating with him.

"You never knew what you were going to get when you worked with Claude, but the more rope you gave him, the better he played. The less you kept a leash on him, the more he would play music with you, rather than beside you. Because he always wanted to play music *with* people. Those moments when I was feeling comfortable with him and would let him just be, let him go, he would really light up."

For Rene Worst, however, there were practical considerations that needed to be taken into account each time out. "What I remember is picking him up, loading his drums into my van, going to the store, getting ice for his gym bag and then buying a case of beer and making sure he had smokes."[11]

Even then, Worst admits, an evening could still go awry. "One of the things I learned pretty quickly was that you only wanted to do gigs with Claude if they were gigs that were suitable to Claude. Otherwise, it was too much work. He would have a bad time, and then everybody would have a bad time."

Indeed, Ranger was no more adaptable to casual engagements in Vancouver than he had been in Toronto. "People would hire Claude to do jobs, pick-up gigs, what have you," Samworth notes, "and there was a certain cachet to having him play on a gig with you. Sure. But I bet that more than half the people who played with him regretted it, because there were a lot of 'non-return' engagements. Claude would just play the way *he* wanted to play. He always took the work seriously because he needed the money, and he tried to play to order, but his 'Claude-ness,' both personally and musically, was more than most bandleaders could handle."

On the other hand, Worst suggests, "If you were on the right gig with him, he'd raise the level of the music exponentially. He was an unbelievably musical drummer, *if* he was having a good time." That was the key, as Toronto musicians had long known and as Worst, Samworth and other Vancouver musicians were learning. "If he was on a gig that he thought was bullshit," Worst remarks, "he was not happy and he would make that plain."

Ranger's four nights with the American trumpeter Jon Faddis at the Victoria and Vancouver festivals in June 1989 were a case in point. Faddis tended to put his extraordinary technical facility — his range in the trumpet's upper register especially — to the sort of showy, grandstanding effect that Ranger inevitably would not have countenanced. The two musicians were at odds from the start, their differences exacerbated by Faddis' insistence that Ranger not smoke on the bandstand.

The Faddis quartet, completed by Worst and pianist Renee Rosnes, rehearsed and performed in Victoria before appearing for three nights at the Landmark Jazz Bar back in Vancouver.

"After the rehearsal," Worst recalls, "we drove back to the hotel and I said, 'Claude, how are you doing?'

"He said, 'I will be better in four days.'"

Faddis requested a change in drummers, only to learn that all of the obvious replacements were working elsewhere at the festival. Left with no other recourse, he called a band meeting, acknowledged

Ranger's animosity and suggested that they try to make the best of a bad situation.

"I think there was quiet disgust from Claude's corner for the rest of the gig," Worst notes. "But he played it. He was there."

Ranger's other significant association at the festival that summer was with Renee Rosnes' own quartet, which also included Worst and Phil Dwyer. Rosnes, originally from Vancouver, had moved to New York in 1985 and by the summer of 1989 had toured with two of the most influential saxophonists of the day, Joe Henderson and Wayne Shorter. Home for the festival, she had four dates under her own name, most visibly at the Commodore Ballroom opening for Tony Williams.

Williams in 1989 was not the same drummer who had so inspired Ranger in the 1960s. His drums in these later years were larger and louder, his hands heavier — the product of his embrace of rock music after he left Miles Davis in 1969. The astonishing sense of risk, surprise and precarious balance that defined his playing as a teenager had given way to a more ponderous display of power and presence.

Not that Ranger's drumming had remained the same. It, too, had opened up since his days with Brian Barley, although the effect was embracing rather than — in Williams' case — bullish. He had tempered its freneticism and eased its combative stance in favour of a more orchestral approach.

And the prospect of sharing the stage that night with Tony Williams?

"It didn't seem to faze him," Dwyer remembers. "He played his ass off."

CHAPTER FIFTEEN

Jade Orchestra

Claude Ranger had a regular routine when he lived on Union Street. Habitually a late riser, he would begin his day by gathering up his empties from the night before and heading off to buy more beer, sometimes scavenging other bottles along the way as he cycled through the side streets of Strathcona.

Back home, beer at hand, he spent his afternoons variously drawing, making drum sticks — short and light, with an oval bead, cut from pieces of dowel and shaped with a file and sandpaper — and working on his compositions and arrangements at a small Fender Rhodes electric piano. He also practiced, using a single pad for the purpose; he could not set his drums up at home.

Occasionally he offered informal guidance in matters of harmony and composition to younger musicians, no doubt drawing on the principles that he had learned from Frank Mella almost 30 years earlier in Montreal. Clarinetist François Houle and guitarist Tony Wilson were among those who benefitted from his help; post-modernists both — Houle classically trained and Wilson more broadly vernacular, and beneficiaries as such of the Vancouver scene's openness to fresh perspectives — they were emerging at the turn of the 1990s as bandleaders in their own right, Houle with Et Cetera, a septet, and Wilson with a sextet. They visited Ranger individually and together; they also played in the orchestra that he introduced in 1990.

"When I was working on my arrangements for my band," Houle recalls, "Tony and I would go over to Claude's place on Union Street — Lili was there — and I'd show him my charts. He would help me with my chord voicings and my arrangements for the horn section, trying to get as big a sound as possible."

As Houle describes it, Ranger's approach at the piano to these challenges showed much the same systematic resolve as his strategy, years earlier, in developing the exercises that he used at the drums. The process was entirely his own and wholly intuitive.

"He would play the same passage over and over again and try different things until he found something that worked. And then he would tell us, 'Oh, yeah, *that's* it,' basically putting his stamp of approval on it. So we brought the ideas and he'd just work on them to make them better for us — without really explaining what he was doing. He'd just find a voicing and we'd say, 'Wow, that sounds really good.'"

Houle remembers taking Ranger a six-pack of beer and "a little bit of money," and invariably leaving Union Street with a plant. "Claude had tons of plants in his apartment, and a cat or two, I think. He loved his cats and he took care of his plants, and he would always give me some plants to take home, because he knew I liked plants, and my wife liked plants. I think I still have some of them."[1]

Wilson's experience with Ranger was similar. "I would go every Sunday and take the music that I'd been writing. We would sit at his piano, look at my tunes and work on them. The lessons were all afternoon. I would bring some beer, Claude would roll his cigarettes and we would sit there, often for several hours. It would cost me, like, fifteen dollars."

One of Wilson's tunes was *Blakey's Beat*, a tribute to Art Blakey in standard 32-bar form. "I had the whole melody down, and I had the harmony for the 'A' part, but I didn't have anything for the bridge. So we started working on the tune, going over and over it — I would play the melody and Claude would try out changes. This went on for I don't know how long, to the point where I was getting tired of doing it. I really wanted to let it go — like, 'OK, another time.' But Claude would hear none of it. 'No, we're going to get it, we're going to get it.' After, I'd say, two hours of working on this eight-bar part, he finally came up with the chords, and they were perfect — all minor 7th chords moving in parallel, which is something I would never have thought of."[2]

Ranger subsequently composed a solo guitar piece for Wilson with sections dedicated to Brian Barley, Lenny Breau, Sonny Greenwich and Don Thompson; both the music and its title have been lost. Many years later, Wilson in turn would write *For Claude* in Ranger's memory.

• • •

Ranger was necessarily limited at home to the Fender Rhodes, but he could play drums with Clyde Reed in the basement of Reed's house, a short walk west along Union Street. Reed, who was teaching economics at Simon Fraser University in addition to playing bass, participated in many of Ranger's ventures as a bandleader between mid-1988 and 1995.

Their first session together in his basement was with Paul Plimley, a pianist adept at free improvisation in a style that personalized Cecil Taylor's influence with softer hands and a lighter heart. "Claude told me afterwards that he didn't think he could play with Paul," Reed remembers, "but he thought he could play with me. This started a friendship, and a musical relationship. I think it's a mystery to people why he hooked up with me, but it was pretty comfortable."

Reed is candid about one aspect of that relationship. "Part of the attraction for Claude was that I had more money than other people, so he would borrow from me. But he never borrowed much and he'd pay it back."

As for the session with Plimley, a pianist — however brilliant — was still a pianist to Ranger's way of thinking, which apparently had not changed since the late 1960s. "A piano can do everything," he told the Vancouver writer and photographer Laurence Svirchev in 1990, "so it should be played by itself. If I were able to play piano, I wouldn't be a drummer."[3]

In fact, Ranger demonstrated that he was actually quite adept at the piano when he and Reed played duets in Reed's basement. "I kept wanting to play *Moment's Notice,*" Reed recalls, citing the John Coltrane composition whose harmonic structure has challenged even the deftest of jazz musicians. "And Claude could play it — he was very good, he knew where he was in the form. But that was harder work than he liked to do, so we played standards. I don't remember playing any of his tunes. He understood harmony, what worked with different chords. He wasn't blindingly fast, but he swung hard. That was the most fun part: he could really groove on piano. It may actually have been easier to follow him on piano than it was on drums."

Following Ranger on drums was not, in truth, easy at all for Reed. As Ranger's primary bassist of choice for his own music — a succession of bassists, beginning with Rene Worst, worked with him in other settings — Reed had to contend with Ranger's drumming at its freest.

"I never felt super secure with Claude's 'time.' He kept using me, but I played with a lot of other drummers where it was easier for me to sync up with them, even though I'm sure Claude was trying his hardest to help me. I just didn't quite know where he thought 'it' was. So I would more likely play off of where the saxophone player was, as opposed to playing off Claude. He would do things to straighten me out — 'Da-da-*dah,*' or something like that, to really make it clear. So then it was clear... for a few seconds."

. . .

Reed's basement sessions evolved into a workshop not unlike the one that Ranger had led on Silverbirch Avenue in Toronto. Tony Wilson was one of the participants. "I think it was Clyde finding a way to help

Claude out financially. That was part of it. But it was really cheap. I think it was ten dollars. We'd go and play standards for a couple of hours."

Laurence Svirchev dated the workshop's beginning to April 1989 and identified Reed as its co-director. "The first Sunday," Svirchev wrote, "seven people came. Each Sunday a few more players would show up, so Mr. Ranger brought in some of his charts and began writing for the group."

Ranger himself told Renee Doruyter of the *Vancouver Province* much the same story in late 1990, with reference to the transformation of the workshop into a more formal orchestra. Doruyter also described Reed as co-director. "The group started from a workshop we had in the beginning of the year," Ranger explained. "There were all kinds of people, everyone wanted to play. At one point there were so many people [that] I said, 'We have to write some music for this.'"[4]

Glass Slipper, Vancouver, January 1990.
Photograph by Laurence Svirchev.

The transition was marked by a move from Reed's basement to the Glass Slipper, which was in fact another basement — this one downstairs from the Cinderella Ballroom, an old legion and dance hall on East 11th Avenue, off Main Street. The Slipper started in the fall of 1988 as a rehearsal space; by the summer of 1989, however, it had opened to the public, taking over and expanding the role that the Classical Joint, soon to close, had played as a base for Vancouver's creative music community.

The transition was also marked by a change in Ranger's relationship with his musicians. No longer were they paying for the opportunity to play with him; in turn, he could not afford to compensate them for his weekly rehearsals at the Slipper in 1990. "In truth," notes Coat Cooke, one of the orchestra's tenor saxophonists, "he was asking 15, 20 people to come and rehearse every week for nothing. I think he was critically aware of that. And we were more than delighted to do so."[5]

That delight reflected the esteem in which Ranger had come to be held after little more than two years in the city. According to Cooke, he responded in kind to his musicians' high regard. "He was always a shy fellow, but respectful in the way he spoke to you about who you were and what your work was. He was very humble and appreciative of you coming and playing with him, playing his music."

Ranger called his new ensemble the Jade Orchestra. "I always liked the colour jade," he told Laurence Svirchev. "I don't mean the stone, I mean the colour. Jade has all the light; it's like water, like fire. It's warm and it's cool." He alluded to Bill Evans' composition *Blue in Green* from Miles Davis' classic recording *Kind of Blue*. "That's a jade colour. My music is something you can see, like Debussy's *La Mer*. You can feel the ocean in the music."

His reference to Claude Debussy was not careless. Svirchev noticed on a visit to Ranger's studio that his record collection included music by the French composer as well as such other early 20th-century figures as Igor Stravinsky and Maurice Ravel, a legacy of his friendship with Brian Barley 20 years earlier in Montreal.

"Brian would talk to me," Ranger once explained, "and he'd say, 'Why don't you listen to classical music?'" Ranger admitted that he had resisted at first. "But I had to learn. Lucky for me. One day, I sat down and I said, 'Brian, yeah, you were right.' And I started to listen to Stravinsky and all those cats. And that really opened up other ways."

Some of "those cats" — he told Renee Doryuter — influenced the music that he was writing for the Jade Orchestra. "We don't play like Hugh Fraser — I'm not as talented a writer as Hugh — but I'm influenced by the music of Ravel, Debussy, Shostakovich, Erik Satie, and I like the harmonies of Billy Strayhorn and Duke Ellington."

Fraser's Vancouver Ensemble for Jazz Improvisation, then in its 10th year, was one of three other large ensembles that were testing the big band tradition's limits in the city, along with the New Orchestra Workshop's NOW Orchestra, which was on hiatus in 1990, and John Korsrud's proudly post-modern Hard Rubber Orchestra, which was preparing for its own debut at the Glass Slipper in October of that year.

There were overlaps in personnel, as well as intentions, between the four ensembles. Coat Cooke, for one, was director of the NOW Orchestra, which shared with the Jade Orchestra an emphasis, in degrees, on free improvisation — NOW ultimately more so than Jade. "Claude's pieces were jazz charts, they were more conventional," Cooke notes. "But he'd have areas with a section where he'd write FROUT for 'freak out.' So there were FROUT sections, and we knew that was open improvisation."

Ranger's composition *Feu vert* was a case in point, now adapted for the orchestra, and for baritone saxophonist Daniel Miles Kane in particular. Laurence Svirchev recorded Ranger's instructions to his soloists at the Glass Slipper one night in June 1990: "You're the driver. When the light turns green, you drive any way you want."

Svirchev exploited the obvious metaphor in his description of the three stages to the Kane improvisation that followed. "Kane strains," he wrote of the last stage, "summoning resources, finding a second wind, a Rocket 88 to musical heaven. Red light! The brake pedal goes to the floor, the last millimeters of asbestos shearing off the pads, metal screaming on metal, the radiator steaming, the burnt-out hulk careening to a stop. There's thunderous applause from the audience, awe-stuck grins on the faces of the musicians, blood on Daniel Kane's reed."

Thus FROUT.

Ranger also adapted at least two other compositions from his Toronto years, *Gefilte Fish* and the ballad *Wood Nymph*, for the orchestra. The full scores for all three, and for the rest of the orchestra's repertoire, have been lost; Ranger did not make copies of the individual parts, preferring to take back the originals from his musicians after each performance. His vigilance in this regard was a practical function of the prohibitive cost of photocopying — given his financial situation, *any* cost would have been prohibitive — and of his penchant, still, for revising his music over and over again.

"Arranging is not tough," he told Svirchev. "Making a decision is tough. If I could just leave it alone! But it has to sound right, and I hear new things every day.'"

● ● ●

In the absence of Ranger's scores and, moreover, of any recordings by the orchestra, only the impressions of his musicians are left to stand for his music. Tenor saxophonist Dave Say did indeed hear Ranger's avowed influence, Debussy, in his tonal and textural palette. "I saw the same colours as I do when I listen to Debussy. The same greens. For me, it came though in the colours. It didn't come through in the compositions themselves."[6]

Clyde Reed, too, credits Debussy's influence, among that of French impressionists more generally, but he identifies another element of Ranger's music that ran counter to impressionistic principles, the play of tension and release at the sort of fundamental level that was also typical of his drumming.

"Claude had a real feeling for drama and juxtaposition. He'd just give you the right amount of cacophony — '*What's going on?*' — then suddenly turn it into something that you could relate to easily."

François Houle also acknowledges Ranger's feeling for dynamics and contrast. "His themes were short, but his arrangements of those themes would explode. I remember his melodies were very modal, very simple, very diatonic — no weird sort of chromatic turns or anything like that. He'd have a lot of horns playing in unison to get the melody really, really strong, and he'd have a few other elements of colour — parallel melodies, straight-up harmonies — for contrast."

Reed and Ron Samworth both remark independently on how "lush" the result often was. "It was very tonal music," Samworth adds. "It was quite romantic. I think it was Claude putting his heart on his sleeve. He liked the big sound — the big, thick voicings."

Ranger clearly was not thinking of the Jade Orchestra in terms of big band convention. When it appeared on Maple Tree Square in Gastown as part of the du Maurier International Jazz Festival in June 1990, it was as many as 13 musicians strong — six saxophonists, three guitarists, trombone, flute, bass and drums, with Ranger also playing electric piano, an altogether unusual and unbalanced array of instruments. For its next concert, in November, it had grown to 19 members in a somewhat more familiar, if still idiosyncratic scheme of three trumpets, four trombones, seven saxophones, flute, guitar, bass, tuba and drums.

Jade Orchestra, du Maurier International Jazz Festival, Vancouver, June 1990.
L-R: Clyde Reed, Gordon Bertram, Claude Ranger, Terry Deane, Jason Liebert, Coat Cooke (hidden), Suzanne Duplessis, Saul Berson.
Photograph by Mark Miller.

The orchestra's evolving configuration was evidently the result of Ranger's benevolence as a bandleader. While some of his musicians remember being invited to join, others arrived of their own accord. "They just come," he told Laurence Svirchev. "If they're good players, and want to stay in the band, they can stay."

Ranger aside, the 13 and 19-piece lineups had eight musicians in common: Coat Cooke, François Houle, Clyde Reed and Ron Samworth, as well as saxophonists Saul Berson and Bruce Freedman, trombonist Jason Liebert and the orchestra's youngest member, just turned 18, flutist Suzanne Duplessis.[7]

Looking ahead to the November concert and beyond, Ranger mused, "It could possibly be 50 pieces next time."[8]

• • •

With Lili Wheatley's help, Ranger applied in September 1990 for his second Canada Council Arts Grant "A," this time to compose a suite in nine movements, *Stars in Tears*, and then take it to other Canadian cities for performances with local musicians. He asked for $33,000 — 12 month's "subsistence" at $2,500 per month, rental for the same period of a "comfortable, peaceful studio with piano" at $200 per month and manuscript paper totalling $600.[9]

In his application, he described *Stars in Tears* as "my ultimate expression on humanity" and set out its theme: "The Stars are the Wise Ones. They see humanity at a loss. They are in tears."

The suite would combine both "new ideas" and "some previous sketches." Ranger had in fact used the title once before for a piece that he played as part of the Concours de Jazz de Montreal in 1986. However, it does not appear among the titles of the nine individual movements of this new work, as listed with brief annotations on his application:

Ballad to the Stars ("Ballad to the Wise Ones")

Croissant ("The Wise Ones are in a thinking process — how to influence humanity")

Entre ciel et terre ("Message from the Wise Ones")

Vasparez Calabar ("Emissary sent by the Wise to encourage beauty and harmony among beauty")

Alveolar ("The guardian of the Vasparez mission")

Flowers of the Spirit ("Acknowledgement")

M's Garden ("Peace")

Temple of Promises ("Reunion")

Valse aux Étoiles ("Rejoice")

The music for *Stars in Tears* — to the extent that Ranger completed it — has been lost along with the Jade Orchestra's other scores, but the narrative suggested by the titles of its sections has something of a theosophical basis. *M's Garden* in particular is an allusion to *Leaves of Morya's Garden*, the title of two books foundational to Agni Yoga, a spiritual teaching that Lili Wheatley had embraced when she and Ranger first met; *Flowers of the Spirit* is a phrase from verse 126 in the first of those books.

More practically, Ranger's proposed instrumentation mirrored the evolving Jade Orchestra — eight brass, seven reeds, flute, guitar, bass and drums. He offered his scores for *Feu vert* and *Wood Nymph* in support of his proposal.

And then he waited. Results from the Canada Council's assessment process were at least five months away, a period in Ranger's career that proved eventful on several fronts.

• • •

With the Jade Orchestra's next concert set for November, Ranger travelled in late October to New York with a troupe of New Orchestra Workshop musicians for two evenings in Manhattan at the Knitting Factory, then in its third year as an important venue for the jazz avant-garde. This, for Ranger, was his New York debut. He was 49.

He had always been ambivalent, at the very least, about the city and its place in the world of jazz. As he explained to Peter Goddard almost 20 years earlier, his objections to the suggestion that he should have moved there were both personal and practical.

"New York, of course, has lots of great players," he argued, "but I'm a Canadian. I want to do my work here. Besides, the work's difficult in New York. I know I can play with them, but there are too many good players, famous names too, who can't make a living."

Ranger made the trip in 1990 as a member of Chief Feature, a quartet led by tenor saxophonist Bruce Freedman and completed by Clyde Reed and an Oregon musician, Rob Blakeslee, the latter filling in for the band's regular trumpeter, Bill Clark. Reed was a member as well of one of the two other Vancouver groups visiting New York, Lunar Adventures, with Coat Cooke, Ron Samworth and Gregg Simpson; the duo of Paul Plimley and bassist Lisle Ellis also appeared under the "New York is NOW" banner.

Ranger and Freedman had met at a session in Reed's basement, where they found something to their liking in each other's playing. Ranger agreed to join Chief Feature and in turn added Freedman to the Jade Orchestra.

"I knew of his reputation," Freedman admits, of their initial encounter in 1989, "but I really hadn't heard him play a hell of a lot. I just knew that this was a 'big time' guy. And from the little I'd heard, I knew he was an Elvin Jones kind of drummer, so when that happened, I was really thrilled. I've always been extremely without confidence as a musician, which to some extent has probably been an asset in the positive angst that comes out in my playing sometimes, so when Claude showed an interest, a big interest, I was thoroughly flattered."[10]

Ranger was the latest in a succession of drummers to play with Chief Feature, following Blaine Wikjord, Dennis Burke and Stan Taylor, as the band evolved through the successive influences of Ornette Coleman and John Coltrane. Ranger did indeed sound like Elvin Jones on *Tibetan Tears of Joy and Sadness*, a piece included in a New Orchestra Workshop sampler, *The Future is N.O.W.*, but it was his raucous response to Freedman on an unissued recording, *Clear the Way*,[11] that captured their rapport in all of its unrelenting urgency.

"Musically it was tremendous," Freedman remembers. "It brought out some things in me that I felt really good about. But emotionally it was really trying."

He recalled a difficult evening at the Glass Slipper. "Clyde was soloing and I went behind the partition on the bandstand. Claude came back, gave me a hug, looked me in the eye, and said, 'Man, this is my favourite band to play in.' Here I am, this young guy looking up to Claude, thrilled to death. But by the end of the evening, Claude was in a black mood you could cut with a knife. And I had to drive him home, because I had a car, and he didn't. It was like, 'Does he hate me? What *is* it?' But he wouldn't talk about it. So we had this silent ride home."

The band's New York sojourn, according to Reed, was also fraught. "The first night, we set up and we played great. Claude was great. And we were feeling really good: here we've come to New York and we're playing just as good as the New York guys. The next night we showed up at the gig, and Paul Plimley and Lisle Ellis had moved the drums for their own purpose, not talking to us. Claude really didn't like that. Now he was far away from the rest of us. It wasn't the same, and the gig wasn't that great. Claude had a bit of a martyr thing and he kind of martyred himself. He could have said, 'No, no, we're moving the drums back.' But instead he said 'OK, we'll do it this way.' But it really came at a high cost."

Freedman has similar memories. "The first night was great. The second night he was kind of moody. He was upset, apparently, because somebody had moved the drum set on the stage. He was also unhappy because I had gone shopping that day and I'd bought a microphone that fits right on the bell of the horn. He was upset about that. He said he didn't like the way it sounded. Here we are, you know, pretty excited, a bunch of Vancouver guys playing in the Big Apple. Who needs a downer?"

• • •

The Jade Orchestra appeared less than two weeks later — Remembrance

Day, 1990 — at the Vancouver East Cultural Centre, its most ambitious engagement to that point and ultimately of its brief history. Ranger was exultant beforehand, telling Renee Doruyter of the *Province*, "I feel like I'm waking up again on this side of the country!" The advent of the orchestra, and now its evolution, had restored his sense of purpose.

The concert was reviewed by Alex Varty for the *Georgia Straight*. Varty began with the suggestion that the musicians in the Jade Orchestra must have found it a "very rewarding experience" and speculated that the time they had spent in rehearsal with Ranger would figure prominently on their résumés.

"Alas," Varty continued, "just *listening* to Jade paid no such pleasant dividends."

He summarized Ranger's music as "curiously lifeless and unattractive," and described his vision as "schizophrenic" in its juxtaposition of composition and improvisation.

"On the one hand, his written parts display a sort of flatly chromatic sheen, like '60s TV sports music gone haywire; on the other hand, he asks his soloists to disrupt the music's gloss with the kinds of bleatings and blasts that typified the New York underground of the '70s."

The result, Varty wrote, was "almost painful," adding that the transitions between the solos and the ensembles — the latter characterized by "a sort of Nelson-Riddle-from-hell slickness" — often came with "a halting, grinding awkwardness that did little to lift either of the music's aspects from banality."

Varty lauded Clyde Reed, Bruce Freedman and tubaist Ian McIntosh for their success in "struggl[ing] up from this morass of bombast and tunelessness," but concluded his review with a final reproach. "Any other moments of merit were simply drowned out in the blare, and the only consolation was that the program seemed a tad on the skimpy side. Thank heaven for small mercies."[12]

Not all of the orchestra's musicians remember Ranger's reaction to the *Straight* review. Those close to him, however, say that he took it very personally — that, as Coat Cooke suggests, "it hurt him deeply; I think it was devastating."

The orchestra had been "wildly successful," notes Clyde Reed, "up until that one review." Ron Samworth recalls hearing that Ranger didn't want to continue, that he was "totally depressed." The review, Samworth continues, "destroyed him, because he put so much into that music, his heart and soul. He *loved* it."

Jade Orchestra, Vancouver East Cultural Centre, November 1990.
Photograph by Laurence Svirchev.

Just as Ranger had turned away from the quintet that failed to win the Concours de Jazz in Montreal four years earlier, he now all but abandoned the Jade Orchestra. There would be just one more performance under that name, an afternoon concert at the du Maurier International Jazz Festival in 1991, again on Maple Tree Square in Gastown but this time with Jane Bunnett and three Americans, Rob Blakeslee and saxophonists Vinny Golia and John Gross, as guests.

Ranger also went out of his way to add trombonist Joe Bjornson for this final performance, evidently against objections raised by some of the other members of the orchestra — objections that likely made

Ranger, who knew ostracism only too well, all the more adamant that Bjornson should be involved.

"Claude called me in for the last rehearsal and invited me to play on the gig. When I was packing away my trombone after the show, he approached me and said, 'Here, Joe, I want you to have my money.' He gave me cash — a hundred dollars or something like that — and thanked me for taking part."[13]

Ranger could well afford to be generous. By then, his proposal to the Canada Council had been approved; he was one of just three musicians among more than 55 Arts Grant "A" recipients, the distinction shared with composer Harry Freedman and violist Rivka Golani, both of Toronto.[14]

As it happened, the music jury included Terry Clarke and Don Thompson, who would certainly have been sympathetic to Ranger's presence among the applicants. Clarke suggests that the guilelessness of Ranger's proposal, among others typically much more elaborate, worked to its advantage.

"We were faced with mountains of material. People would give us their life story, the video version of their life story, the cassette version of their life story, the book and the movie. Claude's application was the simplest: "'I want this, I need this.'

"'OK. Fine. *Next*.'"

In his disillusionment with the Jade Orchestra, however, Ranger did not complete *Stars in Tears*, much less take it on the road. Moreover, he discovered to his dismay that he had to pay income tax on the grant; the same requirement with respect to the Canada Council's support in 1982 would likely have been handled as a matter of course by Ali Karnick on his behalf.

Ranger apparently kept the money from his second grant close to hand — not for him the services or the security of a bank — and simply went on with life along Union Street.

"Even after he got that big grant," his neighbour Graham Ord remembers, "you'd still see him on his bike collecting bottles."[15]

CHAPTER SIXTEEN

"A very tidy guy"

Claude Ranger continued to freelance during the period in which he was involved with the Union Street workshop and the Jade Orchestra. In addition to Chief Feature, he played with several American visitors, including John Handy from San Francisco and Vinny Golia from Los Angeles in 1989, as well as the New York pianist Barry Harris and Oakland tenor saxophonist Glenn Spearman in 1990. He also appeared in 1990 at the Glass Slipper with Jane Bunnett and Ralph Bowen; a recording made under Bob Murphy's name after the latter engagement for the Vancouver label Roadhouse, with Bowen, Murphy, Ranger and Torben Oxbol, was given a title, *Free on the Inside*, and a catalogue number, but never released.

Ranger's informal encounter with Spearman at the Glass Slipper during the du Maurier International Jazz Festival, like his exchange with John Tchicai at Hot Jazz two years earlier, would become the stuff of legend. "You've never heard anything as loud unamplified," marvels Coat Cooke, who was present that night. "They just literally raised the roof.

Glenn was a very competitive guy. Claude started to play with him, and Glenn was like, 'Oh, *yeah*?' Claude was really digging in, and Glenn, of course, could be louder than any saxophone player around, with his hard plastic reeds. It was quite memorable. I think they gained huge respect for each other — not just for their volume but for their playing."

Ranger returned east on two occasions during this same period, the first in early December 1990 to Montreal for a weekend with Guy Nadon at le Grand Café and the second in mid-January 1991 for recording sessions with Don Thompson in Toronto and Charles Papasoff in Montreal.

His reunion with Nadon was filmed by director Serge Giguère for *Guy Nadon: Le Roi du drum*, a fantasy — more than a documentary — in which Nadon, then 57, recreated various events in his career, beginning with a scene on a mock staircase behind an east-end tenement where he plays on the sorts of tins and cans that he had found as a boy in nearby alleyways. He is also captured drumming along with film clips of his early heroes Gene Krupa and Louis Bellson and in person with Ranger.

The Grand Café footage, totalling about two-and-a-half minutes in three segments, is largely unrevealing, its significance lost to anyone not aware of the history between the two drummers. They play individually and together, the excitable Nadon snapping impatiently at the beat, as though it cannot come soon enough, and Ranger — eyes closed, cigarette tucked into the left corner of his mouth — meeting Nadon's nervous energy with a more measured display of power.

Ranger was once again far more in his element with Don Thompson, who had been invited by Roadhouse Records to choose his musicians, as he recalls, "from anybody in the world" and — in addition to Ranger — selected Phil Dwyer, Kenny Wheeler and the British bassist Dave Holland without hesitation.

His compositions on *Forgotten Memories*, which included dedications to Wheeler, Holland and Dwyer's daughter Madeleine, suggest a certain sentimentalism, but the performances have a stirring immediacy. Holland and Ranger prove to be a formidable team, between Holland's low, rolling lines and Ranger's insistent cymbal ride. Thompson draws on the full range of Ranger's resources, from the most discreet to the most explosive; *For Dave Holland*, with its stop-time effects, rhythm shifts and free dissolves, becomes as much a showpiece for Ranger in that regard as it is for the bassist.

The Papasoff sessions, which began immediately after the Thompson date, continued for a number of days and involved a changing cast of players, some of whom were apparently more to Ranger's liking than others. "There was one situation that he didn't like at all," Papasoff admits. "There was a lot of rhythmic rushing involved on the part of somebody else and he just could not deal with it. He didn't want to play after that."[1]

The recording otherwise went well, with Ranger evidently enjoying himself on his latest trip back to Montreal. "Claude was staying at the Ritz-Carlton with an open bar bill," Papasoff jokes, "so he had a good time."

As Ranger's deluxe accommodations suggest, the project was generously financed; its producer had previously met with success selling airplane parts to Iraq. As luck would have it, Operation Desert Storm of the first Gulf War started on the very day that the musicians went into the studio, sidetracking the producer and ultimately leaving Papasoff with a recording — *Emphasis* — that he was able to release only on cassette.

· · ·

The Jade Orchestra aside, Ranger's activities at the 1991 du Maurier International Jazz Festival were limited to concerts with Jane Bunnett and Chief Feature. He nevertheless caught the ear and, inevitably, the eye of the American critic Kevin Whitehead, who reviewed the event for *Down Beat*.

"Everyone credits Ranger, 50 this year, with energizing Vancouver's scene," Whitehead wrote. "Picture a Blakey whose tastes never stopped evolving — a roiling drummer committed to cultivating young talent, exploring new ideas, and kicking ass on the bandstand. At the kit, his patterns and strategies change from bar to bar, but hard swing is as much a constant as the cigarette dangling from his lower lip. Ranger's hard thrusting accents help define the hometown sound. You can hear echoes of his style in young drummers like Dylan van der Schyff."[2]

Dylan van der Schyff was just 16 when Ranger moved to Vancouver — a little young to have heard him at Studio 19, the Classical Joint or the Landmark Jazz Bar. He met Ranger instead at a workshop in Victoria, before leaving Vancouver to study classical percussion at McGill University in Montreal. On his return in 1991, he joined the city's other impressionable young drummers who were following Ranger closely; he was present for the Jade Orchestra's final performance in Gastown, where one incident in particular captured his imagination.

"Claude started to do this drum solo and it was just killing. It sounded awesome. Halfway through, he just stopped and changed his shoes! He used to wear these little Chinese slippers. I guess the ones he was wearing weren't comfortable. So he's playing along, stops, takes his shoes off, gets another pair, puts them on and starts playing again just where he left off!"[3]

Ranger began to follow van der Schyff soon after in turn, starting with a concert at the Vancouver East Cultural Centre by François Houle's Et Cetera. "We were setting up, getting ready to play, and I saw Claude coming in," van der Schyff remembers, "and I thought, 'Oh, shit, Claude's here.' I knew how serious he was, and now he's *here*.

"After the gig, I remember going off to the side of the stage. You know how there are staircases on both sides of the stage at the Cultch? So I look up the stairs, and Claude's coming down. I can tell he's coming towards me. *He's coming right towards me!*

"'What's he going to say? It's okay, it's okay, don't run away.'

"He came up and he was so nice, so complimentary. He was like, 'Yeah, you sounded really good. Your cymbal sounds really good. Your time is good.' Just so encouraging. And he started coming to the gigs that I was doing — I was always going to his — and he'd always had nice things to say, little tips, little things, generally very, very supportive. And then one day he said to me, 'You know you should come over.'

"I'd have gone over and hung out with him all the time, but I was too shy, so he took the initiative.

"He said, 'I've got some things I want to show you, that might be helpful for you.'

"I said, 'Should I bring money?'

"He said, 'No, no, just come over.'

"I called Tony Wilson — or maybe it was one of the other guys who knew him better — and I asked, 'What do you bring?'

"'Well, Claude likes beer. Bring him some Molson "Ex." He'll put it in the fridge for 20 minutes. He's a very meticulous guy.'

"I went over there. I was amazed at his apartment. Everything was in its spot. He had his cigarette rolling thing, his music, his pens. A very tidy kind of guy. We put the beer in the fridge and he started to show me a few of these little exercises that I still use today — I give them to my students. He wrote them out for me by hand.

"I didn't go over and hang all that often, but when I did, there was always some little lesson. He'd seen me do something, and he'd say, 'That was good, you've got to keep thinking about that.' Or, 'I saw you do this; you might want to be careful.' Or, 'Wait, be more patient, you don't need to play all that stuff right away. Just play the cymbal, focus on the cymbal, and build everything into the sound of the cymbal.'

"It was extremely informal. But he was always around and whenever I was playing I had the feeling that he could show up at any time. So that would keep me on my toes because I had so much respect for him."

As much as his presence in the audience was an inspiration for van der Schyff, Ranger's own example on the bandstand was equally a caution. "I learned so many great things to do, and also things not to do. That's what was so fascinating, and frustrating, about Claude — that he was an intensely emotional man who struggled with a lot of things. As a young player coming up, I would see him struggling from time to time, being frustrated, on the bandstand. Sometimes it was for a good reason, and sometimes the way he responded was not the best, but he was never so proud that he wouldn't admit afterwards, 'Sorry, that was not good.' He was very honest."

Ranger served as a teacher or mentor to other younger drummers in Vancouver and Victoria during this period, among them Josh Dixon, Bruce Nielsen and Stan Taylor, but when, in early May 1992 at the Glass Slipper, he introduced a double quartet — to wit, an octet whose instrumentation came in pairs — he invited van der Schyff to be his counterpart.

The two of them played up front, with Clyde Reed and a second bassist, Joe Williamson, behind them, and four horns on a riser farther back. According to van der Schyff, Ranger took this exercise in inversion a step further. "When he started to rehearse the band, we realized he was rehearsing the music backwards. He started at the end. He said, 'OK, I want you to play this chord.' He tuned the chord and got it sounding exactly the way he wanted it, and he'd get the cymbal at the right volume level to have it shimmer. And that was the *last* part of the piece. So we knew where we were *going* from the beginning of the rehearsal. It unfolded in reverse."

Although van der Schyff remembers Ranger being pleased after the performance — "quietly happy and smiling" — the band did not perform again. Ranger thenceforth undertook fewer and fewer initiatives of his own and began to step away — or in some cases find himself pushed — from the scene more generally, his place was most often taken by van der Schyff, notably at the du Maurier International Jazz Festival.

As the festival continued to grow under Ken Pickering's direction, it began to distinguish itself in the early 1990s from other events in Canada by the welcome it offered to Europe's most venturesome musicians, both on their own and in ad hoc settings with kindred Vancouver spirits, van der Schyff, François Houle, Paul Plimley and cellist Peggy Lee — but not Ranger — among them.

"I think one of the reasons why Claude started doing less festival work," van der Schyff suggests, "was because a lot more European free-improv started coming in, and he wasn't interested in that at all."

Ranger's values, though at odds with the Canadian mainstream, were comparatively traditional relative to the various directions in improvised music that had been circulating in Europe since the mid-1960s and that only now were receiving a hearing in North America.

"You'd never hear Claude on 'prepared' snare drum doing a 'Paul Lovens,'" van der Schyff remarks, citing the German percussionist whose playing draws on an expanded range of techniques and textures not explored since the very earliest years of jazz. "In fact, when I started getting more into that, Claude didn't like it. He said, 'You're not playing time any more!' I tried to explain to him that I was doing things more related to sound. He said, 'Yes, you have to do what you think you have to do, but I want to hear you play your cymbal again.' I think he was concerned for me. I was very touched by that."

• • •

After Ranger had set the Jade Orchestra aside, and with it all that it would have represented going forward, his next significant engagement, in mid-August 1991, took him back to his quartet from 1982 with Roland Bourgeois, Kirk MacDonald and Marty Melanson for a reunion at the Festival Acadien de Caraquet in New Brunswick.

The past, in any event, was of no more concern to Ranger, either philosophically or practically, than the future. He remained determinedly in the present, as Kieran Overs was surprised to discover when he and Ranger accompanied MacDonald on a short tour that started in Toronto two days after the Festival Acadien and continued to Kingston, Ottawa — where MacDonald was living at the time — and Montreal.

"Someone came up to Claude in Toronto and said, 'So, what are you into right now? What's happening?'

"He said, 'Well, my main thing right now is this trio with Kieran and Kirk.'

"And we'd never played together before! I thought that was really interesting. He's saying, 'This is where I'm at right now.' It wasn't just a gig. '*This* is what's happening.'"

The trio went from strength to strength as it moved from Toronto to Kingston and on to Ottawa, where the audience at the Downstairs Club on Rideau Street included Nick Fraser, then all of 15. Fraser introduced himself to Ranger as a drummer and explained that he and his friend

Jared Hunter, who was studying with MacDonald, would be following the trio to Montreal.

"That's great," he recalls Ranger saying. "Bring some paper and some coloured pens and I'll hang with you on the break and write out some drum patterns."[4]

The night in Ottawa went particularly well. "We all — including Claude — felt this elation," Overs remembers. "Like, 'Wow, we really *hit* it, we really did!' We went back to Kirk's house, and Claude made steak dinners for us and was sort of celebrating. On the way to Montreal, he was saying, 'You've got to come and meet my mother.' And when we got to Montreal, he said, 'I *love* Montreal!'"

As was becoming increasingly the pattern, however, Ranger's mood soon turned dramatically. "By the time the gig came around," Overs continues, "he was saying, 'I *hate* Montreal.' He wasn't happy anymore; he wasn't enjoying anything anymore. It was all gone. And we couldn't find the spirit we'd had in Ottawa. Somewhere between Ottawa and Montreal it had all turned bad."

MacDonald had seen as much before when Ranger's quartet made the trip to l'Air du Temps and the Festival International de Jazz de Montréal in 1982. "Anytime I worked with him in Montreal, there was always some sort of internal angst going on with him. It was a big deal. I'm not sure why."

MacDonald had arranged to have André White record the trio's two nights at Claudio's, a restaurant overlooking the St. Lawrence River from a loft in Old Montreal; White, who had replaced Ranger as Sonny Greenwich's drummer during the mid-1980s, was also an accomplished pianist and an experienced recording engineer. The tapes from the two evenings were disappointing, however, marred by the intransigence that characterized Ranger's behaviour at its worst. His attention wandered; *he* wandered, leaving his drums to walk around the bandstand and look out the window.

"It was almost like he wasn't on the gig," White recalls, "but then, suddenly, if he heard something that he liked, he'd jump in, maybe play 32 bars, then stop again."[5]

Whatever the cause and extent of Ranger's disaffection on the band-stand, Nick Fraser nevertheless found him to be "a total sweetheart" at the break. "He sat with me, wrote out these figures for me and talked about different ways of interpreting them. Mainly, I remember him writing out the ride rhythm as a triplet and saying, 'That's the way Elvin plays it — "one-trip-let, two-trip-let, three-trip-let." But Tony plays it like this, a dotted eighth and a sixteenth — "ding-ding-da-ding."' And he told me about different ways of practicing. I remember him saying, 'If something hurts, you're doing it wrong. Stop!'"

So it was that Ranger had an impact, however fleeting, on the development of one of the two finest Canadian jazz drummers of their generation. He had already left his mark on the other, Dylan van der Schyff.

• • •

The MacDonald tour complete, Ranger immediately returned to Toronto for a week with Jane Bunnett and Larry Cramer at the midtown Bermuda Onion, a prelude of sorts to a tour of Western Canada in November 1991. Bunnett had moved two CDs further along in her career by then, *New York Duets*, a collection of duets with Don Pullen, and *Live at Sweet Basil*, recorded in a New York club with drummer Billy Hart as her requisite American guest. For the Bermuda Onion, and for the tour, Bunnett and Cramer had invited Dewey Redman to fill that same role.

The empathy that Redman and Ranger had demonstrated on Bunnett's first album, *In Dew Time*, particularly on the title track, only grew as the tour progressed. It was evident when the quintet appeared at the Vancouver East Cultural Centre, where Dylan van der Schyff was entranced by what he heard. "I couldn't keep my eyes off Claude. It was like he was glowing. He'd get this kind of aura around him when he was 'on.'"

It culminated in Saskatoon at the Bassment on 3rd Avenue South, where the audience that packed the small room hung on every note.

"We let Dewey really stretch out and we let Claude stretch out, too," Bunnett explains. "There was no urgency to jump in. It felt great, so we just let them blow."

Years later, Ranger described that night to Ivan Bamford, as "the zenith" of his career. "Everything," he said, "was just right."

As he had with Billy Robinson, Sonny Rollins, John Tchicai and Glenn Spearman, Ranger met Redman more than halfway. "The fact that Dewey liked his playing was a big deal to him," Cramer suggests. "It's that Canadian inferiority complex, whether it's Quebec or it's English Canada: 'They're the real thing, and I'm just a Canadian.'"

They were also African-Americans, and Ranger was white. He had once believed, as he put it, "You had to be black to play." He had proved to himself otherwise.

Redman confirmed his opinion of Ranger three years later when he and Don Thompson were on a break between sets one evening at the Pilot Tavern in Toronto. A young drummer travelling with Redman out of New York, Matt Wilson, sat with them.

"Whatever happened to Claude Ranger," Redman wondered at one point in the conversation, pronouncing Ranger's name as an American would.

"Oh, Claude," Thompson replied, with the correct French inflection. "He moved out to Vancouver."

Wilson, listening in, asked, "Who's Claude Ranger?"

Thompson's answer might have seemed reasonably definitive.

"Claude? He's probably the greatest drummer in Canada."

It was not definitive enough for Redman, who countered, "Make that the *world*."

Three years later still, in the spring of 1997, Thompson mentioned Redman's comment to Buff Allen, who subsequently relayed it to Ranger. "I thought Claude might need a little boost," Allen recalls, "because he wasn't playing anymore. He was in a good space, but he wasn't playing. When I told him that story, he looked down at his shoes, shook his head and said, 'Oh, that Dewey.' But when he looked up, he had this really big smile."

CHAPTER SEVENTEEN

"I think I will never play again"

For much of the time that Claude Ranger lived in Vancouver he worked on a casual basis at Drums Only, the home of Ayotte Custom Drums, a workshop and store run by brothers Ray and George Ayotte, initially on Granville Street downtown and then on Pine Street in False Creek.

"Our shop was the hang," Ray Ayotte explains. "All of the musicians, particularly the drummers, would be there." Ranger and Al Wiertz both benefitted directly from the Ayottes' goodwill. "We kind of supported them with a little side work, a little money. It's what we could do to turn things back into the community. They were our two special cases, our two geniuses. Completely different, but both highly intelligent and likeable characters. Al was the outgoing one and Claude was a little more shy."[1]

Despite Ranger's love of working on drums and the fact that he continued to refinish kits on his own in Vancouver, his duties for the Ayottes were limited to installing lugs on drum shells, among other fairly basic tasks. He also used one of the Drums Only studios as a place to teach and practice, and had a set of Ayottes made to his specifications — a 16-inch bass drum and 10 and 13-inch toms, finished in red.

"He wouldn't have paid for it," Ayotte notes, "but I would have had him do some work in exchange to make him feel that he earned it; the value of the set was far greater than what he put in. And it was an endorsement of a sort, but I had to be careful how I did that, because all of the other drummers would be jealous. So as much as we could, we made it look as though he had worked for it."

Ranger turned his old, refinished Gretsch set over to Dylan van der Schyff. "I gave him some money for it," van der Schyff remembers, "but not what it was worth." Ranger eventually passed his Ayottes along to Ivan Bamford under similarly generous terms. As much as he may have needed money, he evidently did not really *want* it.

• • •

Kate Hammett-Vaughan continued to engage Ranger for some of her projects, most notably in 1992 and 1993 for High Standards, which — as its name suggests — was devoted to the classic American songbook. Her quartet, completed by pianist Miles Black and bassist Miles Hill, appeared at the Glass Slipper and elsewhere in Vancouver and recorded three songs in 1992 for a CBC compilation CD, *Jazz Words*.

Ranger did not often play for singers. *Jazz Words* aside, his discography includes three pop songs with Doug Mallory and Dr. Music in 1974, one with Ernie Nelson as a member of Sonny Greenwich's band in 1979 and one more with Sylvie Perron — the daughter of his old bandmate in Montreal, Léo Perron — from Charles Papasoff's *Emphasis* sessions in 1991.

Ranger paid Hammett-Vaughan a compliment of sorts by playing for her entirely in character — as though, by implication, he knew she could hold her own with him. She describes his drumming on *Jazz Words*, and in her other various bands more generally, as "ferocious." It was certainly insistent on *You'd Be So Nice to Come Home to* and *It Could Happen to You* on *Jazz Words* — not loud, but *pressing,* the intensity of his cymbal work in particular at some odds with the evocative pauses and elongations of Hammett-Vaughan's own, rather more deliberate phrasing.

Hammett-Vaughan nevertheless relished the challenge of singing with Ranger. One challenge was enough, however, and Ranger inevitably presented two. "I felt that I was negotiating with Claude a lot about my role as a leader, about choosing tunes and tempos, in order to have him there. It was a thrill, but I also eventually got to the place where I couldn't play with him anymore, because it was too mercurial. We'd have a really great rehearsal and then we'd go and play that night. Claude would be on Cloud Nine after the rehearsal, he'd be excited, but at the end of the gig itself, you'd drive him home and he'd be chain-smoking — lighting off butts — and saying, 'I think I will never play again.' That just became too hard for me."

Ranger of course did play again, although with increasingly less frequency. Hammett-Vaughan had turned by the end of 1994 to Tom Foster, but not before taking a few more engagements with Ranger, Ron Samworth and a young bassist from Quebec City, André Lachance, including a trip north to Prince George and a Cole Porter program in May at the Glass Slipper.

"We had a good night," Lachance recalls of the Porter tribute. "We actually made some money; two hundred dollars went further then than it does now." Feeling flush, Lachance drove downtown to A&B Sound the next day to buy some CDs. "I turned the corner on Seymour Street, and there's Claude, going though garbage cans, looking for bottles. I'd just played with him the night before! And then I understood: that might have been his one big, money-making gig for the month."[2]

P.J. Perry also called, inviting Ranger to join Miles Hill, as well as trumpeter Bob Tildesley and another Edmonton musician, pianist

Chris Andrew, on a tour of the summer festival circuit in 1993. Miles Black followed suit in the summer of 1994; he, Hill and Ranger had continued to work together after Hammett-Vaughan disbanded High Standards. Perry and Black were both aware of the risk that went with taking Ranger on the road, even as they anticipated the reward. Perry, for one, was prompted to make a precautionary request.

"Before I hired Claude, I said, 'I want you to come on this tour with me, but I want you to give me your word that you won't drink until after each concert is over.' He actually agreed and, furthermore, he kept his word. The result was an exciting tour across Canada, especially in Halifax, where the rhythm section was on fire."

Perry brought the band together again three months later in Edmonton to record the CD *Quintet*, his third album since *Sessions* — also with Ranger — 16 years earlier, and a departure, in some of its contemporary rhythms and synthesized keyboard textures, from the relatively pure bebop of his previous efforts. Ranger was both limited and liberated by the music's various back beats and ostinatos, restricted on one hand as to what he could do within their implicit structural constraints, but free on the other hand to do it as brashly as he wished. The sense of release in his drumming when the band shifted to swing is palpable; his shots and shadings in support of Perry's alto and Andrew's piano on Perry's bop line *Royal Tease*, in particular, are exhilarating.

Ranger and Hill also recorded the cassette *Spin Cycle* with Miles Black and saxophonist and flutist Tom Keenlyside in anticipation of Black's quartet tour in 1994. Black's music was attractively, if conservatively modern in a way that might have put Ranger in mind of working with Moe Koffman 15 years earlier. It provided him with few challenges and he offered few in return, swinging with an expert sort of efficiency and leaving Keenlyside, the band's relative wild card on tenor saxophone, to give the music what edge it had.

In a sense, Ranger had returned with Black, Perry and Hammett-Vaughan to the point, aesthetically, where he had left off in Toronto, playing — and playing well, although not always happily — within the confines of the jazz tradition as others heard it. His only reliable outlet for anything freer or more personal in the mid-1990s was a band that he and Clyde Reed — mostly Reed — took turns leading at the Glass Slipper and elsewhere, with Daniel Miles Kane as its third member and Ron Samworth, as required, its fourth.

• • •

At some point during this period, Ranger began to frequent Murphy's Pub on the downtown corner of Seymour and West Pender, where tenor saxophonist John Doheny had established a regular Tuesday night jam session. There, too, the music moved between mainstream and modern jazz.

"I got in the habit of giving him a ride home," Doheny later wrote. "We talked about all sorts of things, including the difficulty I was having getting someone reliable in the drum chair at that time. Claude started talking about how much he missed having an opportunity to play regularly and I finally realized that he was asking if he could have the gig. Even more amazing was that the 'gig' paid $50. For the whole band. In other words I had to pay Claude *freakin'* Ranger, a guy who has his own chapter in *Jazz in Canada*, $12.50 at the end of the night. A ten, a two (this was pre toonie) and two quarters, still wet from the bar."[3]

Embarrassed by the idea of giving Ranger the quarters, Doheny secured a $10 raise for the band, thereby ensuring that payment, at $15 per man, would be entirely in paper money — and dry.[4]

• • •

Ranger by then was living in the West End. Lili Wheatley had left him two or three years earlier, no longer able to abide his drinking. He remained in their Union Street alone flat for a time, then moved to a high-rise building on Harwood Street, a half block from English Bay, where he stayed for several years with a woman he had known from Montreal, Judith Yamada.

At some point in the early 1990s, he began to seek professional help and to rely on social assistance. He also began his efforts to stop drinking and smoking. Alcohol proved to be the more difficult addiction to break, although neither would have been easy to quit after more than 25 years of abuse. Alcohol, moreover, had compounded the effects on his stomach of a chronically poor diet — generally a single meal each day — and of the aspirin that he had taken so freely for so long to reduce the pain from the boyhood injury to his arm.

By 1994, he had also been presented with a diagnosis that he was suffering from bipolar disorder, a mental illness often, though not conclusively, associated with creative and addictive personalities. However accurate or inaccurate the diagnosis in Ranger's case — his mood swings, while dramatic, were not always enduring — it came, suggests Clyde Reed, as a revelation.

"All that time, Claude had thought it was circumstances that were up and down, and then he recognized that, no, *he* was up and down." This new awareness prompted him to reassess his life to that point — his relationships especially — and to accept and carry the increasingly heavy burden of responsibility, going forward, for the harm and hurt that — he now realized — he had caused those closest to him. His treatment included both medication — in particular, Lithium — and therapy.

Ranger's fellow musicians had tried to take his unpredictability in good grace, even as they attempted to understand its causes and to anticipate the concerns, musically, that would unsettle him.

"It didn't always line up for me when it was good and when Claude thought it was good," Reed notes of their quandary. "Sometimes I thought it was good and he was upset with it. Sometimes I thought it was just okay and he thought it was really good. He had this ability to make everybody apprehensive; after you'd finished playing, you'd really want to hear from Claude that he liked it. It was crazy to make your well-being dependent on something as mercurial as whether Claude liked it, but you did."

Kevin Elaschuk, who had occasionally played trumpet with Ranger in the years after providing him a place to stay when he and Lili Wheatley first arrived in Vancouver, puts the dilemma more directly. "He's such a great player that you're always trying to make the guy happy, but what makes the guy happy continuously changes, so it just may not be possible to do."[5]

• • •

Pierre Tanguay and René Lussier made Ranger very happy indeed one night in February 1995 when they performed at the Glass Slipper as part of a "Hear It NOW" series that culminated in a recording, *Le Tour du Bloc*, with the NOW Orchestra. Tanguay and Lussier, a devilishly iconoclastic guitarist and composer, were stalwarts of *musique actuelle*, the uniquely Québécois idiom in which jazz was but one element of many in a vivid, post-modern montage of American and European musical and cultural references. Tanguay and Ranger had met on Ranger's visit to Quebec City in 1979; Ranger often went to hear friends from back east — drummers especially — when they visited Vancouver.

"People were a bit resistant to us, to René and me," Tanguay remembers, of their initial reception in Vancouver, "because we arrived with these new *musique actuelle* ideas from Quebec. There were some of the NOW Orchestra musicians who were with us, but some were not — they were wondering, 'Who *are* these guys?' When we arrived and started rehearsing, we were missing half of the orchestra. Some members had to leave, some came late. We said, 'Hey, tomorrow everybody has to be here!'

"But then we played at the Glass Slipper, René and me, just as a duo. And Claude was there. And he was happy! Many of the NOW Orchestra said that for a long time they'd never seen Claude laughing and having fun like that. He was enjoying the music a lot and he told all those people, 'Did you hear that? That's *it*, baby.' The next day, *everybody* was at the rehearsal."[6]

The respect that Ranger commanded on the scene was again apparent three weeks later, in mid-March, when he — of all the drummers in Vancouver — was asked to take Pheeroan akLaff's place with the celebrated American tenor saxophonist David Murray for shows in Victoria at Hermann's and in Vancouver at the Commodore Ballroom. In what Ken Eisner of the *Georgia Straight* described as "a raucous set of free-blowing tunes" at the Commodore, Ranger was deemed to have done "a good, if boppish, job,"[7] certainly an accolade by *Straight* standards, but one — according to others in attendance — that significantly underestimated his impact.

• • •

Two months later, in May 1995, a very different story. Ranger was playing with Dave Say, Ron Samworth and Clyde Reed under Reed's name at Café Deux Soleils, a large, open room on Commercial Drive; Say had recently taken Daniel Miles Kane's place as the saxophonist in the quartet.

"This was a band that had been rehearsing regularly for a couple of months and really having fun together," Samworth explains. "Claude was opening up, starting to tell stories about his life, his youth. He was talking about romantic things and about his family. We were playing his music and he was giving a context to people like Marie Claude, whose name I knew as the title of one of his tunes. He said, 'Oh, this was a girl I loved so much back in Montreal. She was so beautiful.' It was anecdotal, it wasn't as though he went on and on as if he was in therapy. I thought it was just kind of a familial thing with us."

On this night, however, Ranger was in a darker and more impatient mood. For once, someone — Samworth — stood up to him.

"Dave was playing this unbelievably great solo on a blues, one of Claude's tunes. Dave couldn't hear himself very well, so he pointed the bell of his horn up toward the ceiling and started to get reflections. Then he started overblowing — started to play free. It went with the posture; it went with the energy level. It was spontaneous, it was ecstatic — a Coltrane/Ayler kind of thing — and it was so beautiful. He'd been tearing up the changes prior to that, so it's not that he was just pulling a runner. But Claude stopped the band at the height of Dave's solo. He said, 'That's no way to play the blues!' And Dave just totally shut down.

"Claude said, 'Okay, we play *Wood Nymph*,' or whatever the song was. And we just kind of shuffled our papers. Everyone was kind of, 'Ah, shit...' And Dave was so rattled that he got lost, missed an ending or something. That was it: Claude threw his sticks down in disgust and got up. I put my guitar down and raced to the back of the stage and said, 'What the *fuck* are you doing?'

"I'd never spoken to Claude in those tones before, but I felt so let down. It was like, 'What the fuck did you do that for, Claude? Dave reveres you. You're like a musical father to all of us. You're mentoring us. And it was like you went up and slapped your son in the face, you publicly humiliated him.'

"He just muttered at me. He said, 'In my band, the drummer's the boss.' And I said, 'Claude, the boss fucked up.' And I just walked away."

Say's memory of the incident is broadly consistent with Samworth's account. "I was in my own space, playing. And then he stopped. I didn't even know that he was talking to me, to tell you the truth. I didn't realize that it was me he was mad at. His complaint, I guess, was that I wasn't playing the tune properly, that I was messing around. Which I wasn't. Maybe I was playing free on a blues; maybe he didn't like that."

Ranger subsequently apologized. "Claude actually phoned me," Say notes. "I've heard people say that was a very unusual thing for him to do. So that made it even better."

The incident nevertheless precipitated Ranger's further withdrawal from the scene. He fulfilled his commitments with Reed, including shows in late June and early July at the du Maurier International Jazz Festival, where he also played with the young American pianist Geoff Keezer, but he seldom worked thereafter.

Guitarist Ken Aldcroft, who had played with Ranger at Murphy's

Pub, took Ron Samworth's place for some of the band's last few engagements. "'Don't listen to the bass player,'" he recalled Ranger saying. "He put me right beside his ride cymbal and said, 'Listen to *that*.'"

The quartet's repertoire, Aldcroft remembered, included Ranger's *Challenge* from 1963 and *Tickle* from 1968. Aldcroft, though just 25 at the time, appreciated the significance of his brush with Canadian jazz history. "That was really weird, like the *best* 'weird' possible, playing with a Canadian icon, and playing *his* music, which was older than I was. I always thought that was pretty cool."[8]

Most of the band's other Ranger tunes dated to the 1990s. Some, including *Do-Bop*, *Two Steps*, *Billy* and an untitled ballad, were as recent as 1995; even as he was playing less and less, he had continued to compose.

* * *

Ranger took the last significant engagements of his career in Victoria, appearing several times at Hermann's, on View Street, in 1995 and 1996 with bands organized by bassist Sean Drabitt. The two musicians first met at a clinic in Victoria when Drabitt was 16 and just starting out. Ranger, at the piano, played with Drabitt and his teenaged friend, drummer Josh Dixon.

"I remember at the time thinking that he sounded like Monk," Drabitt remarks, of Ranger's piano style. "But that's just what I could hear then. I don't know what I would hear now."[9]

Ranger and Drabitt played together again — Ranger now on drums — with Terry Deane at the Glass Slipper in 1992; Drabitt was between sojourns stateside, just back from New Orleans and soon to leave for New York. Home again by 1995, he began to invite Vancouver musicians to Victoria for a night's work at Hermann's. Ranger was a regular; Deane, Miles Black, Phil Dwyer, saxophonist Seamus Blake, guitarist Mike Rud and pianist and trumpeter Brad Turner were among the others who made the trip over.

Ranger would arrive a day or two early and stay with William Stewart, the drummer he had met on his visit to Victoria with Don Thompson 16 years earlier. Stewart shared Ranger's love of refurbishing drums and gave him the run of his inventory for the purpose of putting together a kit to play at Hermann's. He also allowed Ranger to practice at length; in addition to not working with any regularity in Vancouver, Ranger was no more able to play on a full set of drums at his Harwood Street apartment than he had been at his Union Street flat, and instead took a Remo practice pad apart and drummed on the felt insert.

"Claude would show up for the gig," Drabitt remembers, "and it was like he hadn't touched the drums sometimes for months. But he would practice *hard*. He'd put together a kit and it always sounded like him."

Drabitt noticed a gradual decline in Ranger's health, however, and inevitably in his playing. "I could see that he was losing a ton of weight, and he seemed weak. He would be having more and more trouble. Like the first set, he'd be pretty draggy, and then he'd warm up to the point where he'd hit his stride. It wasn't like the first couple of gigs I did with him, where he was so strong off the top. I was having to carry things for a while, then all of a sudden he'd hit that vibe."

It was apparent from Ranger's conversations with Stewart that his priorities had changed. "He was sitting on my couch," Stewart notes, "and telling me that the only important thing to him was his health. Because of the way he lived and had not eaten properly, his doctor had told him that his stomach was the size of a fist and he had to be really careful about what he ate. He was drinking herbal tea, basically, and trying to be really healthy."

Ranger also talked, at least implicitly, about leaving music. "That was part of the conversation about his health," Stewart suggests, "that his health was the most important thing now. He was ready to entertain the idea of stopping, for sure. There was no question."[10]

Ranger made his final appearance at Hermann's on December 28, 1996, with Drabitt, Seamus Blake and Brad Turner. There was snow that night in Victoria, a storm of an intensity rare for a city whose temperate climate had drawn Ranger west nine years earlier.

He insisted that he not be identified in any promotion for the evening. According to Drabitt, he was being audited. He was also increasingly reliant on the support of social services. Under the circumstances, employment of any sort, had it been discovered, might well have jeopardized his standing with the various government agencies involved.

"Claude didn't want his name on the poster," Drabitt remembers, "so I had to put a question mark for the drummer."

Chapter Eighteen

"The groove was so deep"

"Of all the music I've ever listened to," Claude Ranger mused one day during a visit with William Stewart in Victoria, "in my mind I've never heard anyone who sounds like me."

As he neared the end of his career, he was measuring himself — somewhat backhandedly but with evident satisfaction — against the expectation that he had articulated nearly 30 years earlier with respect to the sort of musician with whom *he* had wished to play. To wit, "someone who can improvise their own way, not the way everyone does it on record, but new, fresh."

He was, in short, declaring himself an original. But he was an original within a longer and larger tradition, as originals in jazz generally are. If, in his own estimation, no one else sounded *like* him, he did remind his fellow musicians — and in truth even himself, at times — of one or another of the great figures who preceded him in modern jazz drumming.

"Every once in a while," Kieran Overs notes, "Claude would say to me, 'Man, I've got to get away from that Elvin thing. It's really bugging me.'"

Indeed Elvin Jones is a common point of reference in accolades and observations that other musicians have offered with respect to his drumming.

Steve Wallace, for example. "Because Claude had such a small kit, he could play loud and hard, but it didn't cover stuff up, the way Elvin might have. It was very transparent."

And Tony Wilson. "Claude always swung, and it didn't matter how 'out' the music was, or how free it got, there was always that swing, and that was what set him apart from a lot of drummers, and I don't just mean drummers I played with, but drummers I listened to on records. He just had that thing inside him, like Elvin Jones, even though Elvin probably didn't play as free as Claude. But it always had that swing."

Wilson, in fact, discovered that Ranger was intimately familiar with the technical aspects of Jones' approach to the drums. "I remember once being at Claude's place and we were watching a video of Elvin. Claude just knew everything about him — how he held the stick, how his arm moved, how his wrists moved. It was like a total education, because we're just sitting there and it was like Claude knew every intricate detail of how Elvin played drums. Claude's attention to detail, to me, was quite amazing, whether that was a totally conscious effort on his part, or just that he was the kind of guy that could take in all of those subtleties."

Michael Stuart, who played with both Ranger and Jones in the late 1970s, suggests more abstractly that they shared a mutual love of the unexpected. "There was something loose and unpredictable about Elvin's playing. I sensed that in Claude's playing too, that he would do things — smash his cymbal, or accent something — and you'd be like, 'Whoa, where'd *that* come from?' Elvin, same thing. The groove is happening, but there's an unpredictability about their playing. Pay attention, because at any time there could be a bomb, a cymbal, or *something*."

That same sense of unpredictability was no less an element in the work of Tony Williams, another frequent point of reference in comments about Ranger's drumming.

"When Claude was at his best," Neil Swainson remarks, "I don't think I've ever played with a better drummer. The feel, the cymbal ride, the interaction of the drums with everybody in the band — it was just a beautiful experience. He was a magician, a cross between Tony and Elvin, and equally great when he was on his game."

Of course, to be "a cross between Tony and Elvin" is to reconcile two quite different aesthetics at the drums — Williams' imagination, daring and precarious sense of balance on one hand, and Jones' depth, power and sheer presence on the other. "He mixed up all the accents and broke up the beat like Tony," André Lachance observes, "but he made the backside of the beat *groove* more like Elvin."

Of course there were other elements in his playing as well — other sources, other strengths and other points of reference, both general and specific. "Claude had that thing that usually you have to go to New York for a few years to get," notes Seamus Blake, speaking in broader terms from his own experience of playing with Ranger in Vancouver and Victoria and of living in New York. "He really had that intensity, that beat — that forward motion where it feels good all the time."

Ranger's cymbal ride was key. "His cymbal," Sean Drabitt suggests, "was a lot like Max Roach, right down the middle. Everything else fell off the back, but the *cymbal*, man, if you listen to the cymbal, no matter what else was going on, it was *there*."

His cymbal ride also captured Coat Cooke's imagination. "Claude wasn't a quiet drummer, although he certainly could be, and there were times when he'd play almost a whole piece on the ride cymbal. He would drive the band just with that. His 'feel' was so powerful, and the groove was so deep. He could just play the ride — whether he was smoking or having a beer — and you'd feel the 'centredness' that he could derive from it."

While Cooke speaks of the depth of the groove, André Lachance marvels at the corresponding width of the cymbal ride, a function of its orientation more toward straight eighths, after Tony Williams' example, than to triplets. "It was very accurate, but very free — you could do anything inside of it and he'd make it sound good. He wasn't tight, or stiff, like a lot of drummers now who play with a very narrow beat. It was scary how comfortable it was. There was no friction, no friction at all; his listening skills were so high. I'd never played with anybody who listened to me like that. It just felt like whatever I did, he was going to make it sound good. I just put the beat where I thought it was; I was still trying to hang on to the ride cymbal at that point, and it was easy because there was no friction. I felt this power and support and thunder all around me, and I just did what I did. I hear tapes of us and it's exactly that. He makes me sound good. He just wraps himself around me. If I'm laying back, he'll play a bit more forward; if I'm pulling forward, he'll bring it back."

By virtue of that same flexibility, Ranger was often at odds with bassists who insisted on defining the beat too closely — in truth with any musician, no matter the instrument, whose concept of "time" limited, rather than revealed, the options that might be explored.

"They talk about Rashied Ali, about multi-directionality, about Elvin Jones, and all these different layers of rhythm," Kirk MacDonald notes, "but Claude *always* had that going on. There was *this* idea over here, but there were two or three other avenues over *there* that he might suggest you could go down and explore as well, and he would provide the backdrop to do that. Part of what he would play would go with you, while he might keep other ideas moving with one of the other voices in the band, or even independently, and now you've got *this* against *that*, or you would play against *him*. There were always many ways you could choose to play with the beat; there would be multiple rhythms within — but sometimes seemingly going against — the tempo. Sometimes we weren't playing tempo and Claude would still suggest different routes and pulses. He was an absolute master at this. The door was always open."

Perry White, who was Ranger's tenor saxophonist of choice immediately after MacDonald, heard his drumming not just in terms of direction, or directions, but in terms of dimensions. "Claude's drumming was really as much melodic as it was rhythmic, so even though we were stepping out into areas where there was no form to rely on, it made playing 'free' more of a musical experience, because his thing was so tuneful, you might say, at the same time as it was challenging and searching. There would always be melodies in the rhythm. There are a few drummers who do that — play lyrically — like Ed Blackwell. Claude had that going, and he'd also find dark areas, or very colourful areas, where he'd just make sounds and colours, and then go back into a rhythmic kind of thing where there'd be 'time.' He was just as comfortable and creative whether there was 'time' or not."

Ranger's two albums with Don Thompson — the LP *Don Thompson Quartet* from 1977 and the CD *Forgotten Memories* from 1991 — captured his drumming at its most commanding and stand alongside individual tracks with Brian Barley, Jane Bunnett, P.J. Perry, Doug Riley and Michael Stuart among the finest examples of his work on record.

For Thompson, the inspiration clearly was mutual. "I had the feeling with Claude that I was playing with a whole symphony orchestra," he remembers. "I could play any harmonies I wanted to, any rhythms I wanted to, any time signature I wanted to. I could basically play anything I wanted, and it would always work. Everything he was doing — every rhythm, every time feeling you could think of — he was doing all at once.

"The only time I ever experienced that before was with Rashied Ali. He sat in with John Handy in New York — that was 1967 — and I'd never experienced anything like that before. Sonny Greenwich was playing that night too, and [vibraphonist] Bobby Hutcherson. The music just went to places where you can't believe it could possibly go. Then when I played with Claude, it was just like that again. I had the same kind of feeling. I never worried about anything, because I knew that anything I did was going to be okay. I just felt like I could play anything."

CHAPTER NINETEEN

"He didn't want to leave anything behind"

Dave Say was the last in the 30-year lineage of tenor saxophonists who answered Claude Ranger's call for "one good horn player." Brian Barley had been the first, followed for longer and shorter periods by Gerry Labelle, Alvin Pall, Claude Béland, Ron Allen, Kirk MacDonald, Perry White, Rob Frayne, Phil Dwyer, Terry Deane, Bruce Freedman, and, lately, Daniel Miles Kane. Say in turn had his own history in Vancouver of working with singular drummers, namely Al Wiertz and Roger Baird.

The incident at Café Deux Soleils, though dramatic, did not harm Say's friendship with Ranger. "Everybody there got mad at Claude," he notes, "except me." Ranger subsequently became a regular visitor to the recording studio that Say ran for much of the 1990s in a former

Bank of Nova Scotia building on the northeast corner of Granville and Davie in downtown Vancouver.

Ranger and Say played duets there — for Ranger a throwback to his days in Montreal with Brian Barley — and they gave a concert together in May 1997 at the Nanaimo Art Gallery, making the trip in Say's metallic blue 1979 GMC VANdura, a vehicle, as Say describes it, that was very much suited to Ranger's frame of mind at the time.

"No windows, except at the very back, and there was a curtain over that." For Ranger, who had taken to wearing a hoodie and sunglasses in public, it was the perfect retreat. "It was dark in there," Say explains, "so it was kind of a cozy little hideaway."

• • •

Details of the medical treatment and financial support that Ranger received from local and provincial social service agencies in the mid-to-late 1990s remain subject to privacy laws that govern personal records, leaving only the accounts of friends who saw him — often fleetingly on the street or stageside at free concerts during the jazz festival — to chronicle in the most general and sometimes conflicting of terms his withdrawal from music and his well-being through the years that followed. There were periods of relative calm, and there were periods of distress.

Ranger continued to live with Judith Yamada in the West End and, for a time — well into 1997, if not later — to work at Drums Only, where Buff Allen, who had known him as far back as the late 1970s, was also an employee.

"In Toronto, Claude had always been very mercurial, very irascible," Allen notes. "I'd see him many times storm off a bandstand if he just didn't dig what was going on. Not even a word — he'd just walk off. Whereas during this time at Ayotte, he was the complete opposite. He had a really beautiful smile on his face; he was very happy. And I wondered, whatever they were medicating him with, if maybe he was a little overmedicated, because he was the opposite of what he had been in Toronto."

Clyde Reed, with whom Ranger continued to stay in touch, had similar concerns. "I remember thinking, 'I'm worried that these doctors don't know *who* this is. They don't know that this is Claude Ranger. They don't understand anything. And they're just filling him up with pills to make him docile and not cause problems.' I didn't know what to do about it, but I just think that they were trying to make this guy not a problem. As opposed to, 'No, no — Claude has a lot to offer. He's not a guy that you want to just cavalierly shut down.'"

• • •

As Ranger struggled with his medication and its effects, both positive and negative, he also wrestled with the decision as to whether he should continue playing. By the summer of 1997, he was ready to sell his Ayottes and had found a buyer in Ivan Bamford, with whom he had struck up a friendship at the jazz festival the year before.

"Claude told me he was selling his drums. He desperately needed dental work, so he was selling everything for nine hundred dollars."

Bamford generously offered fifteen hundred instead, pending a three-week engagement in San Francisco. Ranger of course accepted; the sale was completed on Bamford's return.

"Claude said that the shells alone were worth three thousand dollars. And so I knew, even at fifteen hundred, with the hardware and the cases, that I was getting a really good deal."

There was, however, a hidden cost. Some of the instructors at Capilano College, where Bamford was studying, made clear their resentment that he, of all people, would dare buy, and let alone play, a drum set of such distinguished provenance. It was Ranger himself who advised Bamford to pay them no mind.

• • •

Ranger was still trying to sell his cymbals when an old friend from Montreal, bassist Daniel Lessard, arrived for the du Maurier International Jazz Festival in June 1997. More than 25 years had passed since they played together with Brian Barley in Aquarius Rising. "Claude looked different and seemed depressed," Lessard remembers. "I think he told me he couldn't play anymore. You could tell he was depressed."

And yet another friend from Montreal, Charles Papasoff, who appeared at the festival just a couple of days after Lessard, recalls that Ranger raised the prospect of playing together again, and suggested that they approach no less than Charlie Haden to make it a trio. "Claude didn't look bad," Papasoff notes. "He looked his normal self. He was maybe a little bit skinnier than usual. He said he wasn't playing that much, just a couple of things here and there."

• • •

Ranger himself appeared at the jazz festival for one last time on June 28, 1998. He contacted Ivan Bamford about borrowing back his Ayottes for the occasion, an afternoon concert in David Lam Park with Mariusz Kwiatkowski, a Polish tenor saxophonist who had moved to Vancouver several years earlier.

Bamford of course agreed to the request, but he and Ranger failed to meet at the appointed location, leaving Ranger, who had been so exacting throughout his career with respect to the size and sound of his drums, to play a set — likely the festival's backline kit — with which he was completely unfamiliar.

There was also a certain poignancy to the concert itself, according to Kwiatkowski's bassist, Danny Parker. "It seemed to be a bit of a struggle for Claude, and he recognized it." Kwiatkowski's post-bop repertoire was challenging and Ranger, who had not played in some time, missed the band's only rehearsal. After the concert, Ranger felt it necessary to offer Parker an apology for his drumming.[1]

His decision to perform again was at least in part a function of unspecified changes to his medication, as he told André Lachance when they met by chance on the street in the West End one day. "'Hey man,'" Lachance remembers him saying, "'I found the right meds! I went through hell with these other meds, but I found the good ones. Man, I can play on these things!' Claude's problem with the meds is that they made him not want to play, because it just didn't feel edgy enough for him — he didn't feel the music the way he had before."

Ranger nevertheless understood that a return to music was problematic, if only in practical terms. "He said he was afraid to go back to playing because he might like it," Clyde Reed recalls. "I got the impression that somehow the social support he was receiving depended on him *not* being able to work, and he did say something explicit to the effect that he was afraid to play again because, well, what if he liked it? Then what would he do?"

The risk was ultimately one that he did not take.

• • •

A year later, in June 1999, Joe Bjornson caught sight of Ranger in the food court of the Pacific Centre Mall downtown on Granville Street. "He looked crazied right out. A real street person look. He wasn't loud or anything, but he had lost weight; well, he wasn't that big in the first place. You could see the bones of his cheeks. I said hello to him, because I recognized him. He asked what I was up to. I said I had a gig on a cruise ship and I'd be leaving soon."

Ranger joked that Bjornson would have to learn French; the leading agency for cruise work, Proship Entertainment, was based in Montreal.

"And then he asked me for some money. I think I gave him forty dollars."

Another old friend visiting from Montreal in this period, Gerry Labelle, made contact with Ranger by phone. They arranged to meet at a restaurant, where Ranger told Labelle that he had been living on the street and sleeping under a bridge, circumstances substantiated in general terms by the Royal Canadian Mounted Police but denied by

Judith Yamada, who insists that Ranger was never homeless.[2]

He spoke to Labelle of his regret for the pain that he had caused others; to the extent that he said more, he did so under the condition of confidentiality. He did, however, reveal that he had burned all of his music. Labelle understood.

"He didn't want to leave anything behind."

• • •

By the spring of 2000, Ranger had moved on alone from Vancouver's West End to a modest, two-storey public housing complex on 30th Avenue in Aldergrove, a small Fraser Valley community between Langley and Abbotsford in an area of farmland, bush and forest 13 kilometres south of the Fraser River and five kilometres north of the border with Washington.

He asked Dave Say for a ride to his new home; the two of them, accompanied by Say's wife, the singer Candus Churchill, made the trip in Say's VANdura. Ranger took a duffle bag and very little more.

"That surprised me," Say admits. "That he could put his whole life in a couple of bags."

It was a sad, silent trip. "Claude wasn't talking. We weren't having a conversation. He was just sitting in the back with his bags, his hoodie and his sunglasses."

Ranger's room in Aldergrove, Say remembers, was small, sparsely furnished and illuminated by a single, bare light bulb.

Ivan Bamford, who visited him there, saw only a mattress, some incense and a television, even as Ranger claimed, rather mysteriously, to have had $16,000 in savings.

"Claude said, 'That will be good for me for the rest of my time.'"

• • •

Ranger occasionally made his way back to Vancouver, where he once again encountered old friends by chance. Coat Cooke ran into him on Granville Street. "He seemed to be in a really good space — very warm, lots of eye contact, and just a touch to the arm to say goodbye."

Ron Samworth saw Ranger back in the West End, walking alone in the fog on the beach at English Bay. They shared an embrace; they did not speak of Café Deux Soleils. Ranger told Samworth that he had stopped drinking and was living out of town. He also admitted that he would never play drums again.

"He said, 'I'll tell you why. I played with the greatest musicians in the world — Sonny Rollins, Dewey Redman...' Claude loved Dewey. He said, 'I became a great musician. I want to become a great human being.' He expressed a desire to reconnect with his brother and sisters, and with his children. He said, 'This is very important to me.'

"Some of the things he said to me were clearly like he'd been having some counselling; he'd definitely been talking to people about reconciliation and recovery. It felt very valedictory, and I felt I had to say something to him about what it meant to me.

"I said, 'Claude, I never had more ecstatic moments than playing with you. You were like a father to me.'

"And he responded. He said, 'Thank you, Ron, you guys always played really well for me.'

"It was a very sweet moment. And then it was like, 'Okay, man — take care, okay?'"

● ● ●

Ivan Bamford continued to stay in touch with Ranger, picking him up at least once in Aldergrove and taking him back to Burnaby for dinner. Their final visit found Ranger again in something of a valedictory frame of mind.

"That last time," Bamford remembers, "Claude talked for over an hour straight." Such loquacity was neither characteristic of Ranger nor consistent with someone on medication for bipolar disorder. "He was really letting it all out."

Ranger was not bitter but he made it clear to Bamford — more in dismissal than in anticipation — that he was aware of how he would be remembered, why, and by whom. There was no doubt in his mind that he *would* be remembered; he again asked that his remarks be kept confidential should anyone ever inquire about them, as if he fully expected that someone eventually would.

• • •

Spring in Aldergrove turned into summer, and summer into fall. The first days of November, overcast and cool, found Ranger once more in distress. His response to situations that were beyond bearing had always been to walk away. And so it was again.

DISCOGRAPHY

Basin Street, Toronto, October 1983.
Photograph by Mark Miller.

Notes

1 An asterix — * — identifies a composition by Claude Ranger.
2 The following abbreviations have been employed: as (alto saxophone), brs (baritone saxophone), d (drums), db (double bass), eb (electric bass), ep (electric piano), fl (flute), flhn (flugelhorn), Frhn (French horn), g (guitar), p (piano), perc (percussion), picc (piccolo), syn (synthesizer), ss (soprano saxophone), t (trumpet), trb (trombone), ts (tenor saxophone), vcl (vocal), vib (vibraphone).

**

Lee Gagnon
Le Jazztek, Capitol ST-6226 [LP]
Gagnon (as, ts, fl), Art Roberts (p), Michel Donato (db), Claude Ranger (d)

Montreal, April 10, 17 or 24, 1967

Impressions Discothèque
Suite: a) Intro b) Tendresse c) Jazztek
Take Five
Summertime
How Insensitive
Con Alma
Reissued with *Je Jazze* (see next entry) on *Jazze Canadienne*, Harkit HRKCD 8163, in 2008.

•

Lee Gagnon
Je Jazze, Capitol ST-6253 [LP]
Gagnon (as, ts), Ron Proby (t), Pierre Leduc (p), Roland Haynes (db), Claude Ranger (d)

Montreal, September 18 and 20, 1968

Autoroute
Visage

Poussière d'étoile
Espièglerie
Léanna
Ginette
Strut
Reissued with *Le Jazztek* (see previous entry) on *Jazze Canadienne*,
Harkit HRKCD 8163.

•

Michel Donato
Jazz en liberté, Montreal 1969, Just A Memory JAM-9150 [CD]
Donato (db), Alan Penfold (t), Brian Barley (ts), Claude
Ranger (d)

Montreal, May 30, 1969

Intro
Pinocchio
Solar
*Rêverie**
Alone with the Bass
The Ice Pack
As above, without Penfold

Montreal, June 27, 1969

Backseat Generator, How Come It's Taken So Long Because Oh!

•

Herbie Spanier
Anthology Vol.II — 1969-1994 Justin Time JUST-61 [CD]
Spanier (t, flhn), Brian Barley (ts, ss), Sadik Hakim (p), Charles
Biddle (db), Claude Ranger (d)

Montreal, 1969

Waltz No. 2
Summertime

●

Brian Barley
Brian Barley Trio, RCI 309 [LP]
Barley (ts, ss), Daniel Lessard (eb), Claude Ranger (d)
Montreal, June 29 and 30, 1970

Plexidance
Schlucks
*Le Pingouin**
Two By Five
Oneliness
Reissued on CD in 1995 as *Brian Barley Trio: 1970*, Just A Memory
JAS-9502.

●

Herbie Spanier
Forensic Perturbations, RCI 376 [LP]
Spanier (t, flhn), Alvin Pall (ts, fl), Bernie Senensky (p), Michel
Donato (db, eb), Claude Ranger (d)
Montreal, October 26 and 27, 1972

Forensic Perturbations
Ballade for Gina
Rapido
Saints Alive
Précis en bleu
The Colonel's Mess
Waltz No. 4
On the Blues
Précis en Bleu, *Waltz No. 4* and *Rapido* were reissued in 1993 on
Anthology/1962-93, Justin Time, JUST-55.

●

Gerry Labelle
[untitled]
Labelle (ss, fl), Dave Liebman (ss, ts, fl), Richie Beirach (p), Frank
Tusa (db), Claude Ranger (d); percussion, guitar and keyboard
added later

Montreal, August 1973

Flashback #4
Dreamland
Compassion
Don Tavarone
*Rêverie**
Abstract

The recording date for this session has been taken from a
report by Len Dobbin in the March 1974 issue of *Coda*, p. 28.
These tracks have been posted online at www.fusion3000.com/
instrumental-page-3/.

•

Dr. Music
Bedtime Story, GRT 9233-1005 [LP]
Doug Riley (p, ep, organ), Bruce Cassidy (t, flhn), Barrie Tallman
(trb), Steve Kennedy (ts, fl, vcl), Keith Jollimore (as, brs, fl, vcl),
Doug Mallory (g, vcl), Don Thompson (db, eb), Dave Brown (d),
Claude Ranger (d)

Toronto, February-March 1974

I Keep It Hid
That That Rollo
*Tickle**
She's Funny That Way
Gandalf
[Tell Me a] Bedtime Story

•

Moe Koffman

Solar Explorations, GRT 9230-1050 [LP]

Koffman (as, ss, fl, picc) with ensembles of five to 13 musicians including Sonny Greenwich (g) Doug Riley (p, el p), Don Thompson (p, db), Claude Ranger (d) Terry Clarke (d), Michael Craden (perc)

Toronto, July 1974

Earth
Uranus
Mars
Jupiter
Venus
Pluto
Mercury

Ranger and Terry Clarke both play drums on *Earth;* Clarke alone appears on two other tracks, *Saturn and Neptune.*

•

Doug Riley

Dreams, P.M. PMR-007 [LP]

Doug Riley (p, ep), Michael Stuart (ss, ts), Don Thompson (db), Claude Ranger (d)

Toronto, the week of October 6, 1975

In My Life
Chunga's Revenge
Earth
Blue Dream
Dreams

•

P.J. Perry

Sessions, Suite 1001 [LP]

Perry (as), Bob Tildesley (t), George McFetridge (p), Torben Oxbol (db), Claude Ranger (d)

Edmonton, July 11-16, 1977

Sascha Nova
Autumn in New York
Nameless Blues
Torquin' with Torben
Variation on a Blues by Bird
If I Were a Bell

•

Muñoz

Rendezvous with Now, India Navigation IN 1034 [LP]

Muñoz (g, perc, vcl), Bernie Senensky (p), Cecil McBee (db), Claude Ranger (d), Sat Guru Singh Ji (vcl, perc), Faith and Hope (vcls)

Nyack, New York, 1977

The Shepherd's Chant
Blessings
The Word of God Chant
Waiting for Now to Be Forever

•

Don Thompson

Don Thompson Quartet, RCI 480 [LP]

Thompson (p), Michael Stuart (ss, ts), Richard Homme (db), Claude Ranger (d)

Hamilton, September 22, 1977

Full Nelson
Introduction

For Chris Gage
Lament for John Coltrane
Dreams
At least one other piece from this concert, *Softly, As in a Morning Sunrise*, remains unissued.

•

Sonny Greenwich
Evol-ution, Love's Reverse, P.M. PMR-016 [LP]
Greenwich (g), Don Thompson (p, ep), Gene Perla (db, eb),
Claude Ranger (d)

Toronto, week of May 30, 1978

Time-Space
Prelune
Emily
Nica's Dream
Day is Night to Some
Evol-ution, Love's Reverse

•

Lenny Breau
Lenny Breau, Direct-Disk Labs DD-112 [LP]
Breau (g), Don Thompson (db), Claude Ranger (d)

Nashville, February 22, 1979

Don't Think Twice (It's All Right)
Mister Night
Neptune
Claude (Free Song)
Reissued as *Lenny Breau Trio* on LP (Adelphi AD 5018) in 1985 and on CD (Adelphi AD 5018-CD/Genes Records GCD 5018) in 1999. *Mister Night* is a misidentification of John Coltrane's *Mr. Knight*. Thompson and Ranger do not appear on a fifth track, *You*

Needed Me, which is a duet between Breau and Chet Atkins.

●

Sonny Greenwich
Sun Song, Akasha AKH-26 [45 rpm]
Greenwich (g), Ernie Nelson (vcl), Don Thompson (ep), Gene
Perla (db), Claude Ranger (d)

Toronto, week of August 28, 1979
Sun Song

●

Ron Allen
Leftovers, Black Silk ARC 8045 [LP]
Allen (ss, ts), Joey Goldstein (g), Dave Field (db), Claude
Ranger (d)

Toronto, October 26, 1980
See Whole
Generations
Present Day
Ranger does not appear on three other tracks.

●

Dave Liebman
Sweet Fury, From Bebop to Now BBN-1002 [LP]
Liebman (ss, fl), Don Thompson (p,db, vib), Steve LaSpina (db),
Claude Ranger (d)

Toronto, March 23 and 24, 1984
Full Nelson
A Distant Song
Nadir
Tender Mercies

*Feu vert**
Ranger does not play on three other tracks.

•

Michael Stuart
The Blessing, Unity 107 [LP]
Stuart (ts), Brian Dickinson (p), Dave Field (db), Claude
Ranger (d)

Hamilton, February 22, 1987

The Blessing
The Call
Dedication
Celebration
Destiny

•

Jane Bunnett
In Dew Time, Dark Light Music DL 9001 [LP]
Bunnett (ss, fl), Larry Cramer (t, flhn), Vincent Chancey (Frhn),
Dewey Redman (ts), Don Pullen (p), Scott Alexander (db),
Claude Ranger (d)

Toronto, February 25 and 26, 1988

The Wanderer
Limbo
Utviklingssang
In Dew Time
Five/As Long as There Is Music
Ranger does not play on one other track; Brian Dickinson replaces
Pullen on *Utviklingssang* and *Five/As Long as there is Music*.
Reissued on CD in 1991 as Dark Light DL24001.

•

Chief Feature

The Future Is N.O.W., 9 Winds NWCD-0131 [CD]
Bruce Freedman (ts), Bill Clark (t), Clyde Reed (db), Claude Ranger (d)

Vancouver, ca 1990

Tibetan Tears of Joy and Sadness
The Future Is N.O.W. is a compilation CD of single tracks by ensembles affiliated with the New Orchestra Workshop.

•

Don Thompson

Forgotten Memories, Roadhouse Records Route 3 [CD]
Thompson (p), Kenny Wheeler (t, flhn), Phil Dwyer (ss, ts), Dave Holland (db), Claude Ranger (d)

Toronto, January 15 and 16, 1991

September
For Kenny Wheeler
North Star
For Dave Holland
Waltz for Madeline [sic]
Forgotten Memories

•

Charles Papasoff

Emphasis (cassette)
Papasoff (ss, brs), Claude Ranger (d) in several settings, variously with Sylvie Perron (vcl), Charles Ellison and Pierre Sickini (t), Dave Grott (trb), Nelson Symonds (g), Denis Lepage (org), Steve Amirault (p), George Mitchell (db) and others

Montreal, January 1991

Conjuration
Emphasis

The Thief
Will She Ever Know?
Soul Eyes
The Homecoming
The Adventure
Personnel and program as recalled from memory by Charles
Papasoff in the absence of a copy of the cassette itself.

•

Sylvie Perron
Perron (vcl), Charles Papasoff (ss), Steve Amirault (p), George
Mitchell (db), Claude Ranger (d)

Montreal, January 1991

Adventure
This track was posted online at www.reverbnation.com/
sylvieperron.

•

Kate Hammett-Vaughan
Jazz Words, CBC VRCD 1017 [CD]
Hammett-Vaughan (vcl), Miles Black (p), Miles Hill (db), Claude
Ranger (d)

Vancouver, 1992

You'd Be So Nice to Come Home to
Every Time We Say Goodbye
It Could Happen to You
Jazz Words is a compilation CD of recordings by Canadian
singers; Jeri Brown, Trudy Desmond, Ranee Lee, Jennifer Scott
and Joani Taylor are also included.

•

P.J. Perry
Quintet, Unity UTY CD 142 [CD]
Perry (as, ss), Bob Tildesley (t), Chris Andrew (p, syn), Miles Hill
(db), Claude Ranger (d)

Edmonton, October 4 and 5, 1993

Jazz Suite
They Kept Bach's Head Alive
L.L.
Royal Tease
Negligence
No Matter
Doodle
Don't Forget

•

Miles Black
Spin Cycle (cassette)
Black (p), Tom Keenlyside (fl, ts), Miles Hill (db), Claude
Ranger (d)

Langley, British Columbia, spring 1994

On the Street Where You Live
Samoa
Dori
Halloween Blues
Spin Cycle
Quiet Time
Who Can I Turn to (When Nobody Needs Me)?

NOTES

Preface

1. All quotes by Ivan Bamford have been drawn from an interview with the author, December 10, 2013.

Introduction

1. S/Sgt Alex Bolden, Royal Canadian Mounted Police, Langley, B.C., detachment, interview with the author, June 25, 2014.

2. Cst. Amanda Smith, Royal Canadian Mounted Police, Langley, B.C. detachment, email, November 23, 2016.

3. All comments by Kieran Overs have been drawn from an interview with the author, October 30, 2013.

4. All comments by Ron Allen have been drawn from an interview with the author, October 7, 2013.

5. All comments by Michel Donato have been drawn from an interview with the author, December 10, 2013.

6. Unless otherwise identified, all first-person remarks by Claude Ranger have been taken from interviews with the author on April 28, 1978, and March 5 and 9, 1981.

7. All comments by Mike

Milligan have been drawn from an interview with the author, January 16, 2014.

8. Raymond Gervais, email to the author, June 20, 2014.

9. The advertised participants in "Feu vert: A Tribute to Claude Ranger" on November 16 and 17, 2012, were drummers Buff Allen, Bernie Arai, Stan Taylor and Dylan van der Schyff, bassists Paul Blaney, Miles Hill, André Lachance, Clyde Reed and Rene Worst, saxophonists Phil Dwyer, Bruce Freedman, Campbell Ryga and Dave Say, trumpeters Bill Clark, Kevin Elaschuk and Brad Turner, pianists Miles Black and Bob Murphy and guitarists Ron Samworth and Tony Wilson.

10. Dylan van der Schyff, conversation with the author, February 3, 2013.

Chapter One/Rosemont

1. The Royal Canadian Mounted Police missing persons report identifies Ranger's second given name as Gaston.

2. Hugh McLennan, *Two Solitudes*, (Toronto: Collins, 1945).

3. Details of the Rangers' addresses, and of Aurèle Ranger's employment history, have been drawn from *Annuaires Lovell de Montréal* (Montreal, John Lovell & Son), 1938-1970.

4. Greg Gallagher, "The career of a jazz drummer turned composer," *Canadian Composer*, June 1976, 12.

5. All comments by Jacques Masson have been drawn from an interview with the author, August 26, 2014.

Chapter Two/Showbars

1. Claude Ranger, interview [in French] with John Gilmore, Montreal, July 8, 1982; held in the Concordia University Archives, Tape JHC54. All quotes drawn from this interview have been translated by the author. Used with permission.

2. Pierre Béluse, interview with John Gilmore, Montreal, November 10, 1982 (Concordia University Archives, Tape JHC7). Quoted with permission.

3. Keith (Spike) McKendry, interview with the author, May 27, 2014.

4. Len Dobbin, "Montreal modern," *Coda*, April 1960, 7.

5. "Belmont Park opens today," *Montreal Star*, May 12, 1945, 20.

6. Dobbin, "Montreal modern," April 1960.

7. *Ibid.*

8. Len Dobbin, "Montreal modern," *Coda*, April 1961, 6.

9. John Gilmore, *Swinging in Paradise: The Story of Jazz in Montreal* (Montreal: Véhicule Press, 1988), 184-204, 209-210, 213-214.

10. Léo Perron, interview with John Gilmore, Montreal, November 25, 1982 (Concordia University Archives, Tape JHC52). Quoted with permission.

11. All comments by Peter Leitch have been drawn from an interview with the author, April 2, 2014.

12. Gilmore, *Swinging in Paradise*, 172.

13. All comments by Norman Marshall Villeneuve have been drawn from an interview with the author, March 25, 2013.

14. Wes Montgomery, interview with Jim Rockwell, "People in Jazz," National Educational Television, first telecast in 1969.

Chapter Three/*Jazz en liberté*

1. Gerry Labelle, note to the author, August 25, 2014.

2. As dated on a copy of the lead sheet in the possession of Ken Aldcroft, who worked with Ranger in 1995. The lead sheet shows some changes to a version recorded by Ranger with Brian Barley and Michel Donato circa 1968. Ken Aldcroft, e-mail to the author, October 24, 2014.

3. Len Dobbin, "Montreal modern," *Coda*, October 1961, 7.

4. The complete personnel for the Maurice Mayer Septet broadcast in May 1967, as introduced on air, was Mayer (alto saxophone), Réal Gobeil and Herbie Spanier (trumpets), Richard Ferland (tenor saxophone), Jean Lebrun (baritone saxophone), Michel Donato (bass) and Claude Ranger (drums). A recording of the broadcast is held in the Radio-Canada archives. Ranger told John Gilmore that the band also did a week-long engagement under Mayer's name at a forgotten club on Stanley Street near the Chez Paree. This may even have been one of the secondary rooms at the Chez Paree itself.

5. John Norris, "Heard and seen: Montreal jazz underground," *Coda*,

August-September 1967, 37-38.

6. Canadian All Stars: *Canadian All Stars*, Discovery DL3025; Milt Sealey: *A Tribute to Dorothy*, London MLP1001, and *Piano — à la mode*, Trans Canada TC-A 51; Nick Ayoub: *The Montreal Scene*, RCA Victor PCS1042; Pierre Leduc, *Information*, Elysée ELS.5003; Yvan Landry: *Café au lait*, Capitol ST6321, and *Jazz en liberté*, Capitol ST6231.

7. Len Dobbin, "Lee Gagnon: La Jazztek," *Coda*, January/February 1968, 41.

8. Norris, *Coda*, August-September 1967, 38.

9. All quotes by Don Thompson have been drawn from an interview with the author, July 17, 2013.

Chapter Four/ Aquarius Rising

1. John Norris noted Barley's presence there during the summer of 1967. *Coda*, August-September 1967, 38.

2. Barley identified Coleman, Coltrane, Dolphy, Rollins and Shepp as his "favorite instrumentalists" to Ron Sweetman. Liner notes, *Brian Barley Trio* [LP], Radio Canada International RCI 309 (1970).

3. Len Dobbin, "Montreal," *Coda*, November-December 1968, 32. Barley worked with Moffett at the New Penelope on Sherbrooke Street and the Winston Churchill Pub on Crescent Street.

4. Alain Brunet, "Michel Donato en quartette... il y a 34 ans," *La Presse*, September 16, 2003, C6.

5. *Jazz en liberté*, Just A Memory JAM 9150.

6. The quintet was Ranger, Ron Proby (trumpet), Léo Perron (alto and baritone saxophone), Pierre Leduc (piano) and Michel Donato (bass). The trumpeters were Robert Lavoie and Réal Gobeil, and the trombonists, Claude Blouin, Jean-Pierre Charpentier and Gerry Vaillancourt. Lavoie had been Ranger's old boss at the Mocambo Café.

7. Ron Sweetman, "Heard and seen: Aquarius Rising," *Coda*, September-October 1970, 45.

8. Lee Gagnon's *Jazzzzz* (Barclay 80086) was originally RCI 288, Don Thompson's *Love Song for a Virgo Lady* (Sackville C2002) was RCI 302 and

Sonny Greenwich's *The Old Man and the Child* (Sackville C2003) was RCI 303.

9. John Norris, "2: CBC," *Coda*, August 1972, 8-9.

10. *Sun Song: The Music of Sonny Greenwich* (RCI 399); *Paul Bley Trio* (RCI 305); *Pierre Leduc et son quatour (RCI 267)*.

11. Gallagher, "The career of a jazz drummer turned composer," 14.

12. Ron Sweetman mentioned a seventh Ranger composition, *Waves*, in his review of Aquarius Rising at the Shire for *Coda*.

13. Alan Offstein, "The Canadian Broadcasting Corporation transcription story... a conversation with Ted Farrant," *Coda*, August 1972, 7.

14. Geoffrey Young, "Heard and seen: Jazz at the Barrel," *Coda*, January/February 1968, 29.

15. All comments by Daniel Lessard have been drawn from an interview with the author, December 9, 2013.

16. "Nous avons donc décidé de procéder sans thèmes, sans rythmes réguliers et sans accords." Guy Thouin to Eric Fillion, http://tenzier.org/qjlq-entretien-guy-thouin-et-le-jazz-libre-du-quebec,

undated. However, *Stalisme Dodécaphonique*, for one, did have a recognizable theme.

17. Jack Batten, "Where everyone has a chance to create," *Toronto Star*, March 14, 1970, 83.

18. Alastair Lawrie, "Jazz: Meat and Potatoes," *The Globe and Mail*, September 11, 1970, 12.

19. Gregory Gallagher, interview with the author, December 10, 2013.

20. Lilly Barnes, interview with the author, October 18, 2013.

Chapter Five/*La Misère*

1. All comments by Michael Morse have been drawn from an interview with the author, December 10, 2014.

2. All comments by Lorne Nehring have been drawn from an interview with the author, January 5, 2015.

3. Peter Leitch, *Off the Books: A Jazz Life* (Montreal: Véhicule Press, 2013), 51.

4. Michael Morse, "Tribute to jazz drummer Claude Ranger >> Stories — Comments," www.clauderanger.com, online post, April 26, 2006; Steve Hall, interview with the author, June 5, 1914. Also, comments

by Hall, April 15, 2006, and David Gelfand, April 13, 2006, at www.clauderanger.com >> Stories — Comments.

5. John Norris, "Around the world: Toronto," *Coda*, April 1971, 35.

6. "What's on," *Toronto Star*, May 1, 1971, A8.

7. Bob Brough, interview with the author, March 1, 1981.

8. Len Dobbin, "Around the world: Montreal," *Coda*, February 1971, 33.

9. All comments by Gerry Labelle have been drawn from an interview with the author, August 25, 2015.

10. Michael Morse, "Tribute to jazz drummer Claude Ranger."

11. Len Dobbin, "Around the world: Montreal," *Coda*, December 1971, 37.

12. Dave Bist, "Elvin Jones — fine jazz at any level," *Montreal Gazette*, October 27, 1971, 24.

Chapter Six/"Thunder and lightning"

1. Alan Offstein, "Heard and seen: Bernie Senensky," *Coda*, June 1972, 45.

2. Alan Offstein, "Heard and seen: Salome Bey," *Coda*, June 1972, 43.

3. Alastair Lawrie, "Koffman still formidable and reasons are still obvious," *The Globe and Mail*, July 27, 1972, 11.

4. Alan Offstein, "Around the world: Toronto," *Coda*, October 1972, 36.

5. Alastair Lawrie, "George Kelly's tenor sax fits into place among Bourbon's giants," *The Globe and Mail*, July 17, 1972, 10.

6. Heard by the author, August 18, 1972.

7. Advertisement, *Toronto Star*, August 18, 1972, 27. The identities of the other musicians in the quintet are not known.

8. Joe LaBarbera, emails to the author, October 26, 2014, January 27, 2015.

9. "What's doing in Montreal: Nightlife," *Montreal Gazette*, October 27, 1972, 25.

10. Herbie Spanier, interview with the author, March 1, 1976.

11. Alastair Lawrie, "Davern on soprano sax overcomes heavy rhythm odds," *The Globe and Mail*, November 8, 1972, 15.

12. Alastair Lawrie, "Coleman's mighty sax spearheads hard-driving group," *The Globe and Mail*, November 29, 1972, 16.

13. "31st annual Down Beat

readers poll," *Down Beat*, December 29, 1966, 16-22.

14. Terry Clarke, interview with the author, May 24, 1985.

15. Michael Stuart, interview with the author, January 26, 2014.

16. Terry Clarke, interview with the author, September 23, 2014.

Chapter Seven/"It had to be something real"

1. "A summer workshop for music makers" [photo essay], *The Globe and Mail*, August 2, 1973, 41.

2. Len Dobbin, "Around the world: Montreal," *Coda*, March 1974, 28.

3. John Norris, "Heard and seen: James Moody," *Coda*, March 1974, 36.

4. Claude Ranger, "Music vitae," ca. 1990, 4. Author's collection.

5. Barry Tepperman, "Heard and scene: Music is the healing force of the universe," *Coda*, May 1974, 32-34.

6. *Jim Hall Live!*, A&M Records SP-705. Recorded in June 1975.

7. Jack Batten, "Long, talented lineup produces high level concert," *The Globe and Mail*, March 18, 1974, 12.

8. Peter Goddard, "$4,100 raised for ailing drummer," *Toronto Star*, March 18, 1974, D6.

9. Quoted in Ted Warren, "Inside the drummer's studio, Installment 8! Steve Wallace," http://trapdted.blogspot.ca/2012/04/inside-drummers-studio-installment-8.html.

10. Mark Miller, unpublished review, May 1974.

11. John Tank, interview with the author, December 3, 2013.

12. All comments by Bruce Cassidy have been drawn from an interview with the author, October 17, 2013.

13. Peter Goddard, "Saxophone player an underrated star," *Toronto Star*, March 14, 1974, E12.

14. John Norris, "Around the world: Toronto," *Coda*, October 1974, 26.

15. Jack Batten, "Woods still brilliant even with walrus mustache," *The Globe and Mail*, August 29, 1974, 11.

16. Sonny Greenwich, interview with the author, March 10, 2015.

17. Barry Tepperman, "Sonny Greenwich," *Coda*, January 1975, 38.

18. Jack Batten, "Camerata and Koffman meet in Mozart," *The Globe and Mail*,

November 29, 1974, 17.

19. Jack Batten, "Delicious happenings from reedman and bassist," *The Globe and Mail*, November 27, 1974, 15.

Chapter Eight/"*All* feel"

1. Bill Smith, "Heard and seen: Junior Cook," *Coda*, January 1975, 35.

2. All comments by Bob McLaren have been drawn from an interview with the author, October 28, 2014.

3. All comments by Barry Elmes have been drawn from an interview with the author, August 9, 2014.

4. All comments by Vito Rezza have been drawn from an interview with the author, August 20, 2013.

5. All comments by Greg Pilo have been drawn from an interview with author, September 27, 2013.

6. Adele Freedman, "The Sufi: Jim Blackley's basement is a jazz temple," *The Globe and Mail*, August 24, 1977, A23.

7. All comments by Buff Allen have been drawn from an interview with the author, October 23, 2014.

Chapter Nine/"Not nice, not a lot of fun"

1. Nighthawk, "Sonny shows great originality," *Montreal Gazette*, March 17, 1975, 27.

2. Jack Batten, "DeFranco is playing for himself in twilight years," *The Globe and Mail*, April 2, 1975, 12.

3. Barry Tepperman, "Toronto jazz," *Coda*, August 1975, 34.

4. Brian Hurley, email to the author, February 24, 2014.

5. Jane Fair, interview with the author, May 1, 2015.

6. Rising Sun poster in the possession of Steve Hall.

7. Jack Batten, "Superman Moses has a new club concept," *The Globe and Mail*, December 24, 1975, 15.

8. Except as noted in Chapter Seven, footnote 9, all comments by Steve Wallace have been taken from an interview with the author, March 29, 2014.

9. Frank Falco, email to the author, March 17, 2015.

10. All comments by P.J. Perry have been drawn from an interview with the author, April 21, 2015.

11. Ken Campbell, "Thompson Quartet jazz lets soul fly free," *Hamilton Spectator*,

September 23, 1977, 54.

Chapter Ten/"Cynical"

1. Frank Rasky, "Flamboyant musician puts jazz into TV series," *Toronto Star*, October 19, 1977, F5.

2. All comments by Neil Swainson have been drawn from an interview with the author, October 10, 2013.

3. All comments from Claude Ranger quoted or paraphrased by Peter Goddard have been drawn from Peter Goddard, "Claude Ranger plays his way," *Toronto Star*, October 3, 1981, F3.

4. All quotes by Bernie Senensky have been drawn from an interview with the author, August 4, 2013.

Chapter Eleven/"Fifty minutes of pure joy"

1. Mark Miller, "Breau's guitar work evokes reverence," *The Globe and Mail*, April 1, 1980, 17.

2. Ranger's words to Bourgeois were, "Apporte-moi une caisse de bière et je viendrai." All comments by Roland Bourgeois have been taken from an interview with the author, May 16, 2015.

3. All comments by Kirk MacDonald have been taken from an interview with the author, August 1, 2013.

4. The CCMC was formed as the Canadian Creative Music Collective, but used the acronym alone throughout its history of more than 40 years. Its base for much of that time, The Music Gallery, was located in its first incarnation — 1976 to 1984 — on St. Patrick Street, north of Queen Street West. The Music Gallery subsequently moved through a succession of other addresses on or near Queen Street West.

5. *The Canada Council 25th Annual Report Supplement 1981/1982* (Ottawa 1982), 70.

6. Kellogg Wilson, "Ranger's red-hot drums fuelled a flaming show," *Edmonton Journal*, August 21, 1982, H2.

7. Peter Danson, "Around the world: Montreal jazz festival," *Coda*, October 1982, 29.

8. Hal Hill, "Around the world: Jazz City festival," *Coda*, October 1982, 28.

Chapter Twelve/*Feu vert*

1. All comments by Perry White have been drawn

from an interview with the author, September 5, 2013.

2. All comments by Steve Donald have been drawn from an interview with the author, April 1, 2014.

3. Rikk Villa, email to the author, June 13, 2015.

4. Michael White, interview with the author, September 10, 2013

5. All comments by Jonnie Bakan have been drawn from an interview with the author, August 31, 2013.

6. Ray Nance was not a regular member of the Ellington orchestra during this period, but Bruce Cassidy remembers Stone associating Nance with this incident.

7. Freddie Stone, interview with the author, October 31, 1984.

8. Freddie Stone, program note for a concert at the Music Gallery in Toronto, May 8, 1983. Draft held in Freddie Stone Fonds, MUS 224/14, Library and Archives Canada, Ottawa.

9. "32nd International Critics Poll," *Down Beat*, August 1984, 20-23, 52-53, 59.

10. "33rd International Critics Poll," *Down Beat*, August 1985, 20-22, 57, 59.

11. All comments by Phil Dwyer have been drawn from an interview with the author, August 7, 2013.

12. Kevin Turcotte, interview with the author, January 26, 2014.

13. The du Maurier International Jazz Festival ran for just two years, 1985 and 1986, and should not be confused with the du Maurier (later "TD" or Toronto Dominion) Downtown Jazz Festival, which began under a different administration in 1987.

14. Dave Liebman, interview with the author, March 26, 2013.

Chapter Thirteen/"When I play, I own the world"

1. All comments by Lili Wheatley (née Clendenning, the name to which she later returned) have been drawn from an interview with the author, June 22, 2014. For the sake of clarity, she has been identified here as Lili Wheatley, her name during the years that she spent with Ranger.

2. All comments by Rob Frayne have been drawn from an interview with the author, October 28, 2014.

3. Alain Brunet, "Claude Ranger: pompe à rhythme...," *La Presse*, July 4, 1986, B4.

4. Mark Miller, "Ranger gives jazz a bash," *The Globe and Mail*, October 13, 1986, C10.

5. All comments by Larry Cramer and Jane Bunnett have been drawn from a joint interview with the author, December 29, 2013.

6. All comments by Ken Pickering have been drawn from an interview with the author, July 8, 2015.

7. Mark Miller, "Jane Bunnett displays a one-two musical punch," *The Globe and Mail*, December 3, 1986, C9.

8. Dave Field, interview with the author, December 16, 2014.

Chapter Fourteen/"There was a buzz"

1. All comments by Ron Samworth have been drawn from an interview with the author, June 24, 2015.

2. Mark Miller, *Jazz in Canada: Fourteen Lives* (Toronto: University of Toronto Press, 1982), 167-187.

3. The New Orchestra Workshop has employed N.O.W. as an abbreviation and NOW as an acronym. NOW has been used here throughout for consistency, save when N.O.W. appears in the title of the CD *The Future is N.O.W*.

4. NOW in its first incarnation flourished from 1977 to 1981 under the direction of Plimley, saxophonist Paul Cram, trombonist Ralph Eppel, bassist L.S. Lansall (Lisle) Ellis and drummer Gregg Simpson. By 1990, the second incarnation also included singer Kate Hammett-Vaughan, saxophonist Graham Ord and drummer Roger Baird.

5. Gary Pogrow, "Jazz dialogue that makes good listening," *Vancouver Sun* January 9, 1988, C2.

6. James Adams, "Don Thompson's sidesmen [sic] powerful for 70-minute set," *Edmonton Journal*, April 22, 1988, C4.

7. All comments by Clyde Reed have been drawn from an interview with the author, June 25, 2014.

8. Jack Walrath, Facebook message to the author, July 7, 2015.

9. Alex Varty, "Jack Walrath Quartet," *Georgia Straight*, July 1-8, 1988, 25.

10. All comments by Kate Hammett-Vaughan have been drawn from an interview with

the author, September 20, 2014.

11. All comments by Rene Worst have been drawn from an interview with the author, June 25, 2014.

Chapter Fifteen/The Jade Orchestra

1. All comments by François Houle have been drawn from an interview with the author, June 27, 2014.

2. All comments by Tony Wilson have been drawn from an interview with the author, July 23, 2014.

3. All quotes from Claude Ranger to Laurence Svirchev, and all comments by Svirchev, have been drawn from Laurence Svirchev, "Profile of Claude Ranger," www.svirchev. com/?p=124, October 17, 2012.

4. Renee Doruyter, "Jazz adventures: four-day Time Flies fest offers plenty of it," *Vancouver Province*, November 8, 1990, 25.

5. All comments by Coat Cooke have been drawn from an interview with the author, June 23, 2014.

6. All comments by Dave Say have been drawn from an interview with the author, June 29, 2014.

7. The other members of the 12-piece Jade Orchestra at the du Maurier International Jazz Festival concert on Maple Tree Square in Gastown, June 24, 1990, were tenor saxophonist Terry Deane, baritone saxophonist Gordon Bertram and guitarist Ray Khalil. Ranger, at the piano, also performed with guitarist Tony Wilson and saxophonist Rob Armus as a trio, and Wilson in turn joined the orchestra for some of its program. The 19-piece orchestra at the Vancouver East Cultural Centre on November 11, 1990, was completed by trumpeters Derry Byrne, Aron Doyle, Jeff Mahoney and Robin Shier, trombonists Dennis Esson and Brad Muirhead, tuba player Ian McIntosh and alto saxophonist Graham Ord, tenor saxophonist Dave Say and baritone saxophonist Daniel Miles Kane.

8. "Jade Orchestra," *Looking Ahead*, October-November 1990, 5.

9. Details of the *Stars in Tears* proposal to the Canada Council have been taken from a copy of the application in the author's possession.

10. All comments by Bruce Freedman have been drawn from an interview with the author, June 26, 2014.

11. *Clear the Way* was posted online at www.zisman.ca/freedmanjazz/Retrospective/02_Clear_the_Way.mp3.

12. Alex Varty, "Jade Orchestra," *Georgia Straight*, November 16-23, 1990, 34.

13. All comments by Joe Bjornson have been drawn from an interview with the author, July 6, 2015.

14. *The Canada Council 24th Annual Report 1990/1991: Supplement* (Winter 1992), 67.

15. Graham Ord, conversation with the author, June 25, 2014.

Chapter Sixteen/"A very tidy guy"

1. All quotes by Charles Papsaoff have been drawn from an interview with the author, August 25, 2014.

2. Kevin Whitehead, "Vancouver jazz festival," *Down Beat*, October 1991, 61-62.

3. All quotes by Dylan van der Schyff have been drawn from an interview with the author, June 23, 2014.

4. All quotes by Nick Fraser have been drawn from an interview with the author, November 5, 2013.

5. André White, interview with the author, July 25, 2014.

Chapter Seventeen/"I think that I will never play again"

1. All comments by Ray Ayotte have been drawn from an interview with the author, June 25, 1014.

2. All comments by André Lachance have been drawn from an interview with the author, August 18, 2014.

3. John Doheny, comment, Facebook [Bill Clark page], November 17, 2012. Quoted with permission.

4. John Doheny, post, www.vancouverjazz.com, November 6, 2002.

5. Kevin Elaschuk, interview with the author, September 5, 2014.

6. Pierre Tanguay, interview with the author, March 21, 2015.

7. Ken Eisner, "Maceo Parker/David Murray Trio," *Georgia Straight*, March 17-24, 1995, 55.

8. Ken Aldcroft, interview with the author, November 3, 2013.

9. All comments by Sean

Drabitt have been taken from an interview with the author, June 21, 2014.

10. All comments by William Stewart have been drawn from an interview with the author, September 8, 2015.

Chapter Nineteen/"He didn't want to leave anything behind"

1. Danny Parker, interview with the author, October 8, 2015.

2. S/Sgt Alex Bolden, June 25, 2014; Judith Yamada, email, February 6, 2015.

BIBLIOGRAPHY

Books

Gilmore, John. *Swinging in Paradise: The Story of Jazz in Montreal.*
(Montreal: Véhicule Press, 1988).
— *Who's Who of Jazz in Montreal: Ragtime to 1970.* (Montreal: Véhicule
Press, 1989).
Leitch, Peter. *Off the Books: A Jazz Life.* (Montreal: Véhicule Press, 2013).
Miller, Mark. *Jazz in Canada: Fourteen Lives.* (Toronto: University of
Toronto Press, 1982).
— *Boogie, Pete & The Senator: Canadian Musicians in Jazz, the Eighties.*
(Toronto: Nightwood Editions, 1987).
— *The Miller Companion to Jazz in Canada and Canadians in Jazz.*
(Toronto: The Mercury Press, 2001).

Articles

Gallagher, Greg. "Claude Ranger: The career of a jazz drummer turned
composer." *Canadian Composer*, June 1976, 12, 14, 44.
Goddard, Peter. "Claude Ranger plays his way." *Toronto Star*, October 3, 1981,
F3.

Miller, Mark. "Claude Ranger." *Down Beat*, October 5, 1978, 48.

— "Ranger's act on upswing again." *The Globe and Mail*, May 25, 1981, 24.

Svirchev, Laurence. "Profile of Claude Ranger." www.svirchev.com/?p=124, October 17, 2012.

Sweatman, Ron. "Aquarius Rising." *Coda*, September-October 1970, 44-46.

Varty, Alex. "Jade Orchestra." *Georgia Straight*, November 16-23, 1990, 34.

Warren, Carole. "Keeping Time: the odyssey of Claude Ranger," *Coda*, November 2008, 24-33.

Other media

Warren, Carole. "Sticks and stones," CBC radio ("Sunday Morning") documentary, 2007.

www.clauderanger.com [inactive in 2016 but maintained in part at https://web.archive.org/web/20151116224848/http://clauderanger.com/].

Index

Notes

1. Page numbers followed by the letter "a" or "b" and a number — eg, 252a9 — refer to entries found in Notes; "a" and "b" indicate the column— left and right, respectively — and the number identifies the specific note.
2. Page numbers in bold and italics — eg, *179* — refer to photographs.

CPSIA information can be obtained
at www.ICGtesting.com
Printed in the USA
BVHW081326250322
632212BV00004B/516